Archie's Psalm

Christopher D. Burns

C.B. Publishing

Published by C.B. Publishing Company
Memphis, TN. 38125 U.S.A.
Copyright 2009 by Christopher D. Burns

Publisher's Note

Please visit: http://www.cbpublish.com
ISBN 0-9701952-4-9
13 Digit 978-0-9701952-4-1
Cover Design © 2009

Archie's Psalm

Chapter 1

He told stories to pass the time. A simple man, never loud. Carried extra quarters in his pockets, about ten patch made pockets on dingy coveralls, a soft white shirt beneath the faded denim straps over his shoulders. The only look on his face I remember was like the quiet warmness after a summer rain. His half smile marked with crescent moons at the corners of his mouth and lines like folds in brown blankets at the corner of his eyes. His skin soft with bristled hair, even on his hands hair grew. He carried a walking stick sometimes, and walked through the streets each morning and each afternoon. Maybe to see what we was doing, us latchkey kids, us *thugs*. But we wadn't so bad, just bored, and he knew that.

Chapter 2

He told stories to pass the time, stories of uprisings, niggers, Tom's, fools, white folks, but mostly it was stories about the neighborhood that stuck to me.

Me and the guys ran all over the streets bothering and startling the old folks. He just stood when we would ride by, looking at us act up. He never did nothing to us unless he found us being too mannish. Folks used to say he carried bricks, a small piece of brick in each overall pocket. He caught Lil Tony trying to scare Ms. Phillips once. He saw him and from what Tony said,

"I was ridin right, ridin, Buck, I wasn't even messin wit Ms. P. I ain't lyin."

"What'd he do, what'd he do?" I kept asking. Tony's toughskins were scuffed pretty bad on purple knee patches. His palms was dirty with little scrapes on chubby hands. His jaws shook when he got excited.

"I ain't lyin Buck, I ain't-"

"Tony, what'd he do?"

"He threw one at me."

"No he didn't."

"Yeah he did."

"Did it hit you? Did it hurt?"

"You ask stupid questions Buck."

"You the one that's stupid. You know how Old Man Fishstick act when he see Ms. P."

"Yeah but-"

2

"That's why you got hit," I laughed.

"Didn't exactly get hit though, I just saw him raise his hand. So I jumped off my bike. He walked up an-"

"An he laughed at you an walked away, didn't he? Don't lie."

"Yep, he jus laughed an walked off."

"An he lef you sumthin?"

"A quarter."

"Me too."

'Pretty Ms. P,' was what he called her. Old Man Fishstick was what we used to call him. He always talked with Ms. P, but not much to many other folks. I even noticed him take out his folded red kerchief with the white designs on it to wipe his brow, before she would see him. He'd pull off his old blue hat and pull at the tufts of gray hair matted to the sides of his head. He'd even walk a little bit slower with longer strides. Such long strides I think would've been hard with a pocket full of bricks. I had found out that their wadn't no bricks a long time before any body else. What it was, was quarters in small, cloth brown bags. But I didn't tell nobody seein as he only had em every once in a while. Anyways, I asked him why he always fixed up himself, when he see Ms. Pat.

"Ya know what a peacock is?"

"Yes suh."

"Find out why peacocks look like they do, an then ask me why, an I'll tell ya."

Still don't know why peacocks look like they do, but I'm trying to get the answer.

Old Man Fishstick used to be scary to me. He still scare everybody else, but not for *real* scary. We knew he wasn't gonna really hurt us. We would go by his house and yell at him. He'd be on his, one step up, lil wooden porch. Sitting on it plucking strings on a wood box guitar. Singing old songs bout, "Movin on, umm hmmm, movin on down de line. De train dun pass me up, an I's too ol to git on board." We'd run and shout his name, "Ol Man Fishstick, Ol Man Fishstick, Ol Man Fishstick." He'd stand up and run at the gate holding a brick in his hand. We'd take off running an laughing. Twenty minutes later we'd be back.

His house was one of the few really old houses. It sat on the corner of Caldwell, where a potholed street separated it from the elementary school. Both the school and his house was across from the field for the park, where the slidin board, merry go round, monkey bars and lots of old concrete picnic tables was.

That field, in the summer, always had dragonflies floating across and it was lots of them. Like greenish-brown, fat mosquitoes darting back and forth. At night the dragonflies was replaced by lightnin bugs. Small with white butts that blinked on and off when the green, black wings would close and open. Momma said they had to light up or the flowers wouldn't grow.

Ol Man Fishstick had a big backyard that was overgrown by about two inches. But he had a long planting bed where he grew stuff and a honeysuckle vine in there. One long vine that almost made a second fence. We used to sneak back there and get some of the yellow-white stems and pull them out to suck the juice. I had some honeysuckle by my apartment, but it wadn't no danger in getting that.

Besides, me, Lil Tony, Smoke, Skillet, Lizard and Tiger didn't like staying that close to the house. We were the army of UltraMan, too fast to catch, too smart to stay by the house. If we stayed by the house we'd have to do chores for Smoke's folks. So we went to Ol Man Fishstick's place and bothered him.

Every time we went by, he'd be playing the same music with different words, "She don't know babaaah, she don't know my heart hurt sooo. Umm Hmmm. I said she don't know babaah that my heart hurt sooo."

His songs seemed sad, like his stories. But he never seemed sad when he talked. He'd raise his arms and wave his hands drawing pictures of words.

Chapter 3

"Her skin not pink but lighter than daisy yellow. Straight hair, long and brown like dark Gulf sand. She dressed better than everyone. Never a worry for her we thought. But some folks not knowin what she was, didn't want her on Scuttlefield side cause she was too pretty. But she was a good person. Ms. Taddy knew it and thanked her all the time. See, Ms. Taddy's boy was good as dead he was. Good as dead. Had done stayed in Midtown too long. Finished workin the yards for folks but he wanted to look at the big houses. He wadn't doin nuthin wrong, just lookin at the houses. Grand houses they was too, big columns and long front yards. Big stone block gates. Windows draped with big flowin curtains tied up with gold strings, and overhangin balconies with chairs.

I done stopped a number of times to look at them too, but I knew better. But Carl wadn't so smart, fine worker though. Big shoulders, strong legs, handsome brown young man with lovin eyes. No fight in him to be that big. He had done finished with his yardwork and was eyein the houses and walkin. Piece of straw in his mouth and the boy just plain forgot his place that's all. Some of them Midtown Whities saw him walkin, his hand skippin on the bars in front of the Madison House. *Wouldn't hurt a fly.* Three of em walked up to him.

"Kinda late ain't it boy?"

Carl knowin he had messed up, looked down. He knew his place he did. He didn't look none of em in the eyes. Kept lookin down and answered, "Yessuh, sorry suh."

"Thinks you bets be headin back to yo neck of the woods there boy."

"Yessuh."

Carl turned to leave and heard, "Stupid Nigger spit on de ground didn't he?"

"Umm Hmm. Saw it wit my own eyes I did."

Carl hadn't spit he had took the straw out his mouth and dropped it on the ground, just dropped it on the ground.

"Get him."

Carl not knowin what to do, dropped down to the concrete and curled up. He knew he wadn't spose to fight back. So he held his knees and tried to get into a ball. His back hurt, legs throbbed, and his head stung, from heavy kicks and punches. His ears rang, he started cryin, "Sorry suh, sorry suh," till he gagged on thick blood. Yep, them White boys had done kicked him and punched him til he passed out right there on the street. The police had come and the boys told them Carl was tryin to get into the Madison fence. The police took him away.

Ms. Taddy had missed her son before. He had come home late sometime and left early to find work. But after four days she realized that something was wrong. She walked through Scuttlefield askin if anyone had heard from Carl. She even come to me askin had I heard anything.

"You seen my son?"

"No mam, I reckon I ain't seen em for a few days. Usually walk by here an speak for a sec."

"He ain't come home in days, ain't like him. Not like him at all."

"I keeps my eyes out mam, an ears."

Ms. Taddy walked off. I put down my guitar and walked to the gate an watched her for a moment.

"Ms. Taddy, I walks with ya if you wants me to?"

"That be fine."

"I'm sho someone done heard bout him."

"I sure do hope so."

"Aww nah Ms. Taddy don't you worry none bout that boy, he just fine. Just done got hisself into some mischief maybe."

"If you say so, I jus don't like it when he gon for long. He grown I know, but he jus ain't made for these fast folks."

We walked through the old streets over worn dirt trails in the back of the elementary school. The air was thick and drops of water stuck our clothes to both our backs. As Ms. Taddy stepped over loose rocks, dust kicked up and began to cover her shoes. Little black, shiny shoes. By no means was they walking shoes. But she walked on anyway, almost in a waddle. She rocked side to side, her purse over her left arm, a napkin in her hand. Her hat, straw, wide, cast a shadow on her eyes but didn't stop the sweat from running down her cheeks. She dabbed at the drops with her napkin.

"I really do thank you for walkin with me."

"My pleasure mam."

We continued. Past the old yellow brick bakery and other houses down Chelsea street.

"Where you wanting to walk Ms. Taddy?"

8

"We go on down to the courthouse. Lawd knows I don't want for him to be there, but these policemens...Oh Glory," she stopped for a moment. I held her by the arm and walked her to some steps in front of one of the houses.

"Thank ya. It's right hot out here. Umph, this heat catchin up wit me."

"That's alright there Ms. Taddy we can rest here for a moment. Ms. Taddy if-" I stopped before I might have made her worry.

"Go on nah an finish what you gon say."

"Aww wadn't nothin mam. Just worried bout this heat. You sure you gon be alright?"

"Son I'm fine. Dun worked and walked a lot more than this. Jus tired today, this heat is a lil bit more than I expected."

"I know."

We continued down past the old public park and the old Frank's Corner Store, turning right at the edge of the block where a strip of houses had been torn down. Some of the trees had been uprooted.

"Remember when them houses was here? Them was some of the first houses Black folk had. Nah they gone. Them was nice houses."

"Looked like slave houses."

"What's that?"

"Nothin mam? Them houses was okay, but they gone to add more to downtown." We kept walking. The breeze coming off the river was finding its way to the streets. It wasn't a cool breeze but it helped. The trees that hadn't been axed down cast shade on the street.

"Downtown don't need no more."

"Some folks say it gon mean more jobs though Ms. Taddy."

"For White folks, not for us. We still gonna have to work where we allowed. Beale Street, by the Lorraine."

"Well, I think things is gonna start changing."

"It's 1955 son. If it ain't changed by now, ain't gon change. My boy still tillin fields on White folk's county land and lookin for work, day in day out. Ain't changed yet, ain't gon change."

"I know I ain't been around long but I think it's gon change. Folks in Mississippi done started some groups-"

"Black folk in Memphis lazy, they feel fine the way it is."

"I don't feel fine, but what I'ma do? I figure if folk can start doing stuff in Mississippi, it'll eventually trickle down."

"Mississippi tricklin to Memphis?" she asked with this laughing look on her face.

After walking from Caldwell to downtown, we finally reached the courthouses.

"Ms. Taddy you think they gon have him?"

"We gotta check."

We walked round the side of the red brick buildin and knocked on the metal door. The door was made in halfs. They took Black folk in through the front to put em in jail, but if you wanted to find someone...The half door opened.

"How kin I hep ya?" A slender clean cut White boy in uniform asked. His fingers hooked into loops on his jacket.

"Yessuh, I's lookin for my son. His name-"

"Ya know if he here dat he got bail money to be paid?"

10

"Yessuh, I know. His name Carl Taddy?"

"I don't think we rested no nigras lately."

"Sir can you just check-"

"Boy, was I speakin wit you?" He pulled out a stick and stuck it in my chest making me fall back a little.

"Damn nigras, mam like I was sayin-"

"Dammit Charles, can you jus take down the boy's name and check, oh I'm sorry Charles forgot you can't spell." A tall, well-built uniformed white man walked over behind the other. He bumped the first cop out of the way and smiled at Ms. Taddy and tipped his hat.

"Mam, what is your son's name?" He took out a writing pencil and paper.

"Carl suh, Carl Taddy suh."

"Mam, you don't need to call me sir."

She looked at me and I humped my shoulders. I could hear the other one in the background complaining. His keys rattled around and I could hear doors opening and closing. There was a sound of scuffling inside.

"Mam, I'll get right on that... I'll be right back." The taller one slammed the half door. There were muffled words from behind. I could make out a couple of "Godammits," and "Why'd you do thats." The metal door opened again.

"Mam," the taller officer, Anderson was his name, began. "Mam, your boy...is here but his bail is twenty dollars."

"Is my boy okay suh? I got some money, brought all I got." Ms. Taddy pulled out a brown kerchief and emptied it out on the metal counter attached to the half door. The man started counting. I'm sorry mam, all you got is about fifteen dollars. I didn't have nothin to help her with.

"Suh, that's all I has. That's all I has." She looked through the bottom of her purse. Her white gloves were getting dirty from the scraping in the bottom of the bag.

"Suh that's all I has, Suh?"

"Is he okay sir?" I asked lookin him directly in the eyes.

"I'm sorry you don't have enough." He looked back into my eyes as he pushed the coins and crumpled dollars into a pile on the kerchief. Ms. Taddy stood in the door, picked up her money and put it back in the bag.

"My son a good boy, jus a lil slow, is all."

The man looked at me, "I think it be best if he stay here a few more days." He shut the half door.

"Lawd what I'ma do? Lawd."

"I got some money at home. Jus didn't think to bring it wit me."

"Naw, un un, naw. I ain't takin no money from ya. Can't do that."

"You can pay me back."

"Promised, I promised my mama and father that we was gon never owe nobody again."

"Ms. Taddy, I know you been strugglin since Carl Sr. went away."

"Died son, he died. I ain't fraid much to say it. He died with some honor."

"...I know you been strugglin, I jus figured you would take some help right now. I ain't tryin to put you out your way. I ain't tryin to make thangs harder on ya, jus tryin to help."

"I do appreciate it, but I got thangs I can git rid of. Make a lil mo today, an walk back down here an git my boy."

I reckoned that look Anderson gave me said that Carl wasn't okay. I knew those sounds was bad sounds. I wanted to tell Ms. Taddy that she should wait another day an come back. But that wouldn't of made any sense to her. She was intent upon gettin her son.

"We best be gettin back on down the road if we want to make it back here."

"Um Hum, we should make our way back. Sooner the better. I feel worried now. Thought I might be better once I find him, but somethin ain't right," she said.

"Well, Ms. Taddy, ain't much we can do right now. We best be goin."

"I need to see my boy."

"I don't know if that-"

"Look here, I need to see him."

She slipped her glove off her hand and over her fingers revealing paper thin brown flesh, with wrinkled skin on knuckles and heavily scarred hands. Look like her hands was pulled by a rake grabbing leaves over dead grass. The marks moved from the inside of her arms to her fingertips. Like old brown veins in fall leaves, that's what her hands looked like. She knocked on the metal half door. The taps was strong. I could hear the men arguing behind the metal.

Anderson opened the half door to a crack and looked through before opening it the rest of the way.

"Yes mam?"

"I needs to see my boy."

"Mam we can't-"

"Somethin wrong I feel it." She made a fist, with her forefinger extended and touched a place above her heart and repeated, "I can feel it."

"Damn nigras still out there? Hell, tol ya dem damn folk can't take no-"

"Shut up nah," Anderson slammed his hand on the counter. He looked back at Charles.

"Mam, I think it best if yaw'll two come back-"

"No, no, no, suh. No suh, I ain't comin back til I know my son still live."

"Mam, I assure you he alright."

"Yeah Ms. Taddy, I think it best we come back tomorrow. That way we can get the money together."

"I got to see my Carl. Cause I know it, in here, I know somethin wrong," She talked fast.

"Look mam, I promise you tomorrow he'll be fine. Jus be patient an come back tomorrow."

"Look suh let me jus see him, please."

"Go head on Andy, let the nigra see her nigger boy."

Anderson sighed and it seemed as if he was close to exploding. He pulled open the second half of the metal door and let us walk through. To the right, smoke floated from Charles' mouth through his

14

teeth as he smiled at Ms. Taddy and tipped his hat. His feet were propped up on the edge of a wooden desk, papers sat untended in front of him. His shoes were scuffed like field boots. His pants didn't match his blue uniform. They looked green. He flicked ashes into a trash can on the side of his chair, which tilted on the two back legs. Behind him were two other tables that were just as dirty. To my left, was another desk with stacks of paper in neat rows. A newspaper was opened and on it sat a cup. Anderson's uniform was clean and his shoes looked like the lights had got trapped in the leather. I looked down the hall and noticed that the concrete stopped at the bars. The floor was covered with wooden planks in some parts and dirt in others. We walked further into the room and the smell of smoke was mixed with a smell like early morning fertilizer wet with dew. The windows was opened at the end of the hall. There were six cells. They all looked empty. We passed by the first two. The rooms were dirt floors with a sitting chair by the wall and big barred windows about eight feet from the floor. Small puddles with dirt kicked in them sat with flies hovering above. The cells were far enough from the deskroom that the smell was faint in that part of the building. Anderson had stopped at the edge of the concrete and was looking on from that distance. Ms. Taddy reached the last set of bars. She had took off her other glove. She held them in her hand. Her purse still hung from her left arm. She looked into the last one. No shouting, or crying. Her gloves dropped. She wrapped her long fingers around the bars and just looked. I stopped walking and stayed back for a second.

"I sorry suh, I sorry suh, I sorry suh, I sorry suh-" I walked up beside Ms. Taddy. No cryin, no shouts from her at all. I looked in and saw him. Barefoot, pants stained in dark patches, his back bruised, long welts like burnt marks in wood dressers. No blood, just lumps and bruises. His hands covered his head, long and thick, his hands look liked his mother's hands, unhealed. We couldn't see his face, didn't want to see his face. He was huddled in a corner rockin.

"I sorry suh, I sorry suh, I sorry suh, I sorry suh-"

"Shut the boy up, goddamnit." I could hear the other one yelling down the hall. Ms. Taddy turned. Her shoes pushed the gloves into the dirt. She moved down the hall past me and Anderson. Anderson turned and ran towards her.

"Git this nigger bitch offa me."

"Mam-"

"Ms. Taddy-"

She had reached for the other one's neck and was chokin him. Anderson had grabbed her by the waist and tried to get her off. The other one screamed as Ms. Taddy pulled at his hair and scratched at his eyes. Anderson finally pulled her off.

"Throw her ass in that cell Andy goddammit."

"No, I ain't doin none the such."

Ms. Taddy took off back down the hall. Her hat had fell off when she attacked the other one. Her dress was torn at the seam around the bottom. Her purse lay beside the trash can next to Charles' desk. I stood with one foot in the dirt and one on the concrete. Charles was yelling at Andy.

"You gon let her attack me?"

"Shoulda kept quiet Charly. You didn't have to say nothin."

"I'ma put the nigger bitch in wit her boy is what I'ma do."

16

"You ain't doin nothin of the sort."

Charles jumped up and moved towards Anderson. Anderson crossed his arms and looked Charly in the eyes.

"I think you got better sense than to walk at me that way." Anderson stood, clean, sharp. Charles sat back down and began talking under his breath.

"Goddamn nigger lover."

"What was that?"

"You heard me."

A smile stretched across Anderson's face, "Boy you awfully close to a beatin. Awfully close."

Ms. Taddy had gotten Carl to turn and come to the bars. His arms reached through the bars and wrapped around her waist. She had her hands between the iron poles rubbing his forehead.

"I didn't do nothin wrong mama, nothin at all."

"I know baby, shhh, jus be quiet nah. We gon git you outta here."

"I sorry mama."

"You quit sayin that. You ain't got no reason to be sorry. You your father's boy. He fought proud for you. He want you to be proud. Be proud an hush up that cryin."

"Yes mam."

"We be back for ya."

As she turned to walk back, Carl's hand held on to the torn seam of her dress. She bent over and picked up her gloves. She slapped them against her hand till a lot of the dust was gone. Anderson was standing beside me looking at her. She walked on down the hall, when she reached the concrete there was a knock at the station door. A soft knock. Charles walked over and opened the half door and there she was, Her skin not pink but lighter than daisy yellow. Straight hair, long and brown like dark Gulf sand. Sadie Mae stood at the metal door.

"Officer Anderson in right now?"

"Yes Mam," said Charly.

Anderson pulled at his coat and brushed off the sleeves as he walked over. Charles looked on.

"Ms. Mae, good afternoon. If you can wait for a moment, I'll be right out. He closed the door to a crack as not to shut it in Sadie Mae's face.

"Mam I'm sorry for everything. If you can please come back tomorrow I will make sure he doing better, I promise you that." He reached his hand out in a shaking manner. Ms. Taddy looked him in his face.

"I believe you." She looked at me and headed towards the door. I followed behind. Sadie Mae was looking through and watching. As we passed her on our way out, she spoke.

"Afternoon Ms. Taddy."

"Afternoon mam, I sorry Carl ain't been by to clean your lawn this week. He been in the jail for a few days. But he didn't do nothin so please let him-"

"Ms. Taddy, don't you worry he still got a job with me," she smiled and touched Ms. Taddy's shoulder.

Everyone else questioned her living in our part of town, but I could see it in her. I could see it in her skin tone. She wasn't White as

18

Charly but her and Anderson had them features. Her lips wasn't small, they wasn't big either. And everytime somethin happened in the neighborhood, she was there looking on. I assumed she was sympathetic for one reason. Ms. Taddy and I began walking back towards home.

"Thank ya Ms. Cross," Ms. Taddy said.

"Everything'll be just fine, don't you worry, hear," Sadie Mae spoke touching Ms. Taddy light on the arm.

We made our way back by my house. She hadn't said much of anything since we had left the jail.

"I can go in and get my money if you like?"

"No suh, I make due."

We continued for the next block underneath trees down the dirt sidewalk. Folks watched us as we walked, whispering. Why they was whispering didn't make no sense. Black faces was on porches and in front yards. Some folks walkin down in front of Ms. Taddy house, was lookin. I could see a police car in front of Ms. Taddy's house. Anderson stood beside the car. As we moved up pass the chicken wire fence in front of Ms. Taddy's place she finally realized, as I did, what was happenin. Sadie Mae was sittin in front of the house with a shirt coverin Carl's shoulders. In front of the little house, folks was gatherin round. I stood outside the gate.

"Ms. Cross? Mam?"

"You said Carl didn't do nothing so-"

"Thank you mam, thank you Jesus." She hugged Sadie Mae's neck. Anderson looked nervous as more Black folk gathered round. He waved at Sadie Mae. Sadie stood up, kissed Carl on the top of the head and walked to the car. Anderson walked around and opened the door for her. As the car pulled off between a splitting path of Black folk, I could see through the crowd, into that heavy Black car what I knew all along about the White lady that stayed on our side of town.

Chapter 4

His stories, kinda like that old guitar of his, same sound just different meaning each time he opened his mouth. Each story sounded the same, but the words changed. They always changed in a good way. When he'd spend a lot of time on a sad story, he'd do a good story. There he'd sit on his stoop with that guitar strummin, "I seent the fire babaah, Oh I seent the fire in yo soul, Said I seent the fire babaah, done seen it moooore times than you know. An I can't be wrong babaah cause the devil don tol me soooo, wait a minute nah." He'd stop. "Yo big ears too young for that one."

"No they ain't."

"Yes they is."

"No suh they ain't, I done heard my momma in her room some time when Mistah Travis come-"

"Now watch yoself boy." He'd say pointing at me with his fingers clutchin an old pick for the strings on his guitar. The back of the guitar leaned on his chest and the bottom rested on his left thigh. His left hand sat on top of the long part by the tuning knobs. The front of it was sanded down to what looked like yellow wood covered with shine. He'd hum, no words, for a while but they felt good. Good humming, like it wadn't no words that could make up for what he was singing. "Ummm hummm, Aaauuum Uuun unnn a humm, come on sing it wit me boy."

"You ain't singing nothin." The wind picked up and kicked hot air through the yard. The long grass swayed.

"You ain't listenin," he said.

"I listenin."

"I tell you what, yaw'll kids got mo comebacks than anythang. I say you ain't listenin, you should listen, but noooo ya got to be the last to say somethin. Lil Ernest Taylor the same way."

"Lil Ernest Taylor? You mean Mr. Taylor with the lawyering business on Danny Thomas?"

"Naw I mean Lil Ernest Taylor from Caldwell that wouldn't let nobody out talk him."

"What you mean?"

He took out his handkerchief, wiped his forehead and adjusted his hat. I sat on a crate, picking blades of grass and tearing them to little pieces, waiting for him to start. He cleared his throat and stopped playing the guitar. He stood up and walked towards his gate, leaning to one side. His shoulder dipped as he moved. And then I saw her, a lime green dress with flowers at the bottom and around the neck. A straw hat with a lime bow around the base. A shopping basket in her hand. Lime and light brown, like a caramel green apple. Her face full and eyes wide. She looked over our way. Old legs walking slow, she switched the basket from her right hand to her left, and waved, "Hello Mr. Archie."

"Why...um...hello there Ms. P." His voice heavy but smooth, not sounding like it did when he told me stories. He pulled out two quarters and held them in his hand behind his back. I jumped up, took them and walked out the gate to help Ms. P. He followed me out after sitting his guitar down. He swayed like the grass as he walked over. Ms. P. was smiling and he had a big ol grin on his face. I held my hand out for the basket from Ms. P. and walked ahead.

"Mam, I'll help you with that."

"Why thank you sir."

"My pleasure Ms. Mam." I could hear her talking with Ol Man Fishstick. I'd known his real name cause I'd heard it before somewhere but a boy ain't supposed to call an elder by his name without saying Mr. It just sounded so funny coming out her mouth like that, 'Mr. Archie'. He was Ol Man Fishstick, or for me Mr. A.

"Now Archie either you done paid the boy, or he been listenin to your stories."

"Well mam, I right particularly don't know what you referrin to."

"That little Buck ain't got no father at home to teach him such manners."

"His momma purty good Ms. P."

"I do declare she is sweet, but she work too much, I ain't seen her in church in two Sundays."

"But the boy been there huh?"

"Every week. Sunday school, BTU even. But I'm sure he gettin some of that from them stories of yours. They good stories too, real good."

"Why thank you mam."

I looked back and saw Ol Man...*Archie* with his hands behind his back as he walked, still swaying. We had made it to the end of the block and was turning up Sixth Street. Ms. P, *pretty* Ms. P, was walking and still smiling hard.

"Anyway, I think you good for the boy. He stay longer than them other ones that run around here raising Cain."

"Aww them boys jus being boys."

"Well, it look like some of em should spend more time with you."

"Why thank you again, seem like I'm back in yo good graces."

"You never was out of em."

I laughed and looked back. Ms. P. had dropped her head, still smiling. Ol Man Fishstick looked at me with the, "turn around boy look." I laughed.

"I see your yard need a little work?"she said.

"Yeah, ain't don much since you got mad at me."

"I wadn't mad, jus a lil tired. Why you ain't working wit it? I ain't got nothin to do wit you keepin house."

"Well, I felt so lonely that I couldn't pick up no tools or trimmers or nothin. But I get right on it when I get back."

"Oh please, Archie. Maybe I get some rest from this heat an come an help you."

"That would be right nice of you mam."

"We here *Archie*." I yelled.

Ms. P. laughed at me and looked at Ol Man Fishstick. He pulled his hands from his back and put them on his hips.

"Nah Archie, don't you go messin with that boy."

"Don't you worry Mam, I ain't gonna hurt one hair on his head," he said looking me in the face. I opened the gate and put the groceries on the step. I tried to walk by him,

"I gotta get home I think my momma callin me."

"Good ears to hear that son," he held me by the shoulders tight and stopped me.

"Nah Archie," Ms. P began. I laughed, he squeezed. "Don't you go messin with lil Buck." She pulled two dollars from her purse and gave them to me.

"Thank you mam."

"You be good nah Buck. Give one of them to your mama."

"Yes mam." I said.

"I be seein you later then Ms?" I could tell he was flirting when he said *be seein you later?*

"God willin suh," she said.

"He willin ...an able."

"Alright nah."

Ol man Fishstick laughed heavy. I could almost see the color changing in his face.

"We best be headin on back," he said. They stood there for a minute. I knew what they wanted to do. I'd seen my momma look that way at Mr. Travis. I just didn't expect ol folks to act like that. It was kinda gross, kinda like lookin at someone pick they nose. We began walking back towards the park.

"You did it again?"

"What's that son?"

"Wiped your head and started walkin funny."

"You been watchin me?"

"No, I jus notice when Ms. P.-"

"Look here nah Buck," he paused and sat down on a small grass hill. The hill was up like an old house was gonna be made. But then a lot of the street was like that. Two houses, no house, two more houses, no house. There were several trees on the edge of the lot. One was a big enough tree to shade the sidewalk close to where he sat. I walked to the edge of the hill and picked up one of those white flowers that had feathers in a round ball. I guess they wasn't feathers. But when you blew them, the white feathers fell off and followed the wind. I grabbed about six and sat beside Ol Man Fishstick. I didn't look at him as he spoke but I listened as I blew. He took out his handkerchief and wiped his forehead again. He cleared his throat.

"You know why Peacocks look like they do yet?"

"No suh."

"What you learnin in school?"

"School out, that's why I'm with you."

"Book Library open?"

"Yessuh."

"Well... I could tell you, but I wantcha to learn on your own."

"Aww Archie-"

He snatched his hat off and hit me on the top of my head.

"Ow."

"R-E-S-P-E-C-T."

"Huh?"

"Don't get like these other knuckleheads."

"How so?"

"You a good boy, gon be a good man, I can feel it. You call me suh. That's respect, it'll take you a long way. Don't never call no man older'n you by they name, call em suh, or Mistah."

"Yessuh-" he hit me on the head again.

"What was that for?"

26

"That's for when you call me Archie in fronta Ms. P." He laughed. Pushing himself off of the ground, he continued talking. "What time ya Mother gettin home?"

"She gettin home at six, but she got a three hour job after that at the Cafe."

"Lawd she work hard."

"I know."

"That make you sad?"

"Nope. It's like you said... she do it for me to be better."

"That's right. That sho is right. She a good woman."

"Thank you suh." He smiled at me as he rubbed my head. My hair was flat from his hand. His hand was heavy, felt like my neck was shorter after he finished patting.

"Sometime folk don't like you when you good. They think you suddity."

"Sunditty?"

"Sah-Ditt-tee, when folk act like they bettah than ya."

"Kinda like folk thought about Sadie Mae," I asked.

"That's a bit right, but folk didn't like her for her skin."

"But you knew. What you knew?"

"Well, Buck... sometime folk put on airs."

"Suh?"

"They make themselfs into somethin they ain't. In the whole time they hidin behind them lies, they losin they soul."

"Losin they soul?"

"When you wanna play and your momma don't let you go out, how that feel to ya?"

"Make me mad. Then it make me sad and then I get angry again and then I get sad again. Then-"

"Buck, son, How that make you feel inside?"

"Well...I don't know."

"That's what it feel like for folk that hide behind lies. They confused, angry, sad, an jus like you, they sad, angry, an confused all over again. All the time."

"That ain't no good suh. Momma be sad and angry on and off."

"Well Buck, that's different. Lemme finish about Sadie Mae. When folks was in
slavery-"

"Emancipation Proclamation?"

"Not quite, jus listen. Sometimes you see folk drinkin coffee. They puts milk in it, sometime sugar, to make it better. To make it taste different. But when they put milk an sugar in it what happen to the coffee?"

We made it back to the gate. He picked up his guitar and flicked the strings. As he sat down on his chair, I sat on my crate. I could hear the fellas riding up yelling, "Ol Man Fishstick." Then they saw me. They jumped off they bikes and walked to the fence. Lil Tony's afro was full of twigs and grass blades, "We gon play football, wanna come?"

I looked at Ol Archie. He smiled at me and nodded. I took off out the gate and ran across to the park.

Chapter 5

It was only eight of us. Me, Lil T, Stack (cause he was built like a bunch of wide skillet pancakes), Smoke (cause he was so Black), Skillet (Cause he was blacker than Smoke, they was brothers), Man (said like Main street), Tiger (cause he was high yellow with freckles), and Lizard (take a guess why.) Me, Smoke, Skillet, and Tony was on the same team.

"Ol Man Fishstick not mad today?" asked Smoke.

"Nah, he ain't never mad, jus mean is all," said Skillet.

"He hit me wit a brick," Lil T said. "Sho did, right on the back of my foot he did. Made me fall off my bike."

"Why you always stayin there longer than everybody else anyway Buck?" asked Lizard.

"Dang Lizard, tuck your tongue in," said Tiger.

"Shut up, that's why your face different colors."

"So, at least I can talk without lickin people."

"Why you always gotta talk about me?"

"Cause."

"Cause he jealous," said Stack tossing the ball in the air.

"I ain't jealous."

"We all is, but we don't care. You jus mad."

"At what?" asked Tiger.

Stack stood up and walked to the other end of the park. He was bigger and older by like a year or two. He always knew stuff, but he didn't never say nothing until somebody needed help, "Let's play before more dragonflies come."

"Yeah," I said. Ol Archie was lookin on.

Lizard threw the ball high in the air and they all took off. Smoke, Stack and me made a wall so Tony could run it back. Tony caught it and left the wall. He ran between Tiger and Stack, they smacked each other as they tried to tackle him. Lizard set his feet and lowered his head. He and Tony hit, and the ball popped into the air. Grass and dirt kicked out behind Tony's foot and his shoe popped me in the nose. I fell backwards. I lifted my head and saw Stack and Smoke diving. Man, who hadn't said nothing the whole time, let them dive. He waited and picked the ball up. He took off past the whole pile and started kicking his legs, celebrating. I reached my hand up and tripped him. He fell down on top of the ball and it skeeted out. I crawled to my knees and went after it. Once I touched the ball I could feel the earth shaking. All the faces bunched in a mad rush to help and hit. I balled up and tucked. It felt like thirty pats on the head by Ol Man Fishstick.

"I quit," Man said wheezing still on the ground.

"Me too," I mumbled.

"Yeah let's go get some Jungle Juice and honey buns," said Stack.

Everybody agreed. They all stood up, toughskins covered in grass stains and shirts pulled too long on all sides.

"Lizard that was your fault."

"Shut up Tiger," said Stack and Man.

Everyone stopped and stared. Man usually just listened. He never said much of anything like Tony, but he really *never* said anything. We had walked to the front of the community center. The heat was beating off of the concrete walls. Archie's house was at the end of the walk, at the edge of the park. I could have turned around but Man had spoke.

"Tiger you been mad and angry all this week. We know what's going on, but we don't care, so you shouldn't." Man said.

"You don't know nothin."

"My momma said that yaw'll was gon be upset," said Lizard.

"Yo mamma stupid," Tiger replied.

"Hey, look Tiger we ain't got no daddy's either. I know if mine came back I'd be happy," said Stack.

Smoke and Skillet had a daddy and momma. They didn't say anything. Tiger dropped to the ground and started crying.

"You boys come on back down to the house nah," Ol Man Fishstick had walked up. He grunted as he bent down to help Tiger. "Come on nah, got some homemade ice cream in the icebox there. I make you boys some."

"We gotta go home suh." Smoke said grabbing Skillet by the arm.

"Me too suh," said Man and Tony.

"Thank you, but I'ma go in the gym," Stack said.

I looked at Archie, and then at Lizard, then Tiger. We all started walking towards Archie's house.

"Boys, sometimes God put these thangs called obstacles in your life. Nah usually they don't come till ya ol. They don't come til ya tryin to do somethin wit ya life. Yaw'll boys young I know, but you Black."

Tiger looked at him and wiped his hands on his jeans.

"You Black an you gon always have struggles. But-" he opened the gate and threw two more crates beside mine. "Yaw'll stay here nah, I be right back."

We sat outside an picked at grass.

"I'm sorry Lizard."

"You shouldn'tna-" Lizard started to talk and I thumped him hard on his ear and looked at him.

"Watcha do that-" I thumped him again and looked at him harder.

"You should stop being so mad Tiger," he said.

"I don't know what else to do."

"Ol Man Fishstick said that folks got airs."

"Hey nah Buck, slow ya roll there. Lemme finish what I was sayin." He walked out the screen door with a bowl in each hand and one resting between his chest and inside arm. We took the bowls and sat down.

"Think it might be too much sugar in there. But it's still purty good. Look here Lil Ed Weaver, or Tiger, or whatever they call ya. You don't make no long face an eat my ice cream. If ya lookin sad an eatin ice cream, it'll give ya stomach problems. You be pootin all over the place."

We all laughed, even Tiger.

"You ain't so mean, Ol Man Fish-" Lizard started talking. I thumped him again.

"Ow, watcha, nevermind. You ain't so mean suh...Why you always hittin us wit bricks an chasin us?"

"Well son, I make sure you boys learn."

"Learn what?" asked Tiger.

"R-E-S-P-E-C-T," I said. Archie nodded at me.

"That's right, and I ain't nevah hit none of you boys wit bricks."

"Tony said," he stopped talking and ducked, expecting me to thump him again. I didn't, we all laughed. "Tony said you caught him once."

"I did, you jus remember that I caught him and put the fear of God in em."

"What'd you do to him?"

"That's for me and him to know. Besides, I'd rather you run from me an learn some respect than to learn from folks that don't really like ya."

It was hot, but the sun would start setting in about an hour. The dragonflies had started to fill up the field over the park. They darted in and out like throwing handmade paper planes that are too heavy at the front. Soon the lightnin bugs would come and we'd have to go home. I'd be going home to an empty house. Momma always left a meal and books, seein as the big teevee we had didn't work. We had a big wood one with a little tube an a little black and white one, sittin on top of the big one that, "Made light skinned Black folks look white," my mom said. I didn't care much for the teevee anyhow, except on Saturdays. The books was good, they was poetry books. They had pretty words, for ugly things, killings and hangings, slavery stuff. Pretty words describing flowers and trees. One of them was so good I wrote it out and gave it to mom for a gift.

It was the one she read all the time with the words, "Crystal Stair," in it. She cried when she read that one. Sometimes she wouldn't read it for weeks. Then sometimes she read it every night. I knew when she was gonna read it cause I could hear it in the house. The way the door closed, soft and slow behind a creaking screen door. The way the couch sounded when she sat down on it, a light puff of air instead of a heavy push. The way the refrigerator door would sound when she opened it, quiet and humming while the door was stared into, the chair pulled out from the kitchen table. I could hear her words soft, strong sounding, reading, "I'se still climbin Lawd." I lay in my bed not knowing if I should go in and look after her. The floorboards moaned under the weight of her thin legs, tall legs. Those nights I fell asleep dreaming of growing up rich.

The dragonflies dipped down over the grass looking like they could swarm at anytime. Archie continued talking, "Respect important. A lot of folks respect the wrong thing. Sometimes we look at thangs differently for bad reasons. Like you Lil Douglass, or Lizard. You know somethin? Yaw'll boys got too many nicknames. Yaw'll remind me of arguing ol folks, like Dubois n Washington."

"Who're Dubbs an Washington?" Tiger asked.

"I do declare they don't teach you boys nothin in school do they? I'ma get into that a lil later, jus bare wit me. You boys arguin is the fault of jus one of you. An I understand why, but you can't let thangs bother you so much son." He spoke at Tiger. "Sometime folk run out the wrong people. Bout ten years ago, there was this lady. She love her man, but cause folks wadn't ready for that type of love she

34

kept quiet. They snuck an met, an loved. They made a baby an folks talked, an talked, an talked. Wouldn't let her have no peace. Her man, knowing full well that a visit wadn't possible, still came. Flowers in hand, gifts in a bag. Walking slow up Sixth Street, a group of young fellas, ol teenage fellas, followed him. But he didn't run, jus walked, head high. Handsome young fella he was. When he got to the projects them boys lit out on him. Yellin that he raped they sister. He tried to fight, but four on one too much. The boy had purple bruises on his arms, his little blonde head had blood stickin hair to his forehead. She stood at the top of the steps an looked on. She screamed for a moment an realized wadn't nothin she could do. The boys trampled the flowers into the sidewalk. Yellow, red, green stalks was crushed into cracked ground. The bag with the teddy bear sat on the curb. All the neighborhood folks was lookin through they windows. I walked up an ran them boys off.

"Get on nah you lil bastards... get up son, get up nah. You knew bettah." I said.

The boy's lips trembled as he stood wipin dirt off of his shirt an pants.

"Just thought maybe, well love."

"Sometime love don't fix mucha nothin, nothin at all."

"What am I supposed to do then?"

"Love her anyway. She come around, she will come around, believe me."

"How long though I mean, I gotta come back and try to speak and see my boy."

"Watcha name is son?"

"Edward sir."

Tiger looked up from his ice cream and began to listen harder

"The neighborhood look after him until you can be wit em both."

"No sir, I can see my son and wife-"

"She not your wife."

"She gon be."

"An who gon marry you in Memphis? Come on son, jus hear me out. You let thangs be. Yaw'll be together. An if you gotta visit, come early in the morning before sun up, don't come in the afternoon. You get me?"

"Yessuh, I got you. I love you no matter what anybody think, I love you." Edward yelled at Eunice.

We all sat listening and finishing our ice cream. Tiger had stopped eating. Ol Man Fishstick looked at Tiger again.

"Some folks get run off for the wrong reasons. Some good folks get run off son. He a good man. Ya ought to be happy an accept him." A lightnin bug blinked in front of Tiger's face.

"It's time to get home, fore the streetlights come on. Let's go Lizard," yelled Tiger. "Thank you for the ice cream sir," they yelled.

Archie waved his hand at them. He walked over and leaned towards the bowls. I picked them up.

"I got em."

"Why thank you sir."

"Least I can do for the free ice cream."

"Nothin free Buck, you earned that cream carryin groceries."

36

"Yeah, I did." He reached for his hat. "Jus kiddin suh, jus kiddin," I said.

He laughed and we walked into the house. The faint smell of honeysuckle drifted from the backyard.

"You best be gettin on home Buck."

"I see you tomorrow suh?"

"God willin."

"He willin an able," I said. He pointed his forefinger at me and clicked his mouth as he flicked his thumb down like a shooting gun. I did it back.

"You be safe now."

"Yessuh." I pushed the screen door closed behind me. I could hear the guitar as I walked through the gate. His voice full, "Da bright sun don set babaaah, dun set down beneath da land. I said da sun dun set babaaah some lit boys dun become maaaans. Ummm Hummm."

Chapter 6

Sometimes the sun is like a dream, there one moment, hiding the next, behind gray tufts of clouds. Clouds lookin like Mr. Archie's hair under that hat of his. But even when the sun hide behind clouds you can feel it, and see the light from behind. Momma always saying don't look directly at the sun.

"Make you go blind baby."

"I ain't gon blind yet momma."

"Don't tempt fate, jus listen to me is all I ask."

"Yes mam."

Sometimes the sun just like a dream, when you want it good, it don't make it so all the time. Sometime when you sad it shine right on you and make you feel better. So I look at it every now and then. Especially when it go behind the clouds, that's when it remind me of Ol Man Fishstick. When I don't feel so good, just talking to him makes me feel better. But not like the sun, he always there. Wouldn't be right if he up and set behind the land at the end of day, like the sun, on me. But he always let me now that, "God willin," he'll be waiting on me when I need him. I keep him in my prayers before bed, him and momma.

Often times when momma make it home late like she do on Mondays, Wednesdays and Fridays I wait up for her. During summer I can wait up every night, but I stick to Fridays to be on the safe side. I know when she coming cause I can hear Mr. Travis' car engine humming and the door closing. That's when I go get momma a cold glass of milk and a cookie. I don't think she like it, but it makes her smile and I love it when she smiles.

"Why thank you, so considerate, my little gentleman."

"Can I take your bag and shoes mam?"

"Why yes sir, that would be right nice of you. Such manners and respect, that's gon make you rich one day."

"That's right and I'm gonna buy us a house and two cars and-"

"I want a bedroom facing the pool."

"Better than that, I'll give you a big back yard with flowers and a garden like in those books you look at."

"I'ma hold you to that so you betta get them good grades in school."

'Yes mam. Anything else before I retire to the bed mam?"

"No sir. You done made my day complete. Gimme a big hug an kiss." She'd squeeze me tight and kiss me on the cheek. Before I could even get in bed right she'd be in the door tellin me,

"Good night, sleep tight-"

"Don't let the bedbugs bite, Yes momma." She'd click the light off and close the door. I don't know why she said bedbugs cause every night it would be hard to go straight to bed without thinking something was crawling on my legs. I guess the books on lice and mites we read in school didn't help much. For bugs so small, they look like monsters, long, with six hairy legs. Eyes like screen doors and feelers with holes in them to suck blood, some with *mandibles* that hooked on to hair *follicles.*

Those nights I fell asleep late I'd sometimes hear momma and Mr. Travis. He wadn't real loud, just loud enough though, and like I said before, I knew what was happening. He was never there in the morning though. He would come back sometimes and have breakfast like he wadn't never there. He would even come over on those days mom had off and hang out then leave and come back after I was asleep and be gone before I woke up.

"Rise and shine sweetheart," mom would say.

"It's summertime mom, ain't no school."

"There isn't any school...and I don't care if school in or not, you gon get up and move around. Don't have no need for a lazy man in this house."

"Yes mam." I'd get up, my rumpled Aquaman underoos wedged in my butt and my long sleeping shirt was covered with feathers from my pillow. I walked slowly to the bathroom to wash up and then to the kitchen to eat breakfast with mom. The radio would be on playing church music. Momma sang along, voice cracking and all.

"He's my rock, my sword and-" the rest of the words mumbled. I'd grab at pieces of sausage and bacon sitting on the platter. Mom would push eggs onto my plate and scrape the burnt part of toast into the garbage can before puttin butter on them and giving them to me on a napkin. She'd have on her nice clothes for what she called her 'temporary' job.

"Why you dress up for a temporary job mom?"

"Well, what do you think temporary means?"

"Temporary is not permanent."

"Well... That is right, that is right, very, very good. A temporary job is just what it sounds like."

"That mean it ain't-"

"Isn't."

"Isn't your job for good?" I'd spoon more eggs in my mouth.

"Don't talk with your mouth full."

"Yes mam."

"The job isn't mine yet," she smiled and winked at me. Kinda like Mr. Archie winked.

"Yet?"

"If you work hard, look nice and learn what you doing, you can get the job permanently."

"Really?"

"Calm down, calm down. Now I been at that temporary job for a long time now."

"Since I started fourth grade."

"That's right, almost three years now. They finally done opened the position and I may have a pretty good shot at the job. But all we can do is pray, don't go running off telling folks."

"I won't momma, I'll pray too. A permanent job, momma?"

"Yes son?"

"If you get a permanent job, can you start staying home in the evening?"

"Does that bother you?"

"Well, no. I... well, I guess I-"

"Come here boy." She'd hold her arms out for me to hug her. She then made me sit on her lap. I think I was too big for that but, "I'm sorry for not being around all the time. It's just that your momma trying to make due."

"Ol Man Fishstick said you do it so I can be betta."

"That's right. Mr. Archie tellin you the truth. I do it so we can be okay."

"I know. I jus miss you some nights."

"Aww baby I miss you too." Tears ran from her eyes and dropped on her shirt. she hugged me tighter and wiped her face, "Yo momma love you, you know that don't you?"

"Yeah I know mom. I'm sorry for making you cry."

"No sir, you take that back nah. You ain't making your momma cry, them tears come from the Lawd. Them tears let me know I got me a good son that care...Now get up an finish your breakfast."

"Love you too mom," I kissed her on the cheek.

Sometimes the sun is like a dream. Momma walked off into the sun when she left for work. She climbed into Mr. Travis's car. Mr. Travis waved and blew the horn as they pulled off. I got back to the kitchen and finished washing dishes. I ran the push broom over the carpet before I left for Mr. Archie's house.

Chapter 7

It wasn't even five minutes after momma left when Smoke and Skillet was knocking at the door.

"Let's go to Tiger's," said Skillet.

"Why? I gotta finish cleaning and then I was gon go by Ol Man Fishstick's."

"But you gotta go over. Everyone else is there already," said Smoke.

"I don't feel like walkin to the projects right now. It's too early."

"But we have to say bye. Wouldn't be right if they left an we all didn't say bye to Tiger," said Skillet.

"Bye? Who leaving?"

"Stop playin Buck and come on," Smoke grabbed me by the arm. I snatched away to close the door and lock it. It was 8:15 in the morning an we was running over to Sixth Street to Tiger's house cause he was leaving. I didn't feel so bad about him moving but if he was gonna leave the group then we had certain things that had to take place.

When we got there we saw a big Lincoln, with shiny bumpers and a sunroof, sittin outside. Ms. Eunice sat on the steps with a White man. She wadn't that Black, but it still look funny. They was holding hands and talking. Some men was taking furniture, the last of the little furniture Tiger them owned, outta the apartment.

"Morning Ms. Eunice-" we said.

"The rest of em round back with Junior."

"Yes Mam."

We took off an found the fellas in the back of the building with Tiger. Lizard, Man, Stack, and Tony was kneeling in the grass. The bikes was leaning against the brick wall. Stack had his knife out, standing over Tiger.

"Yaw'll know I don't wanna go." I could hear Tiger speaking. He sounded like he was crying some. He squatted and stabbed the dirt and grass with a stick. Kickin earth out like a shovel.

"Let's do it," said Stack. "Buck and them here now."

"Do what?" I asked.

"Make the oath. We ain't nevah don it before, we should've though," said Tony.

I knew what the oath was but I didn't think I was gon ever have to make it with anyone in our group. Wadn't nobody supposed to leave. We was supposed to grow up in North Memphis and then move out at the same time and go to a college. We was supposed to stay together.

"Hey Tiger, I'm sorry for fightin all the time witcha. I didn't mean nothin by it."

"I know," Tiger stood and walked to Lizard an gave him five. He looked at me and we got ready. I could hear his momma yelling from the other side of the apartment.

"Eddie Junior, almost time."

"Hurry up Stack," said Tiger.

Stack clicked the button on his switchblade. The blade shot out like a silver bottlerocket. In the grass between two brick red

44

apartments under the clotheslines, Stack cut his hand first. We could see the blood come out real slow when he held his hand up. Like a package of catsup being pushed. He went to Tiger next. He pushed the blade into his palm, just the tip, about an inch across. Then Lizard, then Smoke, Skillet, Tony, Man and then me. Everyone else stood still when he did it. They didn't flinch at all when they held they hands up and let the blood run out. I felt the heat of the blade touch my skin and I jumped. It sliced me from my second finger to the base. Not deep, but enough to get a good flow of blood before I held my hand up.

Stack reached over and shook hands with Tiger, Tiger to Lizard, same hand. Lizard to Smoke, to Skillet, Tony and Man. I stood holding my hand. The last one had to walk and touch everyone's blood. I stood in the middle of the circle and extended my hand. We then put our hands on top of each others. Stack said the oath.

"Earth, to grass, to trees, to leaves. Fall, to Winter, to Spring, to Summer, to Fall. When leaves fall down and we pass we'll remember each other."

"Eddie Junior."

"Yes Mam. I'm coming." He wiped his hands on his jeans and looked back at us before running around the corner. We all stood, feeling a little lost.

"So what happens now?" asked Man.

"We leave without saying bye. We go towards the sun," said Stack.

"Why?" asked Smoke.

"Cause the sun set. It always come back though. Tiger come back to us one day."

"Let's go," I said. They all walked and rode off. I stayed longer before I walked back towards the front. By the time I reached Tiger's door, I saw the moving truck pulling off. The top of Tiger's head was in the back window of the Lincoln. I thought he waved but I couldn't really tell, the sun made my eyes water.

Chapter 8

I started back home to finish my chores. I had to put up the push broom and check the rest of the house. Over the long block and a half walk I looked at the buildings and the folks sitting on the porches. Big black painted banisters, gray steps and red and brown bricks as far as I could see on the block. Old folks looked tired. Kids looked happy as they ran around before the noontime sun got too high. I made it up to Fifth Street and walked down til I got to the front of my four apartment building. I could see Ol Man Fishstick chasing Smoke and Stack. I ran down to catch up. When I balled my fist up to run I felt the cut break open again. I stopped running and turned back to go to the house. I figure I needed to clean it and put the red, gold stuff on it like momma did. I pulled my shoestring key from inside my shirt and opened the door.

Latching the screendoor shut I walked to the bathroom and ran water on the cut. It wasn't so bad. I put peroxide on it and watched the cut bubble up and tingle. I pulled out the brown bottle and read the label: Mercurochrome. Not thinking I pulled out the stick with the red, gold cotton at the tip and put a bunch of it on the cut. I must've did two backflips from the pain. It burned like hot chicken grease. I threw the stick and blew on the cut, like it would help. It wadn't on top of the skin, it was beneath. It felt like I put my hand in hot water and didn't move. I started crying. I turned on the faucet and put my hand underneath till it cooled off. I figured I had to put the stuff on, and cover it still. I waited for a few minutes and then put a little more and a little more on it. There was a knock at the door.

"Buck, you okay in there?"

"Yes sir." I ran to the door. Ol Man Fishstick stood behind the net screen lookin in, from side to side. I lifted the hook and opened the door. He took his hat off and walked in.

"Heard ya in here cussin and shoutin."

"I was that loud?"

"Yessuh, yessuh, damns, an hells, an all kinda words."

"I'm sorry sir."

"What was wrong boy?"

"Mercoorahcrome."

He laughed and looked me up and down. "Watcha hurt on yourself son?"

"Cut my hand."

"Lemme see." I held my hand out and took off the wrap. He nodded and grunted, shook his head and nodded and grunted again. "You boys sad huh?"

"Bout what?"

"Bout that Ed Junior."

"What about him Mr. Archie?"

"Come nah Buck, the cut on your hand only mean one thang. Its too clean a cut to be an accident. Sides we used to have bloodbrothers when I was coming up."

"Really?"

"Yeah but we did it for a much different reason. I'll tell ya about that one day. Right nah I kin tell ya don't feel so good."

"Yessuh. Wasn't nobody supposed to leave Mr. Archie."

48

"Nah Buck, folks leave all the time. That's what we do son. We born to make a mark, leave somethin here, an then we move on."

"But he didn't even know that White man. You even said White men evil."

"Some of em Buck. I said some of em."

"Then why slavery happen?"

"That's a big question, not easy to answer. If I told you that some people make themselfs bettah, cause they afraid to let thangs be, would that be a good answer?"

"No sir, cause everytime your stories come up they talk about the White folk bad."

"Well, I don't mean it that way. Some of em good, look at your wall. That man next to Dr. King was a good one."

"But he jus one man sir and folk at the school say they didn't have no slaves so it ain't they fault for slavery."

"In a garden some folk jus water they plants. Some folks talk to em. Feed em wit words an water. They both grow the same, but if you ask folks if they different... they say yes."

"Sir?"

"Everybody got a different view on thangs. Everybody got good points, you gotta make up your own as you git older. Right now you jus listen to me. All folks got bad in they roots. Some folks got more bad in the roots an that's what make em weak."

"Like when we stack the crates at your house?"

"Go head son."

"When we stack em like a pyramid they stay up longer."

"Um hun?"

"When we make tall buildings, strong wind make em fall cause they ain't wide at the bottom."

"Well, kinda but it's more like this here: Two big trees, one got termites on the inside. Nah termites eat away at the inside. They don't kill the tree where you can see it. They kills the soul of the tree. While the outside of dem two trees look the same, one of em is weak. That's how all folks is. Black, White, Purple, don't matter, all folks got trees wit termites."

"White folks jus got more."

"I didn't say that son. Listen here...you got somethin for me to drink?"

"Lemonade, Orange Juice and water."

"Lemonade be fine."

"I bring it right back, you can talk. I can hear from the kitchen."

"In some folks eyes there a gleam, a life, you here me?"

"Yes sir."

"Life...Boy named John Jenkins use to live down the street here on Fifth. Long, thick chested boy, dark brown like ripe bananas. Had hair like a sponge big an round, afro style. This wadn't long off nah. Maybe four, five years ago. Early seventies. Boy loved to play ball. Be on the court in the morning fore school and after school til street lights come on. Handsome boy wit a big smile and little, new moustache growing in. Cheeks was like high walls, make him look Indian almost. Boy could dribble tween his legs, on the move, an standing still. Sad thang is, boy couldn't read none. Read like he was in the third grade he did. But he was fixin to get promoted out of school. He'd spent seven school years playing ball and hadn't learned nothin. Folks even said he had colleges knocking at his door."

"Sir I done heard this before. He didn't make it to college. He probably on dope now."

"Tut, Tut, Buck. Hush up nah. I tol ya bout listenin, jus hush up... John stop playing ball one mornin. I was able to see him from my stoop. Sometime I walk by an watch him. Like lookin at fast cars, an big cars that jus float across streets. Sometime I sat an clap for him. I saw him sittin at the park early on a school Wednesday. Dark mornin light framin his big shoulders. He spoke pretty good for not readin well. I ask him why he wadn't shootin.

"Sir, I ain't got no reason to play no more. Us folks in North Memphis don't go to college. I can't go to college. No reason to play no more sir."

"Jenkins, God give us gifts. God give us talents-"

"Mr. Archie, all due respect sir, don't feel much like a story right now."

"Jus lemme finish son. This ain't no story, jus gotta tell ya somethin and I make it on my way."

"Yes sir."

"God give us thangs that make our life turn out bettah. When we don't use em, we turn out for the worse. I wantcha to think on that. God give ya somthin to gitcha outta here. Do right by God son."

I walked off from John Jenkins bout ten feet, cross the grass an headed past the community center. I heard his steps behind me.

"Mr. Archie...Mr. Archie, I'm scared of failing Mr. Archie. God give me talent but no brain sir. What I'm gon do without brains sir. Can't do nothin but work construction or garbage with this body."

"You do whatcha wanna do. God give you a brain."

"I..can't-"

"Read?" The boy look at me hard when I say that. Questionin eyes.

"Right sir. I can't read. They give me grades cause I can play, cause I win for the school."

I put my arm round his shoulder an walk with him. He couldn't stop sayin what he couldn't do.

"I try an read but the words get all mixed up. I can spell but when I spell, the words don't look right. My eyes put em down the wrong way sir. And I jus can't do it right."

"Son what's your name?"

"Sir, I can spell my name fine," he snatched away from me. " I ain't no fool."

"Not sayin you a fool. Jus sayin you can spell."

"Your name easy though."

"Your name jus a word you done heard more than others. You say you can't read, but you didn't say you can't spell."

"I spell okay, it's jus when I write an read. The words jus don't look right."

"You talk to a teacher bout it."

"They don't wanna hear it, them White teachers don't expect much out of us colored boys anyhow, cept Ms... They don't care."

"Who ya bout to speak of? Go head an say it."

"I don't take her class but they say she care bout colored boy's learnin."

"What her name is son?"

"Ms. Newsome, Ms. Newsome sir."

"Let's say ya ask her to hep ya in the morning's before school?"

"It's too late sir I be finished this year. I can't learn to read in a year."

"Son, you said ya spell purty good. Sound to me like you jus ain't concentratin. Think of them words like you think of the court?"

"Don't quite get you sir?"

"When you play other teams don't you know them jerseys?"

"Why yessuh I read em, the names: Hawks, Eagles, Apaches, Wildcats, Tigers, read em jus fine I do."

"Cause you focusin then. You wanna know them, an they names."

"But I know they names cause we play em all the time. I know cause of they mascots."

"I wantcha to start goin to Ms. Newsome an askin for mornin help. You play good cause ya worked at it. Every mornin an night. Nah work at dem books the same."

"I can't do that sir."

"I wantcha to promise somethin."

"Yes sir?"

"You do it for two months, same as you practice ball."

"But season start in two and a half?"

"You still be able to play. Ol Man Archie jus wantcha to do this for him and ya momma. Okay?"

"I try Mr. Archie. I try."

"Nah Buck you listen to me, that boy studied like he studied ball, for two months. That teacher work wit him in the morning an afternoon. Help him learn how to focus in. She find that he had a learning problem an found a way for him to read. Tol him to put a piece of paper underneath each line he was readin. That way he could only see a little by a little. In two months he was readin bigger books an doin his test insteada jus takin grades."

"Mr. Archie, I made myself a D+ all on my own in a English class. Yes sir I did, even took my own math test. But coach say I ain't gon have good enough grades to go to college."

"John you gon be alright, jus keep goin to them sessions in the mornin. You can practice ball in the afternoon right?"

"Yes sir, but what if I don't make gooder, I'm sorry, better grades?"

"Can them Westside Wildcats stop you on the court?"

"No sir, they can't."

"Then how you gon let words stop ya? They jus words."

"Just words."

"Jus keep workin at it."

"I will."

"Nah that boy kept goin to them classes in the mornin an kept playin ball. He even scored sixty three points in one game an seventy eight on one of them math tests of his."

"Mr. Archie, I made a positive or plus fifteen more on my math test, than I did in my ball game. That's the first time that happened. And momma even came to the game. She met Ms. Newsome and cried when she saw her. Ms Newsome cried too. She stayed with my momma until I come out the team room. They both was cryin. She told my momma that I was a lot smarter than folks thought. She even said I could make it in college. My momma yelled Glooreee! and waved her hands. Ms. Newsome laughed an smiled. My coach even done, I'm sorry. My coach even said he was proud of me. I ain't never had no White coach say he proud unless I scored a bucket to win a game. You was right Mr. Archie you was right."

"Bout what son?"

"There ain't no can'ts as long as you try hard."

"You thank that teacher for me too nah son."

"Yes sir. I'll keep workin hard an studying. Make you proud of me too."

"I been proud of you boy, make yourself proud nah."

"So the White coach was proud of him and he went to college?"

"Yeah he went to college but he didn't stay long. He stayed for two years and change his name."

"Why go to college for two years?"

"Cause he play pro ball nah. That's right started playin for the Colonels in Kentucky. Doin purty good."

"But Mr. Archie I don't get what this have to do with White folk. His coach didn't seem to help him at all."

"But his teacher did. You know what color she was Buck?"

"White?"

Ol Man Fishstick clicked his mouth and winked his eye.

"Some folk do right by they skin, some folk do wrong. We all got good an bad in us, jus a matter of choices."

"I still don't think White folk like us much."

"Boy why you got so much meanness in ya? Ya momma didn't teach ya that, I ain't teach ya that."

"Momma said sometimes, every now an then that-"

"Come on nah, talk Buck."

"She say that if White folk hadn't sent my daddy to Vietnam he still be alive. She said it was a White man war against yellow folk that we ain't have nothin to do with. So White men killed my daddy."

Archie sat with a look on his lips, in his eyes and face. I didn't really know what I was sayin. I was jus repeating.

"Your momma a good woman, strong woman. It's a hard world out here an she doin a mighty fine job witcha. She got every right to be mad. This place, neighborhood use ta be full of men. Strong men lookin for work. Men tryin to provide. Seekin work where they could. Lookin to be valuable to they families. Lookin to be equal."

He sat starin forward like he had a lot on his mind. He inhaled deep. His chest filled up and then went down. He shifted.

56

"Yeah Buck, use to be a lot of men in this here area, but nah all you see is mommas raisin sons and lil girls."

"Why they send my daddy though?"

"Buck some of us Black men believed in a greater good. We thought folk would accept us."

"Accept what?"

"I know you didn't know ya daddy, but he was a fine man. Work on cars and anythang that was broke. Could fix anythang I tell you. Was good with them hands, he was." Archie looked down at his hands and was smilin at them.

"Use ta come by an help me git stuff for my yard when I was growin greens and onions. Had don made hisself a mini shovel and hoe outta one piece a wood. He'd flip that lil thang around and dig up onion roots and throw bulbs in the empty ground. He even made a four wheel cart to carry the vegetables to the market wit."

"Nothin special about a four-wheelbarrow."

"Ha, ha, you don't say? How bout a four wheel cart with icebox on top to cool food from wilting in the heat?"

"My daddy did that?"

"Yessuh. Thang was, anythang he did he wanted respect for doing it. Not jus Black respect but White folk to. So he'd show White folk his inventions. They either paid him little bit a nothin for em, or told him they don already thought it up. Which they hadn't. But ya daddy was determined to be equal. He was his own civil right march right here in North Memphis."

"What he do though? I mean why he leave?"

"Well, ya daddy knew the service was draftin for that war overseas. He figure if he fight wit White folk they wouldn't do nothin but respect em. I tol him different. I tol em:

"Nah V I don seen it before. Even did a lil bit a time myself, but ain't nothin change."

"Aww nah Mr. Archie, gon on nah. If a man gon be a man, he got to serve his country. That's the only way I take care of my wife an my boy."

"You doin a good job as it is V. Jus accept that ya doin the best you can. Stop demanding respect from folk that don't give a damn bout ya."

"Mr. Archie, sometime ya gotta do what you feel is right. You gotta dance sometime to take away the pain. You gotta try."

"What about ya Misses? Huh son? Ya leave her in this place wit a boy ta raise on her own? Nah I don't like to think like this, but what if ya die over yonder?"

"If I die, it'll be with respect."

"Goddangit son, listen at yoself, jus listen. You care mo bout your pride than ya lil boy. Goddangit son."

"Mr. Archie believe me, I hear you. I just can't live like this. I feel like half a man. We ain't winnin no wars here. Folks jus keep dyin and hangin and runnin. I ain't runnin or hangin, I'm gon get my respect."

"Listen, we signed up to fight in the World War for the same reason, same reason. When we got back, what we get? Nothin, not a thing. Mo heartache than before I tell ya."

"How so? Didn't folk start civil right marchin after the second World War? It made a difference."

"V dammit, we makin changes nah. We makin changes. They slow but they comin Dr. King-"

"Dr. King a puppet, he don't want no quick change."

"Please son, be sensible bout this. Look round about ya. You see the men round here? We jus shells. We ol, an hurt, one gen'ration removed from slaves, but we still here. Problem is we ain't strong as we use ta be. We need you young men here."

"But we ain't got nothin to show for livin, sir. Jus pregnant wives, run down houses, tired backs, an spare change. We ain't got nothin. An I feels that change comin too slow."

"But it's comin son. Hear me nah."

"I hear you, but listening a different story."

"Victor it ain't no justice out here for us other than how Dr. King doin thangs. He even here for the garbage strike."

"But we still ain't gettin no respect sir. Anyways... sir... it's too late."

"Nevah too late boy, ain't nevah too late."

"I already done signed up, be leavin in a week. Got my orders to head out an all."

"Son, why you go an do that?"

"Jus didn't see no other way. Got my checks to come to Diane. She get my money an insurance if I die."

"You tell her yet?"

"No sir."

"Son-"

"Dammit Mr. Archie what I supposed to say? What I supposed to say to her?"

He start cryin knowin that what he don wadn't right, but for him it was necessary. He ain't think he could do anythang else an maybe he was right, maybe he was wrong, but it was his decision. He found hisself even more certain when the week he was leavin Dr. King got hisself killed downtown.

"Ain't no justice for us Mr. Archie, like I said."

I couldn't speak on it at all. My beacon had don burnt out wit that bullet at the Lorraine. What words could I give him when my faith was gon?

"What ya gotta say Mr. Archie? I need some words Mr. Archie." He touched me several times before he see the tears in my eyes. I wadn't spose to see Dr. King die. Here I was don live through all these thangs. Fifty-nine years ol seein a thirty-nine year ol man lose his life for us Black folk. Wadn't right. No suh, wadn't right at all.

An I ain't have nothin ta say to your daddy. No words seemed fit to change his mind, cause mine had don changed.

"Mr. Archie we be alright, like you said. We be alright."

"Who left son? We ain't got nobody, we jus a doomed people."

"No suh we ain't. This ain't like you sir. Ain't like you at all."

"I'm sorry son... ain't in my right mind... When ya leavin?"

"Tomorrow. Done talked about it wit Diane for the last few days. She done got most of her cryin out, me too. She feel like I didn't ask her the right way."

"You didn't son. Husband an wife gotta talk bout thangs. That way they share, an know where they stand. You get on back down to ya wife; an boy, love em to death tonight, hold em an love em."

"Thank you Mr. Archie. I'll never forget you, I'll be back though you jus be waitin."

"I be waitin for ya son, you make em respect ya. Find they weak spots an make em your focus. You be a man nah, whole man like ya wanted."

"Your daddy walked on cross the park an Spring felt like Fall. Cause everythang had changed, not for life, but for death. Death, an dyin, like leaves on grass, an our Black Jesus had don got crucified an lef us in the wilderness. Young fella, ya daddy chose to go to that war but he had good honor. He had a good idea. He died over yonder wit respect an sent it back here to you. He inside ya right here."

Mr. Archie touched me on my chest and then my head.

"You get that meanness out ya soul cause it'll kill ya and scare your daddy off. It'll hurt ya momma, an you."

"My daddy was a hero?"

"Yessuh, he was a hero, jus like Dr. King. The bad thang is, when they died, us Black folk ain't been right since."

"Sir?"

"Ya finish ya housework?"

"Yes sir."

"Let's get on outta here. Too heavy in this here house, gotta get us some eats an a coke cola. We walk on over to the store. That hand of yours okay?"

"It's fine, it wasn't that bad."

"Look bad to me."

"I'm okay."

Chapter 9

As we made our way out the door, the sun had made it high over the street. Not much shade from the trees or buildings when the sun that high. Ol Man Fishstick had put his hat back on and was rubbing his head with his kerchief. He was walking and looking up and down the block. I walked beside him. I had my coverall's on today. He always had his on. I fixed my pantslegs so they'd hang on the back of my shoe like Mr. Archie's. His was like strings by the heel of his boot. But the cloth was strong and heavy. Mine's was light and didn't feel that strong but they was still coveralls. I had on me a light brown shirt. Ol man Archie always had on a clean white shirt. it was like he thousands of em. They hung on his clothes line in the back of his house, about three of them. He must've had four cause it was always three of them back there hanging up. We walked up the hill of the projects cross the street from my house.

The hill was pretty high, you could ride your bike down it real fast but you had to be careful cause cars would drive by the street below. The project buildings was on the side of the hill and there was a big lot in the middle with parking spaces. The buildings made shade on the lot in the morning and afternoon, but not at noonday. It was hot. About six little kids was playing basketball on a crate they had hung on the electric pole. Sweeping they legs across the concrete, jumping high like shirtless tar with short pants. They was laughing loud and taking turns going to the candylady. We walked down the drive ramp at the back of the projects and started down Chelsea. There was some old houses and empty land by a cleaners across the street.

Beside us there was a chicken wire fence where a bunch of old cars got worked on. There was always two big Doberman Pincher dogs inside, barking. Ol Man Fishstick had his cane and clutched it tight as we walked by.

"I declare if them dogs ever get out, I beat the hell out of em fore they bite either of us. You get on this side a me." He'd move me to his right and put his hand on my shoulder.

"Why you carry that cane?"

"Cause."

"Cause what?"

"Cause a boys like you that ask too many questions." He grabbed me and started trying to poke me in my stomach. I laughed and pulled away.

"Well Buck, I carry this for my balance sometime, an for protection. Jus depend on which I need it for."

"Protection? Wouldn't nobody hurt you."

"Yeah an I'm gon keep it that way." He smiled at me, clicked and winked his eye.

"Don't cut up in this here store."

"No sir, I know better. Momma kill me if she find out I acted a fool in the store. Besides Mr. Travis work in there."

"That's right, that sho is right. So you think ya momma like that Mr. Travis?"

"Yes sir. He come over for supper sometime an stay late-"

"Buck."

"Okay sorry. I think he like her."

"You thank he give us some free goodies?"

64

"Mr. Archie?"

"Jus messin witcha, but it be nice wouldn't it. Nothin wrong wit free stuff."

"Thought you said ain't nothin free?"

"It ain't, but sho is nice when you get some stuff." He clicked and winked again. "Anyways, I got nough money for me you an the rest of them knuckleheads that's been sneakin up on us." He turned around and moved quickly to the wall beside the car lot fence. Man, Lizard and Tony ran around the corner yellin.

"Hey yaw'll what's happenin?"

Mr. Archie stopped chasin so they could answer. He bent over an leaned on his stick a little.

"Need this cane for restin some to Buck."

"We been followin yaw'll since the hill," said Ton.

"That's right seen ya hidin in them steps when we got by the fence." Ol Man Fishstick took his hat off an wiped his head. "I take it you boys ain't scared a me much no mo?"

"No suh, jus make you feel like ya tough. That's why we run," said Man. Man seemed like he was filling in for Tiger. Almost sounded like him. He was right, we wasn't afraid at all, jus knew we was supposed to run. Everybody knew they was supposed to run. Even momma had told me about running from the neighborhood Ol Man. I guess it was tradition. Somebody always kept the kids in line when the parents wasn't around. If it wasn't the folks next door, or down the street it was Ol Man Fishstick for us. I guess it was Ol Man Archie's dad for mom them. I guess.

"I figure you boys wanna go in wit us?"

"Yessuh," they all said.

"Alright then don't be raisin Cain up in there nah."

"We stay right wit you sir," said Lizard. His hand was still wrapped like mine was. Man and Lil T didn't have wraps. They had little band aids on. When we walked in, the cool air rushed out the door and we all took off. So much for staying together.

"Afternoon there Mr. Archie," said Mr. Travis. I stopped running instantly. If he saw me running he would've for sure told mom.

"Hey there Paul. How ya doin on this hot day?" asked Mr. Archie.

"Pretty good, it's fine in here. I ain't got to go out and do much out back."

"Paul, how ya wife doin?"

"I ain't got no wife Mr. Archie, you know that. But I'm working on it, yes indeed."

"So who the lucky lady?"

"Keepin that a secret Mr. Archie. You know, wouldn't want folks talking."

"Is that right? Yaw'll boys got whatcha want?"

"Almost," I shouted back to the front counter.

"That's Buck back there, he the ringleader of that there group purty much. Cept when that heavy boy Stack around."

"That so?"

"Yessuh. Good boy too. Love him like he my own I do."

"That so?"

"Umm Humm. Momma a good lady too. Hard workin lady, good woman."

"That right?"

"Yeah, that's right."

I was standing behind the chips at the front of the store listenin to Mr. Archie. I couldn't really understand what he was doing. I had already told him that Mr. Travis like momma.

"She mighty fine woman. Be a doggone shame somebody hurt her. I find a way to hurt them purty bad if that happened," Archie said picking dirt out of his fingernails and lookin up from under his brow. "Yep, I sho would hurt somebody that do that."

"Well, Mr. Archie I would never do that to anybody, especially Diane. I heard she a damn good woman too. Matter of fact someone told me I should buy her a ring for all that hard work she do."

"That so?"

"That's right, look like this one right here." Mr. Travis pulled a ring from behind the counter from inside his briefcase. I tried to look at what it was. Ol Man Fishstick looked at it hard, cleared his throat and straightened out his shirt. Almost like Ms. P was coming.

"That ain't half bad there for a woman of Diane class. Not half bad at all."

"Well it seem to me it's damn good, pardon my French sir. But this here ring and money ain't the issue. I like the boy, I love her. She make me feel good about myself. I just feel like it's timeout for hidin."

"Jus you do right by Buck an his momma." Mr. Archie extended his hand. Mr. Travis smiled and they shook.

"Thank you for your blessings sir."

"Not blessings, jus takin care of some unfinished business someone asked me to help wit a few years ago."

The guys ran up to the counter, shouting and throwing candy and cookies across the slick top.

"I know that ain't all candy I see?" said Mr. Archie. The guys started taking off all the candy. I brought up a soda, and chips. Ol Man Fishstick patted me on the head. The fellas looked to see what I got and they brought up the same kind of stuff.

"Is that gonna be all gentleman?" asked *Paul.*

"Yeah that's about it sir," I said. He grinned at me and pushed all of the stuff to the front of the counter.

"Yaw'll boys go head on, I'll take care of it all."

"Thank you sir," we all said and walked out of the store. I stopped at the door and looked back at Mr. Travis. He looked me in the face, his eyes twinkled in the store light. He smiled. Ol Man Archie laughed. Mr. Travis put his hand on the counter as he chuckled a bit. Mr. Archie extended his hand again before leaving the store. By the time he walked out the guys had already disappeared.

"Where them other ones at?"

"They gone off already."

"An no thank yous?"

"Well I guess cause you didn't pay they figure they could jus leave."

"Why you ain't go to play wit em?"

"Cause me an you have to talk."

"Oh, is that so son?"

68

"Yes sir. Gotta ask you a few thangs."

"Is that right?"

"Yes sir. First I gotta ask what you two was speakin on when you was at the counter, and what was that thing in the box?" Ol Man Fishstick stopped walking. He stood next to the gate. The Doberman's ran up and started barking. He walked a bit further for the silence I guess.

"You got a good hold on your coke cola?"

"This orange soda, but yes sir."

"You got a good hold on your chips?"

"Yes sir."

He pulled his hat off and creased it in his right hand. He shook it out a bit and looked it over once, then again. Then his hand went up quick, an the hat dropped down on my head like a flyswat.

"Oww."

"Next time you see or hear grown folks talkin, you mind ya own nah. You got anymo questions?"

"No sir," I rubbed my head with the soda. It was cool against the roundness of my forehead which stung from the hit and the heat. He chuckled and put his hat back on.

"That Paul Travis a good man, remind me of a handyman I use ta know. Yep sho do."

We walked on towards his house. We went back through the little projects and saw the same kids playing ball. Some of the older folks was on they porch. Mr. Tucker sat on his porch in a t-shirt and some tight blue shorts. He had a can with a blue ribbon on it in one hand and a rag in the other drinking and sweating.

"Ol fool gon pass out drankin that beer in this heat... Hey nah Tuck," Archie waved. "That's one ol nut there Buck, jus as crazy as, nevermind."

"Hey there Archie. Hi ya been?"

"Purty good, yasself?"

"Holdin on, Lawd blessin me at de dawg track in Arkansaw."

Under his breath to me Archie said, "Lawd don't tell ya to gamble do he?"

"That's mighty fine Tuck, you keep on winnin nah."

"God willin."

"He willin an," Archie cut himself off an said again under his breath, "Aww forget it."

"You take care Tuck," Mr. Archie waved again. We walked down the hill an back up Fifth Street.

"Why you talk under your breath at Mr. Tucker?"

"Some folks ain't worth the loudness of your breath. Sides he jus spoke cause he feel important."

"Yeah huh?"

He popped me with the hat again.

"What you do that for?"

"Cause I kin talk about em, you can't. You still a child an ain't no child's place to speak on a adult."

"Yes sir. I can't wait to grow up, there too many rules you gotta keep straight when you young."

"Don't rush it Buck, you be there fore ya know it."

We continued through the park. The field was pretty clear. Guys was at the court playing ball an drinking.

"They stupid too for drinking huh?"

"Yep sho is. Bout dum as a cat on a flea farm."

" A cat on a flea farm?"

"Cat...fleas? Cat on a flea far...forget it Buck."

"Gotcha Mr. Archie." We laughed. I kept lookin at the guys on the court. I didn't even notice Ol Man Archie pull his hat off and start fixin his hair. I felt him bump me when he started walking though. I looked down to the house and,

"Why hello Ms. P."

"Hello Mr. Archie."

"Hello Ms. Phillips." I said.

I felt Mr. Archie nudge me, so I shut up talking. I knew he was about to flirt some so I just let him do it. I walked on into the fence and grabbed me a crate. They stood at the gate talkin for a few seconds. It was the first time Ms. P didn't have on a dress. She had a pair of working pants, heavy blue. They was pulled up on her stomach real high. Her shirt was light blue and was tucked in an buttoned almost to the last button. Her skin was brown like dark rust on water pipes when all the orange dust been wiped off. She had two long braids, one on each side of her head hanging from beneath her straw hat. She had a basket on her arm. Her shirt sleeves was rolled up to the elbow. In her basket she had scissors, a little claw tool for dirt, a rag and a watering pail with a long spout. Mr. Archie had his hands crossed and was leaning on the fence. His legs was crossed and he rubbed the tip of his shoe on his pants and they looked cleaner.

"Wadn't expectin you to come by today."

"I wasn't expecting to come by, I guess the spirit moved me to come and help you with your yard. And seein how I ain't doing anything, anyhow, it seemed like the neighborly thang to do."

"Well it is quite neighborly of ya and I really do appreciate it." He leaned his stick against the fence and held the gate open for Ms. P. She nodded and walked in.

"I'll go out back an get the walking lawn trimmer."

"That be fine Buck," he threw me his keys. I pulled the screen door open and turned the lock twice before the door opened. I didn't close the door though. I stood behind the screen and looked out.

"Been walking this morning?"

"Yes mam, trying to keep my weight down."

"Lookin pretty good to me," she patted Mr. Archie on his arm muscle.

"Aww quit nah Patty, you make a ol man lose his senses bout hisself."

"Well, it's true."

"You betta stop nah."

I sneezed, must've been dust on the screen door. I knew Mr. Archie knew I was still there cause he stopped talking and cleared his throat.

"I guess we better get in the back an clean up that garden area."

"I reckon so," she said.

They started walking towards the door. I took off through the house, to the kitchen and out the back door. I grabbed the mower and acted like I was trying to start it. Ms. P walked out as Archie held the door.

72

"I been tryin to get this thang started Mr. Archie." I snatched on the cord a couple of more times.

"If you started when I give you them keys, it be running by nah."

"Archie."

"Awww Ms. Mam I'm jus playin wit Buck." He stared at me from under his brow.

"Get that there gas tank an pour some gas in it. Then try it couple mo times."

"Yes sir."

"Archie I'll get started on picking these lil weeds out your garden. Garden lookin a lil smaller than usual? It ain't big as it been?"

"Naw, not much reason to keep pushin myself to turn a profit. I'm purty well off nah."

"Well, just figured you'd still grow them good collard greens."

"I plant a batch for you next time if you like."

"You don't have to go out your way for-"

"Oh wouldn't be no trouble mam, no trouble at all. What else would you like?"

It was horrible all the kissing up Mr. Archie was doing. He had told me, when I thought I liked Lil Liz Mumford from on Sixth Street that:

"Ya ignore em. Show a lil bit of attention, then jus stop."

"But ain't that gonna make her mad at me?"

"No suh. She start wonderin what she doin wrong an then she start askin folks bout ya."

"What if she start likin somebody else?"

"If you act sweet on her an then stop, she'll think bout ya all the time. Trust me son."

"If you say so, I'll listen."

So I listened and did what he tell me to do. I ask my momma if he was right an she said,

"Baby, if Mr. Archie say that's what you do then do it. If it don't work that way, you come back and ask ya momma how to get that Lil Ms. Mumford."

"I'll take some advice now if you don't mind?"

"I thought boys your age didn't like girls?"

"I don't, I jus thank-"

"You just think?"

"Sorry mam, I just think she a nice person is all." I hate when people corrected me but momma,was…well momma.

"Jus listen to Ol Man Fishstick and then come and talk to me and let me know how it goes."

I tried the Ol Man Fishstick way. I should've known a Ol Man name *Fishstick* wouldn't know nothing. It didn't work. She stop talking to me altogether when I start ignoring her. She started liking this fat light skinned kid who gave her half of his Kit Kat's. I figured on asking mom about that kind of stuff next time.

Now here I was with Mr. Archie cuttin grass while he was trying to get him a girlfriend. He wasn't doing nothing he told me to do. He was being real nice and wasn't ignoring Ms. P at all. He even offered to make more greens in his garden for her. I pushed the lawnmower hard over the back grass, missing spots and hitting twigs.

"Buck you be careful with that machine."

"Yes mam."

"Yeah Buck you cuttin like a wild man."

"Yes sir." A 'wild man' alright. I wasn't wild he was just trying to impress Ms. P by making her laugh. She giggled a lil bit an started talking.

"Buck I hear Lil Liz, stay across the block from me done take a likin to someone round here? You know anything about that?"

"No mam, ain't heard nothing of the like. I don't even like girls."

"Umph. That's terrible, she sho is a pretty lil thang. She come over to the house an help me with a little house work. I seen her lunch pail once." She stopped and pulled a string a weeds from the left end of the garden. Ol Man Fishstick's backyard was pretty big and it use to be almost all garden. He had start relaxing a lot more in the last couple of years. He'd put out some grass seeds and grew grass in most of it now. The honeysuckles had always been on the fence like a second wall. There was two big trees at the back that always had empty locust shells stuck to it. On the other side of the fence was some more houses that led to Scuttlefield side, but we didn't much walk over there it was too rough. I liked his backyard, specially cause I didn't have one of my own. Ms. P was still pulling out the last of the weeds when she took out her little claw and start pulling at the muddy soil.

"Yep she pretty. I looked in her lunch pail and she had a buncha papers in it... Archie, she had little hearts with arrows and stick men and women holding hands."

"Is that right? What name she have on them papers I wonder?"

"Start with a B," she said. I pretended not to hear. I kept cutting the grass. I moved the choke up on the mower so it would get louder.

"I think that's a good job there Buck," said Mr. Archie. "Lemme rake up that grass. You go get some of dem bags from the kitchen an bring em out."

He took the rake and started grabbin grass with the rake, and his hand. He threw the bags to the side. I walked them to the front as he finished bagging. After he gave me the last two, he told me to go sit next to Ms. P. on the back porch.

"So you don't have no idea who the hearts was for?" she asked.

"No mam." I turned dirt with a stick.

"Lemme see, she tell me she like this boy. He used to be real sweet on her, then he stop. So she thought he didn't like her. Broke her lil heart it did. Said she didn't wanna go to lunch no more. Said she started hanging with the lil heavyset child that breathe real hard."

"She said she like," I stopped myself. "Do she like the boy with the B name?"

"She sho do. Write his name on scratch paper all the time."

I looked at Mr. Archie. He winked, clicked and nodded at me, "Now listen here Buck, that lil girl don had a crush on you for a long time. But yaw'll jus chil'ren. Don't be round here hidin and kissin and stuff. You treat her like a lil lady. Take her for some candy, an malts."

"Malts?" I asked.

"They don't drink malts no more Archie." Ms. P pulled two dollars from her pocket and gave them to me. "I reckon she over at the community center right now."

"Yes mam." I took the money and jumped up. Mr. Archie cleared his throat and looked on me. I stopped and walked back, "Thank you for the money mam." I hugged her neck and she laughed at me. Mr. Archie nodded again.

"You be careful nah an treat her like ya would your momma, R-"

"E-S-P-E-C-T, yes sir," I finished spelling. I ran through the house and out the front door. As I made my way over to the park. I ran up on the fellas. They were all standing in front of the gym doors. Before they had a chance to see me, I turned and walked to the back of the gym. I ran around the side so I could get inside quicker. What would the guys think if they saw me with Liz? I thought about going back to Mr. Archie's place, but I couldn't do that without giving the money back. I could've hung out with the guy's but then I would be lying to Mr. Archie and Ms. P. I stood outside the gym door in the back leaning against the chipped paint and I picked at flakes of hanging dark blue. Thumping them out into the grass I thought for a minute. Then I heard Tony and Lizard talking, coming around the corner. I ran down to the next door where there was almost a hiding space that sat back far enough that you could see but not be seen. The door in that space was never opened, but it would give me a few seconds. I still needed some thinking time. I stayed there for a minute. Then I heard Stack, Smoke and Skillet. I stayed there for three minutes. I heard Man calling at the others. I stayed another five minutes, my legs began to hurt, but I had to stand. If I sat down, they'd see my feet. I could hear them talking about what they were gonna do. And then I heard one of them mention my name.

"Anybody seen Buck?" asked Stack.

"Not since this mornin. He wit Ol Man Fishstick still I bet." said Lizard.

"Yeah Ol Man Fishstick bought us goodies-" said Man.

"Nuh un, Mr. Travis bought us that stuff, I think he like Buck momma," said Ton. "He always pick her up from work an drop her off. My momma say that he like her a lot."

"You think?" I heard Stack say. "I think Mr. Travis jus like any other man. They see a lonely woman an want em for a minute an leave. Least that what my momma say. Look, ain't no other men round here wit our momma's. Cept for the twins."

"We ain't twins," said Smoke.

"Yaw'll Black the same," said Stack.

"You fat the same," said Skillet. They all said, "Oooh," and laughed.

I couldn't stop thinking about what Stack said. Maybe Mr. Travis was gonna use my momma. Why would he be interested in a lady with a kid. Stack right, ain't no men out there lookin at any of the other mommas with kids. They usually chasing around the young ladies with no babies. I got mad. I wanted to go to the store and ask *Paul*. But I knew better than getting involved in grown folk stuff. Mr. Archie had told me that grown folk thangs is grown folks thangs. But I had to do something. Stack kept talking.

78

"Buck oughta make himself act bad so that Mr. Travis leave his momma alone."

"You don't know what you sayin Stack." said Man. "Some men like women wit kids. I'm glad Buck ain't around to hear all this stuff."

"Man, shut up. You don't know nothin bout mackin," said Stack.

"You don't neither," Man said.

"My uncle look at that movie, The Mack. He say a man ain't got but one use for a woman."

"Stack, yo uncle got one leg an he smell funny. What he know bout women?" asked Lizard.

"My uncle was in the war, he know a lot."

"Awwww," they all said.

I stopped feeling so bad about what Stack was saying. But what if Mr. Travis was just getting what he wanted from my momma. I wanted to walk from around the corner but I didn't. I felt like I couldn't let them know I heard them talking.

"Let's go find Buck," said Man.

"Yeah so Stack can stop talkin stupid bout his momma," said Smoke. His brother gave him five and said, "Right on."

Stack said, as they walked off to the end of the building, "I'm jus sayin is all, ain't none of our daddies that lef come back cept Tiger's, an his dad White. I know for sure ain't no man gon really like a lady wit a boy."

"Stack count to twenty, oops forgot you can't even get outta the seventh grade," said Man. I could see Stack push Man. They all busted up and walked around the corner. I was still behind the wall after fifteen minutes or so. My feet hurt bad and my head hurt.

I heard girls giggling and talking. I looked around again, my feet showing past the wall. I could see Liz with Big Foot Ann, and Rabbit. Rabbit name was Rabbit cause her teeth was big and she could run real fast. Liz was prettier than all of them. They talked loud and sang, "Somebody like Huck a Buck, somebody like Huck a Buck." Liz slapped at them and told them to shut up.

"Yaw'll jus mad cause ain't nobody likin yaw'll," she said.

Rabbit stopped singing, "Buck don't even talk to you no more. You said it yourself."

Liz looked at her and her smile left her face. She was like one of them women Ol Man Archie talk of. Her skin like brown sugar, or something Mr. Archie would've said. She was lighter than me but she wadn't a redbone. Her hair was pulled back with one of those half circle things that hold your hair in place. It made her forehead look big but her eyes filled up her face and they was pretty brown, like light...brown? Anyway, she had on some patchmade jeans and jelly shoes. Her t-shirt had a smiley face on it.

She looked sad when Rabbit said that. Big Foot Ann told Rabbit, "You mean sometimes."

"I ain't mean, I jus tellin the truth is all. What?"

"I didn't say I like him anyway. Yaw'll the ones that say that."

"Well you always talkin bout him when you see Stack an them," said Rabbit. "Jus tell the truth you like him."

80

"No I don't. I don't even like no boys." I could see her cross her arms. I tried to make up my mind if I should come out. I wasn't gonna stand there for another hour.

"Forget boys. Let's make a vow," said Big Foot. Of course she wanted to make a vow. I already knew what she was gonna say. "I say we forget boys an be strong impotent women. That's what my momma say to my daddy. She say she wanna be mo impotent."

"Important?" asked Liz. "Like have more folks listening to her, important?"

"Naw, you know what I'm sayin. Like livin without having to need nobody. My daddy always tell her to go on, but she jus stop talkin an tell him again that he bettah start actin right, cause she do bad all on her own. She can make it impotent."

"Independent's the word. Independent's the word, dang Ann, you need to start doing your vocabulary readin," said Rabbit.

"That's a big word though," said Liz.

"Yeah, it is a big word Rabbit."

"Anyway, what is this vow you speakin of?"

"We in junior high school startin this fall right? I say we be like my momma an be more in-de-pen-dent."

"And?" asked Liz.

"We don't let no boys talk to us."

"I agree with that," said Rabbit. Liz just looked on and put her hands in her pocket.

"Liz he jus gon play with Stack an them. He ain't gon start talking to you."

"Maybe you right. Alright I'm in." They all put they hands together and said, "VOW!"

I thought that now would be a good time to come out an say something. But if they knew I was hiding out and listening, Liz might get mad at me. So I stayed there until they went back inside. I stayed there another fifteen minutes. My feet hurt even worser. They eventually left and walked inside. I sat down again. Then I jumped up. With my luck somebody would've come out again and I would've had to stand up for another hour. I dropped my head and headed back to Mr. Archie's place. They could see me walking from the field. They was on the porch drinking lemonade. They'd cleaned up the front too. The gate looked like new wood. All of the weeds had been pulled up, an the grass was shaded by the overhang in front. Mr. Archie had pulled out a rockin chair for Ms. P and he sat on his bench pushed against the wall so he could lean back. He had his guitar close to him but he wasn't playin at first. Then he saw me walking with my head down. It looked like Ms. P said something to him. He picked up the guitar and started strumming. I got to the street and let two cars pass before walking across. I could hear him singing.

"Got dem walkin blues Lawd, I be walkin all de time. Got dem walkin blues Lawd, my head hung low an to de side. Mmmm hummm. Lookin for my girl Lawd, an she wadn't no where in sight, finally seen her Lawd, wit another man by her side. Mmmm Hummmm."

Ms. P reached over and hit him on the knee. "Back so soon Buck?"

"Yes mam." I opened the gate and grabbed a crate.

82

"What happen son? She don't like you no mo?"

"No sir, I think she like me, but she took a vow."

"Vow?" said Ms. P. "Watcha mean vow?"

"Her, an Big Foo..I mean Ann, and Rab.. I mean Neicy, said they wadn't gonna let boys talk to em no more. They said I didn't like Liz and that Liz should swear too."

"How ya hear all this son?"

"I was hidin behind the wall by the locked gym door."

"Why was you hidin Buck?" asked Ms. P.

"First-"

"Uh oh, *first*. Anytime a man say first he either lyin or tellin a long story."

"Archie let the boy talk."

Yeah let me talk and stop flirting, I said to myself. "First, I was gonna walk in and talk to Liz. But then I saw Man an nem. I didn't want them to see me going to talk no girl, so I went the other way. The long way to the back side."

"Can't get nothin don going in the back door son."

"Archie!"

"Yes Ms. Mam."

Boy Mr. Archie was a mess with Ms. P around. "By the time I got round to the back I heard them comin so I hid."

"Listen to me Buck, don't let nobody stop you from gettin thangs done now. Sometime you gotta go after what you tryin for. If you don't, you end up waitin your whole life for some happiness," she said and smiled at Mr. Archie.

"That's right son."

"Like I was sayin," grown folks really know how to cut off a kid. "No disrespect mam, sir...I was hidin, then the guys walked off. Soon as they left, the girls came out an start talkin. So I hid again."

"Ain't nothin like a man in the shadows," said Mr. Archie. Ms. P laughed and popped him again on the knee. I was glad to see him getting popped for a change instead of him hitting me with that hat. Then I spoke too soon. He stood up and walked over to me and let me have it on the head.

"That's for them bad thoughts ya havin at me." How he knew? Grown folks.

"Archie let the boy finish."

'Yeah,' I thought to myself again. "Well, they said they wasn't gonna talk to boys and that's when I come back." Mr. Archie picked up his guitar again.

"Lawd, lil Buck gotta a problem Lawd, Mmmm Hummm." They both busted up, I felt like going home, but what for? I would've just came back anyway. So I took it, I'ma kid, it's my job.

"Jus teasin ya son, jus teasin ya. Listen at me. Whatcha gotta do nah is get her when she going on home. Then talk to her."

"Ain't you give the boy enough bad advice?"

"Yeah," I said jumping up and running for the gate.

"Get back here Buck and sit down, he ain't gon bother you." Mr. Archie looked at me from under his brow and the lid part of his hat. I knew he was gonna pop me later, but oh well. I moved my crate closer to Ms. P.

"I'ma have noonday brunch at the house Monday. You and Mr. Archie invited. I'll make sho she there wit me."

84

"Yes mam," I smiled. "I'm gonna go to the store and get something to snack on. Yaw'll need anything?"

"No thank ya Buck," said Mr. Archie.

"Thank ya for the offer, but how bout you save that money for Monday?"

"Yes mam. I will. I'm gonna go catch up with the guys. They lookin for me."

"Yaw'll be safe out there."

"Yes mam." Mr. Archie clicked at me and then he waved his hat, and hit it his hand.

"Archie!"

"Jus playing wit the boy is all. You be safe nah son."

I pushed the gate closed behind me and took off down the street and across the park. I ran for a few steps until I heard a shot ring out from the court. I dropped to the ground and covered my head. I looked up and tried to see what had happened. The fence around the little kids area blocked my path of sight. I could see a bunch of the old guys running from the ballcourt. A buncha long legged and long armed blurs, streaking under the food court and off into the projects on the other side of Bickford street. I stayed down and didn't move. I'd heard folks shooting before just not so close and not for no reason other than New Years. I continued to lay down for safety I guess. Then again it was more likely I laid down cause I was afraid to do anything else. I heard Ol Man Fishstick yelling for me to get back over to the house. I didn't move.

"Buck git up an git back over here."

I didn't move a hair. I just lay in the grass and kept my head down. The cut grass was sticking to my arms and face. I wasn't crying or nothing, just couldn't move. Felt like a buncha folks was pulling me into the loose blades of grass. I looked up again and I could see the police cars going towards the front of the park, right next to the court. They had pulled up on the grass. Then I heard the ambulance. Then I saw Stack an them riding up on they bikes. Ms. P and Mr. Archie walked over to me and picked me up.

"You okay son?" He bent down as far as he could and looked me in the face. I opened my mouth and nothing came out. He pulled me close and asked again, "Buck, son, you be alright," he hugged me. On his knees, there in the park after that gunshot, I feel what he told me. I felt something talking to me. Like a whisper, soft, "You be fine son, I'm here." I looked at Mr. Archie and he nodded at me, like he heard it too. Ms. P walked over and held my hand and touched Archie on the shoulder. He looked up at her and then he stood.

"Reckon we should go and see what happened?" she asked.

"I reckon. Buck you okay nah?"

"Yes sir." He held my hand for a moment and then he put it softly on my shoulder. I walked between them up to the edge of the crowd. Everybody had come out and was crowded around. We couldn't really see past the people but Mr. Archie could. He looked over and told us what was happening.

"Lotta blood out there. I think it's the Johnson boy."

"Freddie Johnson?" Ms. P asked.

"Thank so. Can't really tell though, whole mess on his face and all." Ms. P turned her back and stopped looking. Archie put his arm around her shoulder and nodded for me to walk off with them. Stack and them was close to the front staring. People was whispering and one lady ran through everyone screaming.

"Lawd. What she gon have tah face gon be hell on her. Ain't no momma oughta outlive her boy." Mr. Archie shook his head. "Don't wanna know what happened let's git on back to the house."

I wanted to stay though. I wanted to see. I kept looking back over my shoulder.

"Son I know ya curious, but ain't need for you to see that there. No need at all." Ms. P said crying a little. Mr. Archie pulled out his kerchief and wiped his head. I looked back again.

"Sometime you can't look back son," said Mr. Archie. People was still coming out of the gym to see. A lot of folks had start leaving. There was a concrete picnic table over by the court that those guys drank at. On it sat all the brown bags and stuff like sunflower seeds. Some of the bottles was turned over, some sat half empty next to crushed cigarette butts. Freddie Johnson momma didn't go with the ambulance. Guess it wadn't no reason to. She sat at the table. I could see her head in her hands between the stacked cans. By the time we made it back down to the house a minute later, the ambulances and police cars was gone. The park was empty.

Chapter 10

We all went inside of Mr. Archie's house. Quiet. I looked up and down not knowing what to say. Thinking Mr. Archie had words, I looked at him but he was quiet too. Ms. P was sitting next to Mr. Archie holding his hand. He looked straight ahead almost without blinking. When his lids closed they pushed out more tears.

"All folks got bad blood in they roots son. Specially us. Ain't seen nothin like it. Thangs ain't so much like they use ta be, an I'm scared-" his chest raised up an he rolled his head back and looked at the ceiling. "Lawd, Lawd." He walked out of the room into the kitchen. I looked at Ms. P. She moved over by me an sat on the arm of the chair I was in.

"Archie done seen too much Buck. Sometime a man gotta let it all out or he drive himself crazy. He lose it an ain't no use to nobody cause he ain't got it all together." She rubbed my head. I could hear kitchen chairs dragging from the back. The air sounded heavier than moms did, when he sat down. Was I supposed to help him like I did momma? I didn't know what to think. Mr. Archie's house opened after he left the room. The old brass lamps on the end tables aside the couch, seemed dull. The wooden table in the middle was covered with shavings from his knife chipping at wood. His fireplace sat like a pit, a chain net in front holding back the iron black of the hole. Above it sat them pictures of Mr. Archie when he was younger. Except they didn't seem to look like him no more. A sparkle in the eyes on those pictures. No playing and stories, jus a big smile like he knew some stories, but didn't know how to make them come out.

"You let him sit back yonder for a while, he'll be fine. Just gotta get this stuff outta his system."

"What stuff mam?"

"See Buck, when you lived as long as us you see thangs differently, like spring rain."

"Mam?"

"What you see when it rain? After a long winter, cold and gray, dark early every day, then spring come and the sun come out, but it rain. What you see? How it make you feel?"

"I be mad at the rain mam. I always tell my momma that it rain too much here. We need to go where it's summer all the time."

"You know what I see Buck?"

I looked at her listening.

"I see the honeysuckle, the lightnin bugs and June bugs. I see them flowers that Mr. Archie plant coming up out the soil. I see living. You know what Mr. Archie feel?"

"No mam, the same as you I guess?"

"Why no Buck, no. Listen up nah. Sometime thangs ain't always what they seem and folks hide themselfs for a reason."

"Mr. Archie say folks hide an it make them sad, angry and confused, over and over again. He say that some Black folks did that a long time ago cause they didn't wanna be Black."

"Buck there a buncha thangs that make folk keep secrets. Mr. Archie got big secrets and they been eatin him up forever. It kill him not to tell nobody, but he made bargains and promises to make everything right. See son, I love Archie. Done loved him for years, but life don't always come easy to you. It make you wait."

Ms. P moved over to the other couch and patted beside her. I walked over and sat down on the floor in front of her. Mr. Archie had always told me that anytime older folk was talking kids supposed to listen looking up. That way ain't no confusion between who the wiser person is. He explained talking about school:

"In ya school Buck, teacher always stand up an talk?"

"Yes sir."

"Reason for that go back a long way. Same thang in the church. For a person to hold a position of respect he gotta make hisself bigger than ya. Not big wit the body but wit his whole being. Even tho some folk have a lot of booksmarts they put themselfs on the same level as them they tryin to teach."

"Sometime our teacher sit beside us to teach us stuff we having trouble with."

"But that happen only after she don gave the class lecture an made clear her rules. Same thing wit the church. The preacher don't come down from the pulpit til he done finished his sermon or til close to the end. Cause he using his being to earn some respect."

"If folks gotta be up higher than you to earn respect then that mean they ain't really equal to you."

"Well, don't look at it like that. See it as some folks made to be higher than others."

"But you said folks is all equal before."

"They are, jus that some folk use what they got in different ways. You gotta earn your position. That come wit age an learnin.

You jus know when folks speakin wit ya, older folk, you be lookin up. You understand me?"

"Yes sir."

I sat on the floor. Ms. P patted the seat again and told me to sit beside her.

"Why you get on that floor?"

"Cause Mr. Archie say, that kids supposed to look up at elders when they speaking."

"Sometime he ain't quite right, but I understand what he sayin. You spose to give respect when it's earned. But some folk have respect built in, us older folk got that. But you don't never have to be beneath nobody except wit your body. You can be bigger than any man wit your mind. Don't feel like you less. You got that?"

"Yes mam." I heard the back door open. Every time something was happening big in the neighborhood, something bad, Mr. Archie went out to his backyard.

"A while back me and Mr. Archie like each other like you and Liz. Thought we was gon grow up an marry." She smiled and looked at the picture of Archie on the mantle. "Well, thangs seem to be going okay but we had a big argument over him signing up to fight. I tol him I wasn't gon wait around for no dead man. He...went on head an left. I moved off to Jackson for a few years. When he come back and find that I was gone, he met and fell for a lady name Jean. Thang was, Jean was married. They loved each other though, but it wasn't gon work out her being married an all. Well, Buck... that Jean got herself pregnant. Had a lil boy named Victor. Handsome lil boy. I come back round that time. Archie had started tending to his garden growing food to sell and chopping firewood in winter. We talk a lot when I got back:

"Thangs don change a lot Pat."

"They have indeed, but I ain't nevah forget you. Kept you in my heart even when you left."

"I had to go, didn't have no choice."

"What it get you? Nothin. They didn't even let yaw'll Black boys fight much. You jus wash dishes and cut grass, didn't nothin come from it."

"My pride come from it Patty. My pride. Might be nothin to you but for me it's everythang. Nah we ain't gotta talk if this all that's gon come from it."

"You didn't listen."

"You ain't listening nah!"

I couldn't see past the fact that he had chose a White man's war over love. I didn't wanna see past it. It took me over twenty five years, twenty-five long years to forget. But we always talked. Just not the way he wanted. He did tell me about his situation with Jean:

"I loved her, even though I knew bettah. But a man get lonely. I loved her to death I did. But folks start finding out. It killed me to deny thangs, but I had ta, to keep her good name, an mine. But one thang nobody never come to find out. I made a promise I nevah tell anythang. Tol Jean that I take care of thangs anytime thangs got too rough on her an Big Victor. An that's what I did, I give em groceries when they money was low, would help Victor get a job wit Frank's

92

store even. I think he knew bout what happen wit me an his wife. Jus guess he figure if it ain't grow past a rumor, that he let it slide. I thank him for that. But we had our fallin outs over the boy. I knew he was mine. Knew he was, but I couldn't say nothin, and it kill me to this day to see him growin. But I teach him as much as I can. Nah Patty, a man make mistakes and they always come back to get him. It ain't the first time I crossed this line."

"What are you saying Archie?"

"I'm just sayin, I been cross this line before and I promise you that I ain't gon nevah do wrong by no woman again. Ain't right for boys to grow up in such a way as to never know."

"Archie you being a might bit distant with your words. But I'ma respect your thoughts and forget about the past. I just can't deal with so many secrets, it would tear my soul up."

"Nah Buck some folk knew bout Archie, but it nevah got too big. It jus died off. Faded away. Nah everytime somethin happen round here to a boy, it kill him."

"He sound like what he tol me about my daddy. He lost you causa his pride. That's what he say about my daddy. But he say my daddy still here, in me."

"That's right Buck an his son still here in you too. He love you."

"I know."

I heard the kitchen door close. Ol Man Archie's feet drug across the floor and I heard the icebox door open. I heard glasses rattle and clink. A few seconds after, he walked out with lemonade for us. He sat down.

"How you feelin Buck?"

"I'm okay, jus listenin to Ms. P tell stories like you do."

"That so? What she tell ya?"

"That's me an Buck's business. I talk to him bout life."

"And love."

"That's right. That's what I was talkin about Archie."

"That's alright you can be selfish if ya want. I got some stories too."

"And they some good stories Mr. Archie," I said.

"How bout that Ms? I got good stories."

"The boy confused is all. Hadn't heard no good stories til right now. Til I give him some of my storytelling."

"Nah Ms. P, seems you in competition wit me."

"Course I am. That's the only way we keep things straight round here."

"Straight? How's that?"

"We know who's gon wear the pants round here."

"That so?"

Mr. Archie sat down next to Ms. P and they nudged each other.

"Why Archie, that ain't good showing the boy that you hit on a woman."

"He ain't seen none the such. He seen me bump ya. He know bettah than puttin his hands on no woman. His momma, an me, teach him that. We keep him right. You stop all that ol instigatin."

"Me instigatin? Why, I would never do such a thang."

94

"You wouldn't? Jus like I wouldn't eat the last rib at a bar-b-que."

"Mr. Archie I seen you eat the last rib at a bar-b-que," I interrupted him.

"That's my point son."

When Mr. Archie said 'son' I felt it different. But I didn't think on it for too long. It was almost five o'clock an mom would be gettin home soon. She worked way out in Whitehaven. It was like a thirty minute drive in clear traffic like she use to say:

"Sure is a long ride out yonder Buck. But I don't mind much, that ride is worth it. Especially if I get that permanent position. If I get it, maybe we can move out there."

"Momma I thought you said it wadn't no Black folk out there?"

"Sometime your momma stretch the truth a bit. There are some, but they well to do, or much better off than we are."

"How so?"

"Well, less crime out there. A lot more schools, with air conditioning."

"Air conditioning, not fans? I wish we had that out here. When I rode the bus to Frayser, they had air condition. But not over here at Caldwell, or at Grant. We be-"

"We be?"

"We sweat a lot when the summer starts coming an they still don't let us wear shorts."

"We couldn't wear shorts or pants when I was in school."

"For real?"

"That's right. Girls were supposed to wear dresses, long dresses, and boys wore pants."

"I couldn't stand to dress like church at school."

"You would've, cause you didn't have a choice. Our folks wanted us to go to school. They knew how important it was for us to learn. You know... it seems like some of these kids today don't think so highly of school."

"Mr. Archie say that folks done got lazy since Dr. King died. He call it complaced."

"You mean *complacent*?"

"Yes mam. He don't use big words like that until he talk about important stuff."

"I agree with Mr. Archie. Black folk resting on ten year laurels. It's about to be the eighties. We ain't that far removed from what we was, but folks sure act like it. Well, I ain't gonna let you get complacent. That's why I make sure you see me working all the time. Make sure you know what it means to earn your keep."

"I know momma. I learn from you an Mr. Archie."

"I'm glad Mr. Archie round for you." She looked sad when she said that. "He did the same for your daddy. Was always around, cause your daddy's father died young too." She never got into how my grandaddy died but I expect that it was bad.

"I'm glad Mr. Archie round too, but I'm more glad that you my momma."

She hugged me tight everytime she got home from work. It seemed like the same time everyday, like clockwork. At five thirty she'd walk in put down her bag and take off her shoes before going to the kitchen to cook. Sometimes I'd make macaroni and cheese cause it was easy. I'd also make Kool Aid, so she wouldn't have to do so much. I even cut potatoes sometimes, anything to help out.

I left Mr. Archie's house at a little after five. I hugged Ms. P's neck and Mr. Archie's. She clicked like he usually did and I clicked back. I guess her click was more important cause she held a finger to her mouth for me to be quiet. I didn't understand why, so I did it back.

Chapter 11

I made my way across the street and they stood at the door and watched me. There were a few cops still walking around and driving by the park. I walked up past the gym doors and looked in. It was the first time during the summer that it was empty. I guess didn't nobody want to be out after what happened. I trotted up the street faster cause I felt scared. I made it to the house and momma was already inside.

"Where've you been boy?" She said grabbing me by the arms and pushing me to the couch.

"I-"

"Be quiet, just be quiet." She walked back and forth in front of me. She still had her work clothes on and her plastic badge flopped up and down on her shirt. "Where you been Vincent? I come home early after we hear that some boy been shot in North Memphis. I left work early to come here and you ain't home." She pointed her finger in my face.

"I-"

"Shut up, Vincent. Don't talk when I'm saying something. I can't stand it. I'm sick." She finally sat down, wiping her head with her hands. Drying tears with the cuff of her shirt. "I'm sick of living out here, tired."

"Momma I'm okay, I was with Mr. Archie and Ms. P."

"I know you okay son, but you gotta come home when thangs like that happen."

"I was scared momma," I looked up at her and her tears made me cry. " I didn't wanna come to the house by myself."

"I'm sorry, I'm sorry." She pulled me close and hugged me. I couldn't understand why I was crying but I felt like it was my fault. I should've came home.

"I'm sorry too mom. I know I was supposed to come home. I'm sorry I made you cry and I worried you."

"Naw nah, it ain't your fault. You done the right thang. You okay for staying wit Mr. Archie. I wouldn't want you nowhere else. I am not mad at you. I'm jus tired son."

"You want me to fix you something to drink?"

"I want you to stay here beside me, that's all."

And I did stay beside her. I didn't move. I knew something had happened that day. Momma didn't feel like herself. She had a look on her face that said she was fed up. With what, I wasn't sure but I felt like she was fed up. So I didn't talk about nothing until she started talking. I think she needed some peace.

"Did you see it?"

"No mam. Jus saw the crowd. Mr. Archie saw it though. He started explaining, but Ms. P wanted to leave."

"Don't much blame her. Folks gotta be tired of seeing young folks pass."

"Mam?"

"Vincent, I'm gonna get us outta here. Gon move us on outta here. I ain't gon let this street swallow you up. I ain't gon let it."

"I'm okay momma, I know bettah."

"I know you do. I just ain't gonna let this street take my only child. Buck what, what happen with your hand? Lemme see it."

"Just a cut. From out playing this morning."

"Playing?" She gave me that 'don't be lying,' look.

"Mom, I can't tell you how I did it. I made a vow."

"Boy ain't no vow bigger than your momma."

"Yes mam. We blood brothers. Stack and Smoke and-"

"Boy you went and cut your hand? Take that wrap off." She started taking the brown bandage off. Then she saw it. She started laughing. "What the hell did you put on here?"

"Mercoorachrome. Same as you woulda done it." She lay back on the couch laughing.

"Did it hurt?"

"Mom?"

"Is it okay son? It don't hurt none do it?"

"No mam."

"You ain't supposed to use that much. Just dab around the cut. Did you clean it with water first and then put that on?"

"Yes mam." She stood and started walking down the hall. You wanna help me make something to eat and tell me what else happen today other than that other stuff?"

"Yes mam. First, when you left this morning, Tiger them moved."

"I knew about that already. They moved out there by my job."

"We did the blood brother thing cause he was leaving, but I can't tell you no more than that."

"Don't get into no habit of keepin stuff from your momma. I'm your family. Don't get into a habit."

"Yes mam. Then we went to the store with Mr. Archie. He was gonna buy us some snacks, but Pau- Mr. Travis gave us stuff for free."

"Is that so?"

"Yes mam."

"Well, I guess I'll have to thank Mr. Travis on tomorrow."

"You going to church tomorrow?"

"Sure am. I ain't gotta work for a change."

I continued, "After the store I went to find..." I didn't want to tell her about me trying to talk to Liz and what the fellas was saying about her and Mr. Travis.

"Go head an finish I'm listening." She was buttering bread for cheese sandwiches.

"Nothing mom, I went to Mr. Archie's house." She looked at me again.

"I went to the gym to talk to Liz, but the guys were there so I didn't talk to her and I hid and heard the guys talking and then I heard Liz talking and then I went back-"

"Slow down and talk like you got some sense."

"Mom, do you like Mr. Travis?" She put the last cheese sandwich in the skillet and flipped it before answering. She brought the other five sandwiches to the table and took two glasses out with the pitcher of lemonade. She started to speak and stopped to take out the other sandwich. She sat down and touched my hand.

"Vincent, now-"

"I know Mr. Archie tell me that some thangs grown ups business and that I ain't supposed to talk on such stuff."

"That's right, but I don't mind. Not at all. Mr. Travis is a really nice man. He help me a lot you know?"

"Yes mam."

"Your momma thinks very highly of him. He's very respectful, got his own business and no family. He's an awfully good man, and yes, I care for him."

"Do he care for you?"

"Such questions Buck," she laughed. "Why you got so many questions?"

I put my sandwich down before telling her what Stack was saying. "Mom, Stack said his uncle said that women only good for one thang."

"Who? Stack's uncle? You mean the man with one leg that don't bathe?"

"Yes mam. Stack said his uncle look at The Mack and that a woman good for one thang."

"And what would that one thing be?"

"I don't know, Stack didn't never say that part. He just said that don't no man want a ready made family."

"Well, seeing as that man ain't been right since he come from Vietnam, I'll let his thoughts roll right off. He ain't got everything together upstairs. And you shouldn't listen to folks. Folks always got something negative to say. I don't listen to folks rumors, I listen to my good judgment and my heart. That's the same thing you need to do. I think Mr. Travis is a fine man and I'm quite sure he feels the same."

"That's what I thought, cause he showed Mr. Archie something at the store, in a box but I couldn't see it. But Mr. Archie told me to stay outta grown folks business."

"And that's what you should do."

"Yes mam."

We ate our cheese sandwiches at the table and I thought about the whole day. What if I would've been the one that got hit by that bullet? What if we would've moved away, would the guys have been blood brothers for me? Sometimes being a kid is tough, I'm tired of all the problems. Kinda like mom say she tired. But I think her's is more important. Grown folks got more rules than kids, at least when I do something wrong I get a do over. Whatever happened in the park today was grown folks stuff, it wasn't no do overs.

Chapter 12

Sunday morning I woke up an smelled cooking. I could hear bacon sizzling and smell biscuits. Mom made these cheese eggs that was real good. I got up to shower and get ready for church. Mom usually came in to say, "Rise and shine sweetheart," but she didn't today. I could hear her talking over the gospel music.

"Never you mind how I make it. I do just fine." Mom said.

"Oh do you now. Look at it like this, if we put our money together and work out a few things we could get outta North Memphis. We wouldn't have to hide no more."

It was Mr. Travis. He sounded like he was begging. I heard a little more before I got in the bathtub.

"Look, I thank you for the proposal and all, I just don't think I'm ready for that right now. Paul, I care bout you a lot, but that's such a big step."

"You need to let go."

"Of what? What do you mean let go?"

"He's been gone for over twelve years now, and ain't nothing gonna change that. I'm here now and I love you."

"Paul, it ain't got nothin to do with that nah. I'm just trying to make my own way is all. It ain't got nothing to do with that. I need to wake up Buck." I could hear her walking down the hall. It wouldn't take a second for her to be in my room. And I knew she hadn't heard me walking I was being quiet. I turned the water on and start running it in the bathroom before she walked outta the kitchen. I heard her stop. I think she knew I heard them talking but she just yelled through the door, "You gettin ready baby?"

"Yes mam." That was all she asked. I finished and walked back to my room. She had already taken out my suit to wear. It was the one she thought was nice. I didn't like it. It was gray with thick stripes all over, stripes you could feel. The stripes wasn't even made into the cloth like the old men wore, they sat higher than the gray material. She made me wear this burgundy shirt with it and a black clip on tie. But those wasn't the things that made the suit bad. It was the bell bottoms. They was way too big, bigger than normal for a suit. The pants leg fit tight around my thighs and then flared out at the bottom. I looked at the suit laying there on the bed and all I could do was exhale hard.

"I got your favorite suit out."

"Thanks mom."

"Hurry up now, fore your food gets cold."

"Yes mam." I had an idea. I put the suit on and went into the kitchen for breakfast. Mr. Travis was sitting there with his head hung. Momma was standing and making plates.

"Hey Buck. You boys enjoy those goodies yesterday?"

"Yes sir. Thank you for that sir."

"My pleasure." His smile looked fake. Not like he didn't enjoy talking to me, but like he was sad. "Well, I best be getting on. Just stopped by to say hi to your momma. Let her know I love her." He looked at her when he said that. I looked at mom and mom stopped putting food on the plate. She turned around and looked at Mr. Travis.

"Paul, I love you too. Don't you see that? I just don't want-"

"What? Diane, what?"

"Vincent please take your food to the living room."

"No Vincent, please stay."

"This ain't no place for a boy. He ain't in this and you don't tell my boy what to do." I stood up and began walking down the hall.

"He got to know, he got to. I'm tired of hiding from everybody. A man shouldn't have to keep his feelings inside. Now I may not be the boy's daddy, but I care for him and he need to know how I feel about you. Vincent please come back."

"Paul! Dammit this is my house. It ain't much but it's mine and I make the rules in here. When I tell my boy to leave, them is my rules. You ain't got no say under this ceiling," mom started crying. I dropped my plate and ran back into the kitchen.

"You makin my momma cry," I swung at Mr. Travis with my fork. He jumped backwards and bumped the chair. "You ain't gon make my momma sad." I charged again.

"Vincent what are you doing?" mom grabbed me by the shoulder.

"He hurtin you momma and I gotta stop him." She put her hands on my shoulders and faced me towards her.

"Boy I ain't taught you this. You put that fork down and sit in that chair. Right now." She wiped her tears. "Paul sit down please." Paul hadn't said anything even when I charged at him. He sat down. Mom paced back and forth on the floor, her house shoes making a sweeping sound.

"Vincent apologize to Mr. Travis."

106

"Sorry sir." I stood and walked over to shake his hand. He shook my hand and I returned to my seat.

"Paul, forgive me for everything. I don't want you to think I'm ungrateful, cause I'm not. I just can't have no men coming in and out of my son's life. I much rather raise him on my own than let somebody bring us both down."

"But Diane, I want to marry you. I don't want to be in and out. I want to be in. I want you and I want everyone to know."

"I understand, but... I just can't do it."

"Diane, he is gone, and ain't nobody can take his place. That ain't what I'm here for. I wanna make you happy."

"I'm happy the way it is."

"No you're not. I can see it. Buck, I love your mother and you. I don't get to spend much time with you, but I know you a good boy. I would never hurt your mom." He walked over and kneeled down in front of me. One of his knees was on the floor and his face was below mine. I looked down at him. "I can never be your father, but I can be your dad. I'm not askin you to call me daddy or nothing, I just want your respect and I wanna help."

"Vincent, Mr. Travis asked me to marry him this morning."

"The thing in the box was a ring yesterday?"

"Yes, that's what it was Buck," said Mr. Travis.

"Mom you said you love him. I heard you say it before. I heard you say you care for him."

"I do son, but that ain't the issue."

"Then what is Diane, please, tell me."

"I married one man. Never got divorced, never thought about marrying nobody else. When he died over there in that war, I promised I would never forget him. I promised." Mom put her hand up to her face. She breathed in real deep, and straightened out her shirt. "I said I'd always hold him fast in my heart."

"Mom, Mr. Archie said-"

"Vincent," she put her hand up at me. But I couldn't stop I needed to talk.

"Mom I gotta finish." She looked at me and sat down. "Ms. P say that she loved Mr. Archie a long time ago, but she let things hold her back from loving him. She said it took her twenty-five years to be happy. Sometimes you gotta let things happen mom."

"Well, look at the time Buck, Paul. Almost time for church we better get a move on." Mom walked to her room and put on her hat and shoes. She left me and Mr. Travis in the kitchen.

"Thank you Buck."

"For what sir?"

"For talking." He walked down the hall and into the living room to wait. I looked at the food on the table and the mess in the hall. I grabbed the broom and cleaned up. I covered the rest of the food and stuck it in the refrigerator. I never got a chance to use my idea, which was to drop food on my pants. I fixed my suit and walked up front. Sometimes big things can get small and small thangs can get big, it all depends on which way you look at it.

Mr. Travis took us to church. He dropped us off right in front. Before mom got out the car he held her hand.

"Just give me a chance Diane. Sometimes you gotta let things happen."

I smiled at Mr. Travis and winked my eye. He winked back. Mom climbed out of the car and waited on me by the curb. Some folks still stood outside waiting to go in. Sunday school had just finished and everyone was getting ready for eleven o'clock service.

Chapter 13

"Fire and Brimstone, that what folk call it that don't know what we praising. They thank I'm raising hell in the pulpit cause us folk," Rev. Herman paused and inhaled heavy into the microphone. He wiped his forehead with a shiny white napkin. His big white robe flowed back and forth as he waved his hands when he talked. The robe looked like a picture of dancers holding silk clothes as they jumped into the air. Sweat dropped from his chin like every five seconds. His glasses was little on his head. He had a big round head, molasses brown and a tiny moustache. The pulpit was wooden with a purple sash covering it, a brass plated light over the Bible cast a light on his chest. Behind him the choir sat, women nodding in agreement, men nodded off. The balcony folks clapped in rhythm with the folks in the pews on the bottom. I sat beside mom. I wanted to sit in the balcony over the back of the church, cause that's where the kids sat, Smoke and Skillet and the rest of the guys were there. But mom said all we did was sleep and sneak out during the sermons...and we did. But isn't that what kids do? Mom would cry during the sermons. I think it was the Holy Ghost. She'd wave her hands and tears would come out, every week. I think she had a lot inside her that came out when Rev. Herman spoke and the choir sang.

Rev Herman banged his hand on his stand and repeated, "Fire and brimstone? I'm jus praisin the Lord here an you can't be still when God got a hold on you. You gotta shout, scream, dance, you gotta do the spirits will. How can I," breath, "preach fire and brimstone," breath, "when the Lord," breath, "Jesus Christ," breath,

110

"Gave his life," breath, "For us, so that we," breath , organ blast, "could have," breath, organ blast, "Everlasting life," everyone said in conjunction with the pastor and the organ. "You don't hear me," breath, walking out of the pulpit with the microphone. He usually did this when he was going to raise the offering or call folks to come up and join the church. I joined two years ago. "You don't hear me," he said. "Sometimes you gotta believe in the Lord, that he gon make it alright. You got to trust in the Lord," Rev Herman started singing as he called for people to come up and join. "Ahhh will trust iiin da Lord, Ahhh willl truuust in da Lord, Ahhh will trust in da Lord til I diiiiee, Ahhh willl trust in da Looorrrd. I wiilll trust in da Loord til Ahhh diee. Will there be one," his hand outstretched. The white napkin, like a peace flag hanging from his fingers. He asked for one person to come. No one came that day, but mom kept repeating, "Sometimes you gotta believe, sometimes you gotta believe." She wiped her eyes. I sat staring.

As service ended I saw the guys and walked over. Mom was back shaking hands with the pastor and other folks. I knew we would be going downstairs to the back to eat dinner. But I hoped we wouldn't have to stay late for everything else. I walked outside with the guys.

"Why come you don't never sit wit us?" asked Smoke.

"Momma say yaw'll don't listen."

"You don't listen either," said Stack. "My uncle say men ain't supposed to go to church anyway. Church is for women."

Man came from behind his mom and walked over. "I betcha Stack said somethin stupid again huh?"

"How you know?" asked Lizard.

"Cause yaw'll jus starring at him like he said something stupid." We laughed at what Man was saying.

"Stack, if church ain't for men, then why is there a man preacher?" asked Skillet.

"My uncle say, a preacher jus a pimp-"

"I think my momma calling me," I said. I didn't want to be around when somebody caught Stack talking. "I'm going to the kitchen."

I walked off. I turned to ask if any of the guys were gonna stay for dinner. Just as I looked around, I saw Stack's mom pop him upside the head. All the guys busted out laughing. I knew it was coming. I made it to the back and mom had already found a table to sit at. The Mothers of the church were always first to get their dinner plates, then the Elders, then deacons, then us and then the ushers. We had greens, cabbage, hot water corn bread, pork chops, neckbones, black eyed peas, rice, mac and cheese, and sweet potato pie for dessert. Sometimes they served ribs, if there wasn't any more church after eleven o'clock service. It was a lot of food to eat for three dollars a plate. Mr. Travis usually came at four o'clock to pick us up. I never realized how much he went out of his way for mom. He was early today. It was three thirty-five or so, when he walked in. He was all dressed up like he had come to church. Stack and them were all with their folks. The pastor was sitting close to the kitchen, I thought to myself that was why he was so big. He let out throat busting laughter as he ate. Mr. Travis looked over the whole place. Mom had just stood up to take her trash to the garbage can. She was walking back. I saw him and waved. He raised his hand and I could see the box.

"Ms. Diane Sams," he called to her. Everyone stopped eating. Smoke and the guys ran up to the front by me. Mom placed her hand on her hips and looked confused.

"Ms. Diane Sams, before all of these people I profess my feelings for you," he dropped to one knee, held the box out and opened it. "I love you Diane. Will you marry me?"

Everybody was quiet. They all looked and waited. One of the Mothers spoke up, "Hell, if she don't marry him I will." Everybody laughed. Mom continued looking with her hand over her mouth. Mr. Travis was starting to move around on his knee. Pastor Herman spoke, "Hurry up nah Ms. Sams fore the boy knee become a part of the floor."

"Paul, I-"

"Just say yes Diane."

Mom took off out the back of the church. I thought about going after her. Mr. Travis pointed at me to stay. I sat back down. He took off after her. Folks started whispering. I finally understood what Mr. Travis meant when he said mom was still holding on to the past. I heard several people, "That girl ain't over Victor yet." One heavy lady said. Her friend beside her replied, "I don't think she gon ever get over him and marry again. Terrible thang ain't it."

"Indeed it is, but I understand," said another lady at my table.

Pastor Herman stood up, "Folks idle minds...let's not make comments on such thangs that don't concern us." He looked at me. "Folks have to move at they own pace. When the good Lord see fit to judge he will, but yaw'll can't judge." Everybody stopped whispering.

The back door opened as mom walked in holding Mr. Travis's hand. I looked for the ring, and so did everybody else. There was no sign of it. Mr. Travis walked in and mom waved for me.

"Everyone I'm sorry for the distraction. Please forgive me." We turned and left.

She hadn't taken the ring, but they talked a lot on the slow ride back to the house. I felt like I was the reason for mom not marrying Mr. Travis. I guess if I wasn't around she could be happy. He was a nice man, and she even said so. She even said she cared, but she wouldn't marry him cause, "She could do bad all by herself an wasn't no man gon walk in and out." If I walked out maybe she would go head on and marry him. I'm the man of the house and I'm supposed to take care of everything.

"Diane, I do apologize for doing that and putting you on the spot, but I've asked you in every way possible."

"I can't believe you did that, I really can't"

"It ain't like people didn't know we was together. Ain't no secrets round here. Somebody know something all the time."

"That ain't the point." Mom looked out the car window as she talked. She never turned towards him for the first few minutes. I guess she was embarrassed. I knew what I had to do. I had to leave. I was figuring on packing up some stuff and then saying goodbye to Mr. Archie and Ms.P first, then I could leave while mom was at work. I could leave her a note and just go, that way she could marry Mr. Travis and start a new family with him.

"Well, Diane... I'm all outta options here."

Mom finally turned her head and looked at him. "What do yo mean by that?"

"I won't ask anymore, I'll back off."

"What are you saying back off?"

"I won't ask you for anything anymore, nothing at all. You keep all that anger and confusion to yourself sister, cause I don't need it. Ain't no reason for me to be putting myself out like this for no one. I'd rather..."

"Say it dammit. You've said enough already. We can finish this right now."

He looked at me through the rearview mirror. I was almost in tears. For what reason I was crying I didn't know, I just felt like I had messed up everything. He stopped talking. I guess she heard me sucking in air. She blew out real hard and shook her head.

"How about we finish this later? We both are saying stuff that we don't mean right now."

"I think we're saying things that shoulda been talked about before, *with* Vincent around. Like you said this morning he has a right to know things. I can't treat him like a child no more with folks dying and acting they way they are out here, please." She turned in her seat. The leather squeaked a bit as she moved.

"Vincent, I don't want you to feel bad or hurt by what's happening here. Ain't nothing wrong or bad happening, you hear me?" she asked.

I shook my head yes, but I knew something was wrong. It felt like a big room filled up with air from a hot fire. I was sweating and the car was cool. It felt heavy.

"I'm gon talk to Mr. Travis when we get back to the house. I want you to go to Mr. Archie house and sit with him for a bit. We'll come back down and get you."

"Yes mam."

As we rounded Sixth Street onto Caldwell, I told myself I would never go back to the house. My momma shouldn't never feel no grief cause of me. I understood that for certain.

They pulled up to the curb. Mr. Archie was sitting on his bench, on the porch. He stood up when he saw the car, he walked towards the gate and opened it. I climbed out and he patted me on the head. He walked closer to the car and mom rolled down the window.

"Hey now, Mr. Archie."

"Paul, Diane," he looked them in their faces as he leaned. "Hmm, I guess yaw'll best be gettin where ya goin. Too much heat in this here car." Mr. Travis turned his head. "Sho is...too much heat, I do declare. Get goin an finish what you started." He turned from the car and smiled at me. I sat on the porch instead of my crate. Not cause of church clothes, but because I didn't feel like sitting low.

"How was service son?"

"Figured you an Ms. P would be there today. I ain't use to not seeing yaw'll."

"We stayed up pretty late talking and stuff. Anyway boy, you ain't answer me nothing yet?"

"It was pretty good. Rev. Herman sang again today."

"Did he talk and breathe."

"Yeah, and he even humped his shoulders some when he was preaching."

116

"Sorry I missed that one. Ya got anythin you wanna tell me?"

"No sir." He moved his bench closer to my chair and looked me in the face.

"Somethin ya wanna tell me son?"

"Mr. Travis asked momma to marry him."

"That so? I reckon she say no. I can feel that. Well, some folks take a long time to feel different bout some thangs."

"I know. Ms. P said she took a long time to love you again. I told momma Ms. P told me that."

"Yeah son, it took a long time. Mighty long time. But the Lawd find a way to make thangs right. We right nah. It feel mighty fine." He kind of brightened up when he was talking. I felt even worse. I just felt like I messed up all kinds of stuff with momma. I dropped my head and played with my hands, making small circles with my pointing fingers. I felt like crying but I didn't want Mr. Archie to know how I felt. But I knew better, he always knew everythang.

"Nah Buck, son, ya momma, like I told ya, she a strong lady. An strong folk find a way to be what they are cause they know thangs need to be a certain way. An they keep thangs that way. That's why ya momma's doin what she doin. She tryin to keep thangs simple."

"But how did-"

"Son, I seen all this coming twelve years ago. Seen it steady like a candle flame in a dark room I did."

"Sir?"

"When your daddy passed on...listen up cause this ain't easy for me. And it ain't gon be easy to hear, but you gon be a man soon. Too much happenin for ya not to hear."

"I'm listening sir."

"I told ya daddy to be a whole man, find they weakness an use it. Use it to make hisself smarter. So he could live. But them Black boys over there seen more fighting than every other folk. Us Black folk got sent into everythang. Ya daddy volunteered an wanted to fight. He jus really thought that would make him equal, but I told him. I told him..." Mr. Archie closed his mouth and clenched his teeth. "I told him to be smarter. When we got news of your father dying, they sent a man with dog tags. One metal dog tag an that's it. Nothin else left to bury. Your momma, she was strong though. Didn't cry much at all. Kept it all in. When they had the funeral wadn't nothin in the casket but his spirit. Son, ya momma, she said she would be strong for him an wouldn't never leave his memory behind. Ya momma findin it hard to divorce the past." He stopped talking, stood up, and walked over to his guitar leaning on the tree. He picked it up and brought it over to his bench. He flipped it over and laid it on my lap.

"This here guitar was made for ya daddy. Look here on the bottom." I looked across the bottom of the honey colored wood. In the round of the back, it had some etchings. I couldn't tell what they said cause some of the words didn't look right, they wasn't spelled wrong, but the etching had worn a bit. 'IF FOLK ONLY KNEW HOW YOU THE SUN IN MY SKY. THEY KNOW WHY I HOLD YOU SO HIGH.'

I read the words and looked at Mr. Archie. He rubbed the guitar.

"I was gon give that to ya daddy. Teach him some songs on it when he come home. Teach some good blues. That thang ain't known

118

no good blues since he passed. Cept when you come around. You remind me of em so much." He stopped and took the guitar from my lap. "What's goin on wit your momma don been twelve years in the makin. It ain't none of your fault. So don't think on it like that. Think good for your momma, cause it's gon be your spirit that help her through."

"I do my best sir."

"No. You gon do it. You gon help her through it. I don't want ya best, I want ya spirit. Ain't no tryin when you give it yo all. Ain't no best, no good, no better, you give her your spirit."

"Yes sir." He held the guitar in his hand an picked at the strings slow. His head was bowed, tears was dropping on his coveralls leaving dark blue spots in the material. Then he held his head back and let it all out crying. I had never seen no man cry like that. Like he was laughing, but his tears was like rain on a window. Like looking out into the dark when it finished raining, they rolled down his cheek. He took out his kerchief. His big hands held the sheet and dabbed at the corners of his eyes and face. I left the porch and sat on my crate. I pulled the old crate right in front of the step-up porch.

"Tell me a story Mr. Archie." I couldn't think of nothing else to say. I just didn't want him crying on account of me. "Tell me a story." He stopped crying and smiled.

"Thank you son." He smiled at me, his eyes like icicles sparkling with water still falling, "In the morning you could hear him. Right at dawn when the sun look like it was climbing from under blue, gray clouds and the last star seemed brighter from the shine of the light, you could hear him. Loud like field songs shouting high to glory for the chariots to carry us home. You could hear him. Even when he got old, like... you seen him, he still rose up and yelped for the day to come. Some thangs like clockwork and don't never change. He run down them high steps over in the old apartments an chase yaw'll lil boys around. He use ta be a strong dog. Watch out for folks comin in the neighborhood that wadn't right. Folks that come to do harm. He could scare em off. Big jowls opening and yelpin and barkin. Big gold coat shinin like dew done settled in it. He wasn't so bright by the time you boys come along. But he still had them smarts. Lemme see, yaw'll call em Stomp, right?

"Yes sir. Stomp the crazy dog."

"He wadn't crazy though. Not at all. A dog got four good legs, right? Human got two lil slow legs like you boys. Even when yaw'll would stomp at him an yell. He sit for a spell fore movin, right?"

"Yep cause he was too old and sleepy to move. He use to just sit and look for a minute."

"What you think that dawg was thinkin on?"

"Dogs don't think much. He was just tired."

"Nah yaw'll stomp, an yell, til he finally get up an chase you down the street. Everyday yaw'll mess wit that dawg, stompin an yellin. An he chase ya everyday. But he never caught yaw'll huh?"

"Well, sometime he did, but he ain't never bite us. He made me cry one time though cause he caught my shirt and it ripped. I ran even faster."

"That sho do sound familiar. Somethin chasin ya but not hurtin ya. That dawg had done lived a long life when yaw'll start teasin him. But outta habit he chase yaw'll till he was too sick to run. Outta habit

120

some folk keep doing thangs, cause that's all they now. Now a dawg ain't gon change unlessen you teach him. He ain't got the power to decide to unlearn thangs. But us human folk we unlearn thangs. Change thangs. Folks can change, for good, or for worse all dependin on how they feel like livin."

"Yes sir. I know folk can change." It was the first time I got what Mr. Archie was saying in his stories. The first time I got it right away. "My momma scared to change?"

"Your momma got her reasons. Right nah they seem like the right reasons to follow. And she feel like that's what she sposed to do."

"So momma ain't gon marry him you think?"

"Don't know that Buck. I jus know it ain't you that make all this happen. This thang started long before you even could walk. So don't be hangin yo head an feelin sad. Alright nah?"

"Yes sir," I said but I still felt like I was the problem.

"That ya momma them pullin up here?"

"Yes sir." I walked to the gate then turned. I ran back hugged Mr. Archie. "I love you Mr. Archie."

"I love you too V." I ran to the car.

"Vincent, I didn't mean to put you off on Mr. Archie."

"I understand mom."

"Just that me and Mr. Travis had some thangs we needed to talk over." Mr. Travis was quiet. "Mr. Travis and I have decided that we won't be seeing each other anymore."

"But mom-"

"Vincent."

"Yes mam."

"We figured that right now isn't the time for us to be making decisions. Life changing decisions. But I want you to know that what me and Mr. Travis doing ain't got nothing to do with you."

"That's right Buck. It ain't over you. I know kids take thangs different than grown folks. I know you been thinking on it and it bother you."

"Yes sir. Mom, you remember Stomp?"

"That old dog over there on Bickford?"

"I remember that dawg, was crazy wasn't he?" Mr. Travis put in.

"Well, Mr. Travis," I said as he pulled in front of our apartments. "That dog use to chase us cause he felt what he was doing was right. He didn't know no other way cause he a animal. He never hurt us, and he knew he wadn't spose to. Sometimes, animals can do thangs on they own." He turned from the wheel and looked at me, mom did the same. "A dog is a dog no matter what, and they can't change less you teach em to. Human folk make up they own minds and change when they feel it, but sometime people act like animals and don't never change. It's all in the way they see thangs." I climbed out of the car and left mom behind with Mr. Travis. I pulled my key from inside my shirt and opened the front door. I walked down the hall into my room and closed the door. I wasn't gonna run away now, cause I understood what Mr. Archie was saying. Wasn't no sense in running from grown-up problems. They made they own decisions. But I still thought about leaving.

Mom come in the house about five minutes after I walked in. She came and knocked on my door.

"Mam?"

"You alright in there. Need some juice or ice cream or something?"

"No mam."

"Can I come in?" I couldn't say no even if I wanted to, she usually just walked in anyway.

"Yes mam." I sat on my bed with my coat and tie laying next to me. She moved the clothes and sat down next to me.

"Vincent, folks can change they mind when they feel they have to, this is true. But sometimes you make agreements. Kinda like the blood brother vow you guys made. Son, I made a promise."

"I know."

"You know?"

"Mr. Archie told me. He told me everything."

"But he ain't me Vincent. I ain't never know a love like I had with your father." She walked to my dresser and looked at my picture I had of him. She wiped the dust off the frame and wiped her hands on her dress. She flattened out the square cloth I had the picture sitting on. She picked the picture up and brought it to the bed. It looked almost like the picture of Mr. Archie when he was young. "Mr. Archie a good man, but he ain't me. I had to live with never having my husband after he left for that damn war, never touching, smelling, seeing his smile... nothing. An all they had to give me was a damn medal and a dog tag. Wasn't even a body inside the casket to grieve over, nothing. And I made sure I hold him fast forever." She took a breath. "Some folks can change, in time. I just ain't ready to let go. And I can admit that. I can say that, but it don't make it okay. It just makes it harder."

"But momma, I think daddy would want you to be happy. You cant be happy crying all the time."

"Then I'll stop crying. You the only man I need to care for now. I don't need...I can't handle loving someone again, like that, and then losing them. I want you to know that. I wouldn't bring such grown up thangs to you otherwise. I need you to know that this is my problem, and not cause of you."

"I think I understand now."

"Get them church clothes off and join me for some ice cream." She put on a smile.

"Yes mam!" I jumped up and started getting undressed. We ate and she told me about my daddy. More stories than I ever knew. I took them all in.

"What's that girl's name you sweet on?"

"Liz."

"Liz what?"

"Elizabeth Mumford is her name."

"You already better off than your dad was. He had chased me for a whole summer, but wasn't smart enough to ask what my whole name was. I figure if he didn't get my name from somebody, he couldn't have been too serious."

"Sometimes folks don't like givin out they last names though mom."

"Well everybody knew each other in North Memphis. If you wanted to know somebody's name, all you had to do was ask the next door neighbor, or one of the elders. Anyhow, your daddy was a senior in high school. He was about to graduate and wanted a date for the prom. I knew him cause he played football and was real good. But I was a year lower than him. I figured he had all the girls."

"My daddy was The Mack?" She popped me on my knuckle with her spoon. It hurt bad and left a ice cream bruise, a chocolate swirl on the knuckle. "Owww mom."

"Your father was not The Mack. He was a man, a handsome young gentleman, very respectful and proud. He was a man. Don't you never let me hear you say nothing like that again."

"Yes mam." I rubbed my hand.

"Your daddy was a lot like you in some ways."

"How so mom?"

"Well, he asked a lot of questions like you do," she said touching me on the nose. "He always helped out around the house with your granny."

Every time mom mentioned my grandparents her eyes fell. I could see her changing like something about my grandparents was wrong. I always assumed that most grandfolks died when you made it to eight or nine years old because of they age. Considering I didn't have any of my grandfolks and neither did a lot of the guys. I never saw it as being out of place. But it had to be different cause anytime mom said something about them she choked up a bit. This time instead of moving on to something else she talked about my daddy's father. She said things I'd never known.

"Your dad lost his father when he was thirteen."

"That's almost the age I am know."

"I know. He use to be with Mr. Archie all the time, all the time. I guess he wanted to replace..."

"That's okay mom, you don't have to talk about it. We can just eat ice cream." She teared up but she never really cried.

"It's like this Vincent, Black folks...Your daddy lost his father to... to a kangaroo court."

"What's a kangaroo court?"

"That's a really tough question. I'm surprised Mr. Archie ain't tell you about it." She tried to brighten up some.

"He ain't never mention it. Neither did Ms. Phillips."

"Son, I know you hear me say a lot of mean thangs about White folks."

"Yes mam."

"White folks done a lot a bad-"

"But all folks ain't bad, Mr. Archie told me that."

"That's right, so don't think your momma hate White folks, cause I don't. But I got a lot of reason to."

"But it ain't good to hold hate inside you."

"That's right Vincent."

"I understand mom."

"Your granddaddy was what you call a sharecropper."

"I heard Mr. Archie talkin about that before."

"I'm sure you have. Mr. Archie did it a bit from what I understand. That's how he got so good with the backyard of his."

"Mom? I heard Mr. Archie talkin bout sharecroppin but he ain't say-"

"He didn't say." She cut me off, correcting me.

"Yes mam... He didn't say what it was exactly."

"What did he tell you?"

"Mr. Archie said croppin was just a good way a keepin Black folks as slaves."

"He about right. He sho is." Mom hadn't finished her ice cream. I had already put my bowl up. The chocolate in her bowl looked like milk. The heat from the kitchen light was strong. The sun was starting to set, and through the kitchen door, I could see the grass and the dirt walking path in the back of the apartments. I could see lightnin bugs glowin and the 'rrrrrr' sound of locusts drowning out crickets. The fan in the kitchen window pulled out most of the heat but at dusk it got hotter before it cooled off. Mom continued telling me about my granddaddy and dad.

"Mr. Archie say it wadn't legal."

"Now, really, sharecropping wasn't spose to still be happening but...folks still worked land and paid too much for it."

"Mam?"

"Folks had to pay for the items they used to take care of the land. I'll give you an example: I pay rent here, for this apartment. But I don't own it. I'm just living here. Now all the money I pay on this apartment go to Mr. Banks. The old White man that come pick up the rent each month."

"With the big nose and moustache."

"Buck?" she popped me on the hand.

"Yes mam."

"Now I'm paying for this apartment but it ain't never gonna be mine and when we move out we can't take nothing but our furniture. Now with sharecropping Black folks rented the materials and land, but they paid more for it than it was worth, which meant they always owed the owner."

"Why would White folks do that?"

"Don't ask that son. Ask why would anybody do that. Your grandpa was a sharecropper, he worked some land out in Jackson. He worked there all fall, and come home for a week in the winter to give money to your grandma, to take care of thangs. He did the same in the spring. When your daddy turned thirteen the spring of 57, his daddy never came back home. Mrs. Sams had heard through some folks at the church that he'd been lynched out in Jackson. They say he stole from his boss and came up short on his money for that spring. But from what everybody else believe, it was just a kangaroo court lookin to keep folks in they place."

I sat wondering what my mom was saying. I thought if my granddaddy was killed by White folks, and my mom said my daddy was killed by White folks, then where did that leave me?

I wanted to talk to Mr. Archie. Mr. Archie would know what to tell me and how to fix things. I didn't want to sit at the table anymore. I didn't need to know everything. I didn't want to know. I felt like I was mad at mom for telling me. I think all things don't need to be said, especially to a boy. Like Mr. Archie said, some thangs is grown folks stuff.

"Mom can I be excused."

"Vincent, I need you to know something else."

"I don't wanna know nothin else."

"Excuse me? You don't wanna... Boy if you-"

"Mom some stuff is grown folks stuff, I don't wanna know." She grabbed my arm and I pulled away. I ran down the hall to my room and slammed the door. I sat on my bed and looked out the window. On the side of the building I could see bedsheets draped on clotheslines barely moving in the wind. The lightnin bugs had disappeared but the light form the moon was clear. Through the trees I could see the outline of leaves and branches with almost a bluish black canvas of buildings and sky. I looked out hoping that it would rain. Mr. Archie said that the rain wash away all the bad stuff and bring back happy sunshine. He said it in one of his songs. I wanted rain to come and make all of the stuff from the past two days go away. Tiger and mom, that boy in the park, I wished it would all go away. I could hear mom moving in the kitchen. She didn't come down to the room at all. No, "Sleep tight, don't let the bedbugs bite," no nothing. It was the first time I could remember her not saying good night.

I wanted to sleep but I felt as if I had hurt my mom. I couldn't sleep. I lay in the bed with my hands, underneath the pillow, raising my head. I could still see moonlight making tree figures on my wall through the window. Then, after what seemed three or four hours, I heard the first drop. It was like a heavy drop from a water faucet. Then there were two more, then three, then a whole bunch of them.

Hitting the metal gutters, the silver part of the windows and the glass itself, like guitar plucks from Mr. Archie, the rain made music. I listened for a while, rolling onto my stomach. There was a flash of light that lit my room for a brief second and then a rumble.

The rumble was low like a groan and moan, "I said de rain dun come Lawwwdeee, and it sho is heavy on my mind. I like de rain to come Lawwdee, cause it make everythang feel fine." The grumble of thunder rolled through the house and instead of being scary, it calmed me and put me out. I slept hard until I heard my mom turn the knob of my door. She didn't say the usual, she just walked in and sat on the bed. Her work clothes were on and the plastic badge hung from her shirt. It was still dark out. Mom didn't usually leave until the sun was up and Mr. Travis blew his horn. She shook me.

"Vincent, momma has to leave a lil bit earlier from now on. I have to catch the bus this week until I can go ahead and get us a car. So you rest up and don't worry, okay?"

I sat wiped sleep from my eyes and sat up into the dark room.

"Mr. Travis not coming by this morning?"

"Afraid not son. But your momma made due before him, I'll be fine."

"Sorry bout hurtin your feelings last night mom."

"You didn't hurt my feelings. I slept on it and you was right, some thangs are better kept til you get older. I just felt you needed to know about your granddaddy. Vincent you are a smart, beautiful boy. I'm proud of you and I love you." She reached her arms out. I hugged her.

130

"I'm proud of you too mom."

"Well thank you, thank you very much. I can go to work happy now."

"Be careful out there at the bus stop."

"Aren't we full of advice this morning?"

"Yes mam."

"I'll be careful Mr. Buck. You don't go off cuttin yourself and gettin in no trouble today."

"I won't. I'm supposed to have brunch with Ms. Phillips and Mr. Archie."

"Brunch? Only rich folks have brunch?"

"I'm practicing." I smiled.

"Keep practicing then. When you make it what you gon do for your momma?"

"I'ma get you a house, a car, a Cadillac and coats and some more kitchen stuff and-"

"Okay, okay... I gotta go now. You finish telling me later whatcha gonna do for me."

"Yes mam." She kissed me on the forehead and left. I sat in the bed and noticed the sun coming up. There were still raindrops on my window. Mr. Archie was right, the rain does wash all the bad stuff away, at least for a little while.

Chapter 14

After mom left I sat in the bed until I couldn't stand the sunlight coming in. If mom would've been there she'd have made me get up with her and stay up. But I figured I deserved the extra sleeping in. I'd had a long weekend. When the heat from the sun got to be too much, I got up and got ready for the day. I took a bath and checked the kitchen to see if there were any dishes. Mom must've stayed up long, cause the kitchen was all clean. I took the push broom out of the cabinet and ran it through the house, over the wooden floors and the carpet covering the living room floor. I checked the garbage and opened the door. It was already hot. My t-shirt stuck to me as soon as I walked out the door. The rain made the air thick and wet. There were a few small puddles left that I stomped in the front of the house. I figured that the fellas weren't up yet but I knew better. No sooner than I got out of the house and emptied the garbage, I saw Smoke and Skillet riding down the street shouting for me to hold up. I thought to myself I'll be doggone if I'm cutting my hand again. I looked at the big scab that had formed, knowing that mom would've cleaned it again and put more stuff on it before she wrapped it. I shook my head and started walking back to the door.

"Buck, Buck," called Smoke.

"What?" I said opening the door.

"Wait for us." said Skillet taking one leg off his bike and coasting to the steps. His brother jumped off and they pulled their bikes up. I let them in. They sat on the couch.

"Whatcha doin Buck?" asked Skillet.

"What does it look like?"

"Can't see you in the back." They giggled.

"I'm wrapping my hand. Why yaw'll coming down here shouting all loud?"

Smoke stopped laughing, "You need to hurry. Man, T, and Lizard are at Stack's house. His folks gone and Stack's uncle left out his books."

I knew what books he was talking about but I didn't need to see those. I really wasn't interested. Then Smoke yelled, "They got White and Black women in them." I thought again and figured, I didn't want to let the guys down. Besides I had to know if Black folks and White folks look different naked. I finished wrapping the hand and I took off to the front. The guys had already went down to their bikes. I slammed the door behind me. I yelled as I ran down the steps. I climbed on the back of Smoke's bike and we shot down to Stack's house.

Stack stayed on the other side of Chelsea. We had to cross the big street and pass the bakery to get there. He lived closer to Greenlaw than Bickford, but he didn't like the guys over there. So we let him hang out with us, plus he was older. He kinda made us feel more important.

When we made it to his house. The grass was a lot higher than it usually was. The fence had been torn down and there was a Black Firebird on the front lawn. The house wasn't that big, but at least they had one. I just wasn't used to it looking so run down.

"Dang, what happened to the house?"

"Stack momma got laid off and his uncle been spending up his checks," said Skillet.

"Yeah, my momma said she been lookin for a job for bout four weeks and that Stack uncle is a junkie," added Smoke.

"What kinda junkie?" I asked.

"Daddy said he usin needles," said Skillet.

"Dang, I wouldn't put no needle in me. I don't even like shots."

"Forget that," said Smoke. "Let's go in and look at the books."

We walked in. The house was dirty. Shoes and pants were in the living room and little bottles of beer were in different corners. Cigarettes filled up gold colored, tin ashtrays. I could hear the other guys talking. We walked into Stack's Uncle's room. His uncle usually had a padlock on the door. But considering how the house looked I guess it didn't matter. The guys were sitting on the edge of the bed. The bed didn't even have legs or rollers under it. It just sat on the floor. The sheets were dirty and the room smelled like old cans of sardines.

"Dang why don't yaw'll take the books outside? This room smell like dookie," I said.

"Cause what if my uncle came back? At least we could put em down and get out before he made it through the door."

Stack looked comfortable in the room. It looked to me like when you live in a house like that you don't think much about it being messed up. They flipped through big books with foldouts and bright pages, filled with Black and White women. Lizard was quiet when he looked, he stared and had his mouth open. Man looked at the book

134

from every angle and said, "It don't look right to me. Look like some slices of meat. It just don't look like nothin to me." He dropped the book.

"Don't look like nothin to me neither Man," said Smoke but he kept looking and so did Skillet. I picked up the book and flipped through the pages. All the women had these looks on their faces like they were eating really good food, but I didn't get it. If they were so happy why did they take pictures so everybody could see them? I flipped until I saw a White and Black women. I guess I wasn't looking at them for the same reason as the guys, mainly Stack. I wanted to see if there was any difference.

"Look yaw'll ain't no difference."

"What?" asked Lizard. Ton reached for my book, I jerked it away.

"Whatcha talkin about Buck?" he asked.

"Look at the picture. It's a White woman and a Black woman and ain't no difference."

"Cept one dark and one white," said Man.

"And one got nappy hair and one got curly hair," said Stack.

Lil T added, "Yeah and they both look like they smellin this room."

We all busted up. Then we heard some yelling. "I thought you said nobody was home?" I asked Stack.

"It ain't, I think."

"Then who car that is out front?" asked Smoke.

"Don't know for sure. That car come here when my uncle home, but I don't never see nobody going in or out of it."

"Thought you knew everything," said Skillet.

"Guys quiet. You hear that, sound like footsteps?"

"That can't be yo uncle," said Smoke laughing.

"Shut up punk," Stack yelled. He reached over to punch. I stopped his hand.

"Listen." It sounded like running. I froze, nobody moved. What if it was a robber or something? I heard the door slam and the engine to the car rev up. The car squealed away. We all looked at each other. Nobody moved. I sat trying to hear any sound. I heard what sounded like a bad moan. But it was coming from under the floorboards.

"I'm ready to go," said Man.

"Shut up," we yelled. Man was usually the first one ready to break out when something wasn't right. I was inclined to follow him cause I figured he knew something. Instead I said,

"Let's find the sound."

"I don't know," Lil T shook his head and stood up slow.

"Stack you go first it's yo house," said Skillet.

"I will. This is my house," he tried to be tough.

He walked towards the door and looked out around the corner. He nodded for us to come. The moaning stopped. We walked towards the front door and saw that the Black Firebird was gone. The moaning started again. I wanted to walk straight out the door but that would've made me a sissy. I stayed with the group. We walked down the long hall, straight ahead was the back door. The rooms branched out like trees on the right and left side. At the darkest part of the hall was the basement. It had one way up and one way down. There was a big

136

door that was locked on the outside. I'd been inside and I knew the basement wasn't that deep, but it was always dark, always. That back part of the house was shaded even during the day. I really didn't want to go but... We kept walking.

I was between Smoke and Skillet. Lil T was behind Stack, and Lizard followed him. Man was behind us all, as usual. We walked real slow looking into each room. We tried to be quiet, but the floorboards spoke up from our weight. We tried to walk on our tiptoes and nothing worked. With every step, the moaning got louder. I started to sweat. I touched Smoke's arm and he jumped, "Don't do that Buck," he said.

"Shhhhsh," everybody held their fingers up to their mouths.

"My bad."

The moaning got louder and there was heavy breath that followed it, the closer we got. Everybody began to hold each others shirts. The further we walked back, the less light there was. We peeked into the bathroom and then into Stack's room and then into the kitchen, then into Stack's moms' room, nothing.

"The light's on in the basement," Stack talked low.

"I think we should go outside and play," said Man.

"Stop being a punk Man," said Lil T.

"A punk live to see tomorrow old folks say."

"Stop talkin Man and come on," whispered Smoke.

I felt scared. We finally made it to the door and it brightened up only a little. The light behind the door was low and peaked out between the floorboard and the lowest part of the painted brown surface of the door. It also showed through the hinges. The moaning got louder and then the breathing. Stack pulled at the door without turning the knob and the door sat still.

"Turn the knob you-" Skillet said.

"Shhhhsh," Lizard said moving to the back of me and Skillet. Stack turned the knob. Underneath the light, between old mattresses and bundles of clothes sat his Uncle's wheel chair, but no uncle. We heard the moan and then the wheez. We all walked down the short, two step drop and looked in further. We saw a foot and and a flat pants leg. Stack's uncle was leaning against the wall holding a needle in his right hand. He had a big black rubber tube clenched in his teeth. He was moaning and breathing through his straining mouth. Covered with sweat, in camouflage pants, a green-brown t-shirt and what looked like a fishing hat, he lay against the wall pushing a needle into the crease under his arm muscle. We all stood. He looked up, his mouth opened and the tube fell out. The needle dangled in his arm. A lighter and something like a hotplate sat beside him. He shook, and then jerked, and sank even further down the wall. His face look swallowed up and sunk. His skin was pasty Black. He laid his head on the wall and started talking.

"Dem lil bastards gon nah, yep. Gon dey is. I kill em good, runnin lil rice bastards dead dey is. You boys see em? Run out pass ya. Right on pass, an tried to keep runnin, but I took my aim an plucked em off like the lil baby VC's dey is. I seen em an dey gon. Dey won't be back fer a while nah. Not fer a while dey won't." The needle dangled in his arm and his head bobbed like a hit boxer. We looked, quiet.

138

"Let's get outta here." Stack turned and began walking out. He stood behind the door until we all left the room. Once we was out, Stack closed the door. The light was still sneaking from under the door, and something moved in the corner of the dark. I jumped slightly and turned my head. We all walked back to the front of the house.

Stack walked with his head down for a second. Then he picked his head up, "Yaw'll I gotta start pickin up round the house. I'll be at the park later."

We understood. We all walked through the front door not wanting to look back and see Stack, but we couldn't help it. We looked over our shoulders and saw him closing the door to the house. The sun had start pushing past the clouds. It was getting warmer. I wanted it to rain. I wanted it to rain for Stack.

Chapter 15

As we walked back towards Fifth Street we didn't say much. I hadn't seen nothing like it before and really didn't get what had happened. I guess none of us knew anything about it. I thought about Tiger and how he knew a little bit about everything. He would've known what was happening. But he was gone. I asked Lil T, "What was he doin?"

"Not sure, but I know he was doin drugs."

"My momma said he used needles. I tol you that earlier, remember?" asked Skillet.

"Yeah, but I didn't think that's how it look. That wadn't even like a shot. That looked worse, like he was in pain from the inside out."

"Guys I'm going home," said Lizard.

"Me too," Man added. "I don't feel so good. I didn't like seeing that."

I agreed. Lil T stopped walking his bike and rode off. He didn't say anything he just rode off. I walked with the twins for a minute until they climbed on their bikes and rode away. I walked by myself, by my house and down through the park. It looked like it was about to thunderstorm but it didn't. The gym was closed. There were only a few guys at the court drinking and shooting. I decided to walk around the backside of the gym so I wouldn't have to pass the courts. I walked straight on to Mr. Archie's house. He wasn't outside on the porch, but his door was open. I heard some different noises coming out. Like pots rattling and stuff. I'd seen him bar-b-que before, but

140

not really cook a lot, although there was always a lot of food in the kitchen. I walked through the gate and up the step.

"Mr. Archie, you in there?"

"Come on in son."

I pulled the door open and walked in. The house smelled good. It smelled like fresh biscuits, pepper and just plain sweet. I walked through the living room and into the kitchen. Mr. Archie had on a pair of brown trousers and a blue shirt. The sleeves was rolled up, and his hair wasn't covered by a hat. He was leaning over a big bowl stirring, humming, "Lil food for de soul, yes indeed. Lotta soul for dis food, yes indeed." I looked around and there were two covered platters on the table. The pale sunlight slid through the curtains and the kitchen door. Mr. Archie even had on some shoes. Some big brown ones, shiny with a buckle.

"Hand me that there pepper an stop ya starin, mighty rude that is."

"Yes sir."

"Act like you never seen a man this sharp before." He stopped stirring and stepped back to show off. He turned and spun. "You like that there don'tcha? Mr. Archie sharp today." He stepped back again and then start stirring.

"Dang Mr.-"

"Whatcha mouth there."

"Yes sir. Why you all dressed up?"

"Well Buck, you found out why a peacock look like he do?"

"No sir, not yet. But I did ask mom and she said she think only the male got all them colors."

"That's almost the answer there. I figured you be dressed a lil bit better. Not sayin you ain't. But figurin on how that lil Mumford girl gon be at Ms. P's I thought-"

"Dang, I forgot-"

"That mouth."

"Yes sir, I forgot all about the brunch."

"Must not be too high on that girl then?"

"I am, it's just that too much been going on lately."

"Well you got bout fifteen minutes to thank on some good stuff ta say."

"Fifteen?"

"Yes indeed." He kept stirring his potatoes. "Fifteen minutes ta practice ya lines."

"What lines?"

"You listenin? You gotta have somethin nice to say. I mean a girl love to hear something sweet. Make her feel like a pretty flower."

"That's what I'll say."

"What's that?"

"I'll call her a pretty flower and give her a pretty flower."

"I do declare you got a jones."

"A jones? What's that?"

"Here, taste this for me." He handed me the stirring spoon and it had lumps of white potatoes with sprinkles of green and red pepper, with bacon pieces in it. It also had some Black pepper on it. I licked the spoon a bit. Then again. Then again and then I put all of the spoon in my mouth. It was like cold mashed, spicy potatoes. I don't even like bell peppers but I ate those too.

142

"I cook them peppers in my special sauce fore I put em in that salad. I know you don't like potatoes much, but you ain't nevah had none of mines."

"Dang, this is-"

"Mouth."

"This is good Mr. Archie, real good."

"I know it. This big plate here full of homemade macaroni and cheese. This one got some of my baked honey ham in it." He pointed at the plates with his spoon after taking it out of my hand.

"We got about five minutes fo we start walkin. You feel like speakin to me bout anythin in particular?"

"No sir. Not really wanting to speak about thangs right now. Maybe later."

"How's ya mom?"

"She took the bus to work this mornin. Said she and Mr. Travis ain't much of a item no more. She ain't really say it, but I knew that's what she was hinting at."

"That so? Well, yes indeed. Hmmph. Come on help me carry this stuff on into the front room." He looked like he had something to add, but he didn't. We put the plates in a big basket. I put the salad in a brown bag. We took the stuff into the front. I excused myself and went to wash up. After coming back I figured we'd be ready to walk. Mr. Archie was still sittin down in his spot on the couch.

"Son, I useta know these folks that live back yonder there in Scuttlefield. Wadn't no big family, maybe three or four at the most. Good folks. Nah this was maybe late fifties early sixties. I tell you all this while we walking." He stood up and grabbed the basket. We walked out the door.

"Momma say she don't know how you leave your door open all the time."

"Cause Buck, if'n you live in a place, an it's yours what you need to close the door for?"

"She say folks done changed too much. Don't nobody leave they doors open no more."

"I ain't other folks." We began walking up Caldwell towards Sixth. He had rolled down his sleeves some but they were still up at his forearm. He had a clean white t-shirt on underneath the blue shirt. He had a blue kerchief that matched the shirt, stuffed into his back pocket.

"If folks gon lock themselfs up in they own house... If you gotta bicycle-"

"I ain't got a bicycle."

"Listen nah. If you had a bicycle, would you lock it up an walk everywhere?"

"No sir, I'd ride my bike with the fellas and go to the store and jump hills and-"

"Buck."

"Sorry."

"Nah, if'n that's yo bike, you wouldn't lock it up right?"

"Only when I ain't around it."

"Then why you lock your door when you home inside yo own property? Folks bring fear in they home when they do that."

"But mom said people ain't right no more. You can't do thangs like you use to. Cause people don't respect nobody no more."

"She got a point. But I'm too old an set in my ways to worry bout thangs like that. I make do okay. Sides ain't right to be no prisoner in your own house. That's what people dun become, trapped in they own homes. Long time ago we needed ta do that."

"Why so?"

"Cause folks that didn't care for Blacks would come an take you away from your family while you sleepin. I jus figure I ain't gon be lockin myself up from my own people."

"I guess I understand."

I did understand, but after the last two days I see why mom said those things. Folks ain't right. That boy that got shot and Stack uncle prove me that. I guess wasn't nobody gonna mess with Mr. Archie though. We cut across some vacant land onto Sixth street. An old house had burned and nobody had come to tear it down.

"Look at that, I declare. A while back, us young men woulda finished the job and got rid of that sight. Nah folks jus walk by an let it be. Ugly it is too."

"Can we tear it down?"

"Be nice if we could, but it take almost six men to do it. Mighty hard for a boy an a ol man to do a job like that."

"I could get the guys and we could try."

"Well, maybe, let me thank on it some. Sho would be nice to try an make this neighborhood better lookin."

"Sure would," I said. Mr. Archie switched the basket from hand to hand. The heat wasn't so bad but the wetness of the air was.

Sweat didn't roll down, but it made drops on our faces. The sun had pushed back into the clouds giving us a little relief. We had a block and a half left.

"I was gon tell ya bout somethin earlier Buck."

"Yes sir?"

"Nevahmind, somethangs ain't for ya ears."

"I know sir." He patted me on the head. I ducked away. "You gon mess up my hair fore we get to Ms. P house."

"Well, excuse me son," he laughed. "Wouldn't wanna cause you no problems wit Ms. Liz."

"That's Ms. Mumford to you."

"Really nah?"

"Yes sir."

We laughed and continued on. Walking under the shade of trees overhangin the sidewalk, we could see Ms. P's house. Some kids were riding their bikes and playing street football. One kid was hiding in the bushes yelling 'Car time.' The other kids ignored him. I saw Rabbit and Big Foot Ann sitting on Ms. P's doorstep. We walked into the gate.

"Good Morning there ladies." Mr. Archie bowed.

"Mornin sir." They answered back. I looked at them and they turned their noses up at me.

"Liz you ready to go," screamed Rabbit. Liz ran to the door and looked out. When I saw her it was like looking at those books, I felt embarrassed. She had gotten bigger over the whole summer. I didn't notice it at the park cause she had on a baggy shirt and pants. But now she had a nice shirt with some dark green shorts on. Her legs look like they went on for half of the door. She stood behind the screen and looked out. Her shirt was light brown with no sleeves. The side of her shirt stuck out. I probably would've never noticed if I hadn't looked at those books. Big Foot pulled Rabbit by the arm and they walked towards the gate. Mr. Archie looked at me and humped his shoulders.

"Don't ask me bout nothin. This yo business."

"I'm just ready to eat," I said. We both laughed and walked up the steps.

"Come on Lizzy. We goin to my house," said Big Foot.

Liz looked at me. I guess she was thinking.

"You know the vow," Rabbit spoke up. I was mad at her, but I didn't say a word. Liz looked again and finally said something.

"Ms. P want me to help her with some stuff."

"What kinda stuff? Can we help?" said Big Foot.

"Wait a minute, I'll ask." She disappeared from the screen door. I eyed Mr. Archie.

"Uh oh son. Look like you gon have a bit a company."

"Why don't yaw'll go play or somethin? Ms. P got enough help, dang," I said.

Mr. Archie popped me on the top of the head just enough to mess up my hair. The girls started laughing. I knew Ms. P was gonna say yes to them. She never said no. Liz ran back to the screendoor and opened it.

"Yaw'll can help too. She got some greens and potatoes that need cuttin. Then we gon hang out some clothes in the back."

"Tell Ms. P my momma want me to be back at the house before twelve," said Rabbit.

"Mines too." Big Foot and Rabbit turned to walk out the gate.

"Yaw'll sure? Ms. P can always use some help?"

"Naw, that's okay Liz. You go head an finish we see you later," said Big Foot Ann. They turned and ran off. Mr. Archie walked into the house laughing loud. I felt relieved. I didn't wanna be embarrassed talking to Liz in front of her friends. I walked in while Liz pulled the door closed behind me. She lifted the hook and dropped it in the hole to lock the door.

"Hey Buck."

"Hey Liz." I put my left hand in my pocket and swayed. I walked to the side like Mr. Archie did when he saw Ms. P. She walked beside me. I kept bumping her arm as we moved down the hall toward the kitchen. I had the brown bag in one hand, and then I let my left hand swing a little. She looked at me and smiled. She had pretty teeth. They were big and white and all sitting in a row. When she smiled her cheeks made her eyes squint. She still had the half circle thing on her hair, but this time it matched her green pants. I looked at her skin and tried to think of something to say.

"You look like a flower in dirt." Dang, I said to myself. I stopped swaying and looked down. I knew I said something stupid. I can't for the life of me figure out why I couldn't make my words come out right.

"Thank you Buck, that was sweet. You look like a flower in dirt too," she laughed. I felt dumber.

"I didn't mean to say that. I was tryin to be like Mr. Archie and say some nice stuff."

"That why you was walking and bumpin me?"

"My bad."

"It's okay, I thought you looked kinda cool."

"Really? Oh, I know I was okay. You know me and Mr. Archie made all of this food."

"You helped cook?"

"Sure did. I cook at home too. My momma be tired sometimes, so I take care of things."

"That's nice Buck." We walked on into the kitchen. I put the bag down. Mr. Archie was standing beside Ms. P talking about the greens and laughing.

"So you cuttin up greens and doin laundry right nah?"

"I be doin that sometime today, or tomorrow, or sometime or another."

"You somthin else. Tellin them lil girls that big ol story."

"Wadn't no story, I *will* be doin those thangs sometime or another," she laughed.

Her hand was inside of a big oven mitten. She reached down to pull out a sweet potato pie. Mr. Archie started taking the food out of the basket and the bag. Liz and me walked out to the back of the house. Ms. P's yard wasn't as big as Mr. Archie's, but it was nice enough. She had about half of it covered with clotheslines and the other half had a small garden with all kinds of colored flowers and green grass. It stretched for about eight feet to the back fence. Behind the fence was a back drive that went to some apartments hidden off of

Bickford. There was trees lining the drive that dropped leaves into Ms. P's yard during the fall. The trees didn't right belong to no one so she'd have to sweep them from the fence border every fall. There were two chairs underneath an overhang on the five step back porch. Two of the old iron kind with rounded legs so that they could rock. I sat down in one and Liz kept standing and looking over the backyard. I had never asked Mr. Archie what you were supposed to say to a girl when you were by yourself. So I just sat there looking at what she was looking at.

"Watcha lookin at?" Another dumb question.

"The flowers... in dirt," she laughed and came and sat down.

"I didn't mean that for bad, you know?"

"Yeah I know, flowers look pretty good, even in the ground." She smiled. "I've never had anybody say I was pretty like that before." She kept looking out.

"I bet people tell you you're pretty all the time."

"No they don't, Rabbit and Ann-"

"They jus jealous cause you look better than both of them. They don't know nothin."

"I was fixin to say that they say I'm pretty."

"Oh, my bad. Well, I think you're pretty and sweet like the honeysuckle in Mr. Archie's backyard." I sat upright and held my head high after saying that.

"Thank you Buck," she dropped her head.

"I ain't mean to embarrass you."

"I'm okay, jus that you makin a fuss and I thought you didn't like me. Now you say you do. I'm a lil confused, but I guess it don't matter."

"Mr. Archie told me to do that. He told me that I should ignore you and you'd like me more."

"It hurt my feelings."

I felt bad about what I did. Mr. Archie was right but he was wrong too. I didn't know what to say except, "I'm sorry. I won't do it no more. Not never again."

"You swear?"

"I can't swear. My momma told me you ain't supposed to swear. But I can bet you that I won't say it again. That's more important anyway."

"Okay."

I reached my little finger out and she did too. We hooked fingers and said, "Promise." Her finger was warm and it felt soft and spongy. Like the stuff in the sink after you wash the dishes. I felt icky, but I also think I felt good. I giggled and let go.

"What are you giggling at?" she asked.

"Nothin."

"Yes you are."

"Okay, okay, your hand felt warm and funny."

"Yours too Buck. It felt like a warm muffin."

"Muffin? I'm gettin hungry, you?"

"Yeah, let's go back in." I walked over and held the door for her. She thanked me and walked through. I shut both doors behind me. I didn't care what Mr. Archie said, I don't like leaving the door open.

The house smelled like Sunday after church. All kinds of food everywhere. Ms. P had made some salmon croquette and green bean casserole. We made our way to her dining room. She had a big table with a light hanging over it. The table cloth was dark white with dangling strings hanging off of it. The food was all around the table. Ms. P and Mr. Archie were still laughing and talking as we passed through the kitchen and into the dining room. I figured I better go back and help with something. Liz stayed in with the food. There wasn't much sun out yet but it was enough. The daylight filled the room through the two big windows on the side. I walked into the kitchen and almost freaked out. I stopped and let out a big gasp. Mr. Archie was holding Ms. P around the waist and pushing his mouth up against hers, like two old fish in a pond going after the same bait. I couldn't stand to look, but I did. Why? I don't know. I just hadn't seen old people act like that. Mr. Archie heard me, and pulled his hands down real quick and opened the icebox. Ms. P brushed her shirt down and put her leg down. Why was it bended anyway, I thought. She pulled her mitten off.

"Uhh, Buck, you uhhh, got the um lemonade? Here take this lemonade. I be right on out shortly."

"Yes sir." I took the pitcher and looked him in the face.

"Gon nah and take that on out there an stop that staring, mighty rude that is."

"Sorry Mr. Archie." I kept looking and standing there.

"Gon nah, git on in there and put that down for you drop it."

152

"Yes sir I'm moving." I left out looking back over my shoulder a number of times before going past the kitchen door. I walked into the dining room and Liz was snatching her hand back from the salmon. Her mouth was still chewing in little bitty nibbles.

"I saw you."

"Saw what?" she asked.

"I saw you snacking."

"Nuh Un."

"Yeah I did. I ain't gon tell though, cause I want a piece too." She laughed at me and broke off a piece of fish, put a drop of hot sauce on it and passed it to me. After I sat the lemonade down, I gobbled the bite. We both sniggled quietly.

"Guess what I saw in the kitchen?"

"What?"

"I saw Mr. Archie-"

"Whatcha see there Buck?" Mr. Archie and Ms. P walked in together.

"Nothing sir, I thought I saw you looking at me sneak some food."

"Sneaking food huh? Couldn't wait for us to finish in the kitchen," said Ms. Phillips.

I started laughing cause I couldn't help it. I wanted to say, '*Whatcha mean finish?*' But I didn't say nothing.

"Boy you jus plain ol nutty."

Liz laughed at his words. We all laughed.

"This don't look much like brunch do it?" Ms. P said looking over the spread. She hadn't made much but her two dishes along with

Mr. Archie's food was a lot. I sat on the side of the table with Mr. Archie. Liz and Ms. P sat across from us. The settings at the head were there but we wasn't expectin nobody as much as I knew.

"Naw, this don't look much like brunch, it looks like Sunday dinner don't it?" I asked.

"Sure do." Liz answered.

"Alrighty nah, evrybody git yo hands out so we can pray, gotta say grace." We all reached out. Me and Liz had to lean up some cause the table was kinda big. When I touched her hand it felt warm. She smiled at me and was looking from under her bowed head. I was lookin too. Mr. Archie lowered his head and got ready to pray.

"Dear Lawd, make these chilren close they eyes durin this prayer so that this food will be blessed, so that we might use it for your work. In Jesus name, Amen."

When he finished Ms. P slapped him on the hand. He let out a deep laugh like a car starting up loud. I felt embarrassed again and Liz laughed, that made me feel better. We got into the food, passing plates and pouring lemonade. Mr. Archie was telling jokes and Ms. P laughed at all of them. Even the ones that wasn't that funny made her laugh. But it wasn't much talking as we cleaned our plates and worked on seconds. The sun came out for a moment and just like that it left and then it sprinkled. Not hard but just enough to let you know it rained. I felt good for Stack.

"Aww gloreee, I am stuffed. Archie... that potato salad, you outdone yourself."

"You put your foot in them salmon too Ms. P, sho did. You sho ya didn't go down to the river an catch them salmon."

"Ain't no Salmon in the Mississippi?"

"It was a joke Buck. Even I knew that," Liz said.

"I did too. I was just jokin back." I leaned back in the chair holding my stomach. Liz sat back also, even though she didn't eat that much. Mr. Archie had a tooth pick and was switching it back and forth in his mouth, and sucking on his teeth.

"Where's yo manners Archie?"

"Sometimes ya manners up and go when you so full you can't think right." He chuckled. Ms. P shook her head and laughed too. She got up from the table.

"Guess it's bout time we start picking up."

"Guess it is," Mr. Archie said still sitting down rubbing his stomach.

"I take it you can't move right now?"

"Well, Ms, I reckon if I did move somethin wouldn't smell right in here."

"Archie!"

I laughed my butt off. Mr. Archie was showing out and I liked seeing it. I liked seeing him real happy. No stories about sad stuff or happy stuff, just him eating and being comfortable. I figured I'd better start helping out if I wanted Liz to be impressed.

"Take a break Mr. Archie. I bet your arms are pretty tired. You was shovelin that food in your mouth like throwin mulch."

"That so? I guess you purty tired yourself there. Mighty hard to eat and stare across the table. That musta put a hurtin on your neck."

"I wasn't starin across the table."

"Nothin wrong with that, just thought you might be kinda tired is all," he said to me still chuckling. Liz got up and started helping. She was quiet and listening most of the time. I wanted to talk to her, but not in front of Ms. P. We carried the plates and leftovers to the kitchen. Ms. P had ran dishwater and was cleaning plates. We could hear Mr. Archie in the dining room breathing, sayin, "Woooweee, I do declare."

"Archie gonna get that Black-itis in a minute," Ms. P laughed.

"What's Black-itis?" asked Liz.

"Well, some folks eat an then they pass right out, right where they sitting when they finish. Sometimes they move to the couch and get a book, act like they reading something. But usually they ain't reading, they sleep."

I laughed and Liz laughed for a second.

"Liz baby you ain't eat much. You feeling okay?"

"Yes mam, I'm fine. I ate enough, I'm okay."

"Well, we fix you a plate to take home to your father, mother and little sister."

"That's okay mam. I thank you for the offer though."

I kept putting away the food and listening. Ms. P stopped washing dishes and looked at Liz. "Elizabeth, anythang you wanna tell me?" Liz looked at me, then back to Ms. P, and nodded her head no. "Something you wanna say baby go head and say it. We ain't no strangers and you know I consider you my own." Ms. P wiped her hands on her apron and sat down. Liz looked at me again and nodded her head no. I knew it was time for me to leave. I didn't need no other hints.

"I'ma go check on Mr. Archie."

As I walked out, Liz And Ms. P sat down at the little table in the kitchen. "Talk to me sweetheart," I heard as I made my way into the living room. I couldn't hear much else and I knew better than to listen in from the other side of the wall. I walked through the dining room and no Mr. Archie. I made it to the front room and he was sitting on the couch with a paper in his hand. His head dipped and then popped up. It dipped again hard, like it was about to fall off, then he held his head up and started smacking like he was eating on something. He opened his eyes looked at the paper, turned the page and said, "Mmmm Hummm, I declare."

"You declare what Mr. Archie?"

"Lemme see, I was looking at this here paper and reading bout some thangs."

"You look sleep to me."

"Wadn't sleep, no suh. Wadn't sleep at all. I was resting up my eyelids, to finish this here article."

"Ms. P said you got eye-tis. She say you was gon be in here sleep."

"That what she say? Well I guess I better go in there and let her see that I ain't sleepin." He stood up and wobbled. "Woooweee, I guess I'm a lil lightheaded." He sat back down.

"You okay Mr. Archie?" I asked walking over by him.

"I'm fine Buck, jus stood up a bit too fast. I'm alright."

"Okay." I could see he was alright after he cleared his throat and tucked his shirt back in. "For someone that wasn't sleepin you sure do look like it."

"Aww hush ya mouth." He tapped me on the head as he began walking towards the back.

"I think they talkin."

"About what?"

"Don't know, Liz was lookin pretty bothered bout something."

"Hmph, she wadn't eatin much neither. Like she was thinking the whole time. Well, we give em some peace. What's on yo mind son?"

"Nothing." I walked over to the couch and sat down. He came back and sat where he was.

"You sho?"

"Well, I'm wonderin what's wrong with Liz."

"Probably nothin much. She might be askin what to do when a girl like a boy."

"You think, really?"

"Naw boy. I jus figured on gittin ya hopes up. Of course she like you or she woulda went on wit them other lil girls. She jus askin how ta talk wit you."

"Mr. Archie, I like her too. So what am I supposed to say to her now?"

"Jus be yoself and be real nice to her. A boy likin a girl don't mean much of a change. Ya carry her books. Give her yo milk when she forget her school lunch, jus be nice wit her is all."

"Do I have to do what you was doing with Ms. P?"

"So you saw that huh?"

"Kinda sir. I saw yaw'll touching all close and stuff."

"Well Buck, that kinda stuff for grown folk. You jus hold hands wit Liz."

"That's all I wanted to do anyhow."

"Good, and very good. That was a meal huh?"

"Yes sir. I think I'ma take a plate for mom."

"That be mighty fine. Yes indeed, fine that would be...Yep." His voice started trailing off. I could hear, but my eyes couldn't stay open. I tried to hold my eyes open wide, but it didn't work. I looked at Mr. Archie and his head was tilted back, he was asleep. I said to myself that I wasn't gonna get the eye-tis, but some thangs are just unstoppable.

"Look at there, jus like I said, Black-itis." I could hear Ms. P talking but I couldn't see her. Then I heard a loud pop. My eyes shot open and I jumped. I wiped my eyes and saw Ms. P and Liz standing in front of us laughing. She clapped her hands again, but Mr. Archie was snoring. He didn't hear a thing.

"That's a doggone shame. Look at him. Little slob on the corner of his mouth and all."

"I looked at Mr. Archie as he finally woke up. He started smacking again, like he was eating as he rolled his head forward. "Ummm Hummm, I do declare."

"I declare you a mess Archie. Ain't bit mo and the first help me clean that table and kitchen. This ain't the fifties, woman ain't gotta do it all," she laughed.

"Patricia, a man got a right ta rest up some don't he? Me and Buck walked a long way over here nah."

"Yaw'll walk half a mile and Buck wasn't sleep," she said.

Mr. Archie looked at me, "Boy you bettah learn how ta fall asleep after dinner, git you outta a lotta housework." He smiled at me.

"Just a mess Archie, Just a mess."

Liz was smiling. I felt glad that she wasn't looking sad anymore, but I wanted to know what was wrong. I told Mr. Archie I was sleeping.

"Nah Patricia, why ya gotta tell a story on the boy?" He stood up and walked toward Ms. P reaching for her stomach tickling. Ms. P laughed and slapped his hand away a little.

"You need to quit Archie."

"I quit when you gimme some sugar."

"I ain't doin nothin of the sort." She put her hands on her hips and looked at him. Almost like mom did when I was talking too much. Mr. Archie stopped and fixed his shirt again and cleared his throat. He smiled as he sat back down on the couch.

"So Buck what are you two doing the rest of the afternoon."

I didn't know what we were doing but I remembered the money Ms. P had gave me. Liz sat on the smaller sofa with Ms. P. I didn't say anything for a minute and then it happened, again. Another dumb outburst.

"I don't know. I'ma go play with Stack and them." Dumb, dumb, dumb. I wanted to say that I was gonna take Liz for ice cream, but it just didn't come out the right way.

Mr. Archie looked me in the face and I came to my senses. "Well, I don't know if Liz would wanna go for ice cream, but that's what I wanna do."

"I'd like to go for ice cream," Liz said smiling.

160

"Thought you said kids don't go for malts?"

"Archie, don't start with me... I said kids don't know what malts is no more. You just don't listen do you?"

"I listen, you jus don't say much worth hearin."

"Excuse me? You the one, story after story, you been tellin stories since we was kids. I know em all now. You ain't gotta tell me them stories no more."

"So whatcha sayin?"

"You need some more stories."

"You too." Mr. Archie said raising his voice. "Doggone woman still stubborn after thirty years. Jus as stubborn as you was-"

"Watch it Archie," Ms. P sat up in her chair straight.

"Uh, I think we gon be going to the store now. Come on Liz."

"Look at you, done scared off the chilren. Done scared em off."

"That's yo loudness. If you ain't come out shoutin an carryin on-"

I took Liz by the hand and we walked towards the door. Liz held her head down. I guess the shouting made her sad again. We walked out and I could hear Mr. Archie stop yelling. We stopped on the porch and listened through the door. I heard Ms. P say, "That work like a charm."

"Sho did. Got em right on outta here. Nah you gimme some sugar." I heard this loud smack and Liz and I lost it. "Uuggh, yuk," we yelled listening to the gross smacking. After saying that I heard footsteps coming to the door. Liz and I jumped down the steps and took off. I looked back and saw Mr. Archie peaking through the screen door. He had a huge grin on his face. We laughed as we ran off up Sixth Street.

We made it halfway up the block almost by her apartments. She lived in these orange and red brick buildings that faced the street. The windows were big and they all had bars on them. Her apartment was on the corner about two blocks from Ms. P's. She looked over towards them and grabbed me by the hand. She started running towards one of the old houses across the street from the start of her building.

We cut through the yard and walked up the chipped concrete drive into the backyard. There was a fence that was partially pulled up at the back of the lawn. It was bent backwards enough that I could squeeze through it barely ducking. It led to the alley behind this really old house that nobody lived in. I never walked that way cause there were too many trees. But it led to the store faster. I just didn't like going that way.

When we made it through the pulled-up-gate, it seemed as if somebody hid the sun. It was like dark green. I could see the back of the old house. The front of that house wasn't so bad. It was on Fifth Street, but nobody ever went into it. It sat up on the hill on the same side as the little projects across from my street. The house was old wood. With two windows on the front, two on the sides, and one in the back. The wood was gray, not like regular good brown. Paint was chipping off of it in pale, white, flat, chunks. There was always a cat, or two, or three, sitting on the steps in the front. There was a fence around the back of the house too. It was pulled up at the corner in the same way as the one we cut through.

The back of the house had dirty curtains that moved when the wind blew. I wanted to run. Who knew if that was the wind. Besides, it was ninety degrees out and the wind was barely enough to make it okay to walk in, let alone blow curtains in a closed up house.

If the sun wasn't going in and out behind clouds, and making it cool, then I would've ran. Liz held my hand as we continued down the alley. I could see a break in the dark green as we were getting closer to the end of the alley behind the apartments.

"Why'd you wanna come this way?" I asked.

"Cause?"

"Cause what?"

"Cause, um, it's quicker."

"Yeah but ain't you scared of that house?"

"Naw, that house ain't nothin to be afraid of. Some other things scarier than that house."

"I don't know none. That's where Mr. Archie say some folks got caught in a fire."

"What kinda fire?" Liz stopped walking right before we got outta the dark part.

"Why don't we just get into the apartments and keep on to the store? I'll tell you."

"No, what fire?" She crossed her arms, like a little Ms. P.

"Come on and stop actin. Let's go get ice cream." I could feel the wind picking up. It sounded like the doors was closing on that house. I walked on across the dirt into the projects. She stood there and looked at me. She turned and took off towards the house.

"Liz!" I called after her. Her arms pumped in the air as her legs turned over the grass and dirt kicking up dried leaves. "Liz," I shouted again, standing on the opposite side of the dirt. I couldn't see her anymore as she ducked under the fence. I heard the door slam shut.

Now, the manly thing to do would've been going back to see what happened and why she ran to that house. But I'm not a man, I'ma kid, and some things better left to grown folks. But it was Liz and I liked her. So I stood on the opposite side of the dirt and yelled for her again. Nothing. The sun had start moving behind this big gray cloud. I could see through the branches the beginning of rain. When it looks like the sky is coming down in the distance, it rained. I could see that it was coming down. I walked back over and continued yelling.

"Liz it's fixin to rain... come on Liz the rain is comin." I looked up again and it was starting to get dark. My momma and Mr. Archie called it tornado weather when it got cool on a hot day and the clouds started falling. It was getting cool. The wind in the dark green pushed around loose twigs, scraping on fallen leaves. The branches waved back and forth like hands telling me to come. I stopped walking again.

"Liz, I'm gonna go back to Ms. P's. You should come too." 'Please come Liz,' I was thinking to myself. I walked closer to the opening in the fence. I looked at the hole for a few seconds before I ducked down and crawled beneath it. The dirt was thick like hard mud under my feet. Brown and orange colors filled the back yard between stumps and overhanging tree limbs. There were locusts shells stuck all

164

over the base of one tree, and fire ants in a big pile beside the biggest stump. I looked all over and thought against yelling anymore. So I whispered loud.

"Liz I'm here, come outta the house and let's go. Please." I moved towards the back of the house. There wasn't a real porch there but there were steps that went up to the door. It was about five steps, gray wood. The screen door, had no screen and it was open a little bit. 'Why in the hell did she run back in here,' I wondered.

"Liz...Liz," I called trying to tip up the steps, they creaked and moaned. I saw lightnin and then heard the rumble through the blanket of thick green blocking out the sky. I stopped on the steps.

"Dang Liz, stop playin and let's go before it start raining." Still, no answer. I had to go in. I walked up the steps and opened the screen door and then the big heavy back door. Black. I couldn't see past the wall of the kitchen. For a shotgun house it had a lot of walls. I figured I'd be able to see straight down a hall into the front room, but I'd have to go all the way in to even see the light coming from the front, if there was any. From Fifth Street you could see that the shutters in the front were closed. But there had to be more light closer to the front than it was in the back. I walked in and something ran over my foot, heavy. I jumped and saw that it was a mouse. It ran out the back door while it was still open. I didn't close the door cause I needed the little light it gave.

"Liz, I'm here, tell me where you are?" I was in the middle of the kitchen and was running out of light, it was getting darker the further I moved inside. When I stepped over the edge of the kitchen, I could see each room in the house. The hallway was the center of the house. It connected each room with six feet of old floor. We were a little ways from the back door when it made a wooshing sound and slammed shut. I was about to cry, but I needed to find Liz.

"Quiet Buck, they don't like noise." I heard coming from the dark space on the right. Liz clicked on a lighter and held the flame so I could see her. She moved the flame over two candles and lit them. I looked on and couldn't say a word. "Come and sit down." The light was enough to show a room with a mattress on the floor covered by sheets. There was an old dresser with a mirror on it and a box, that looked like it was for jewels, sitting on top. I walked in and sat beside Liz on the side of the mattress. I could hear what sounded like small footsteps coming towards the room. "Shhsh, don't say nothing. They don't talk to nobody but me." I was starting to sweat. I wiped my hands on my pants and moved, putting my back against the wall. Liz just sat and looked at the door, smiling at the blackness. I didn't see anything. "They gon now."

"Who? and what'd you have to come in here for. It's about to rain hard. We shoulda went back to Mr.-"

"Shhsh. They trying to sleep some. The rain make em sleep better for a while."

I looked around and saw a pile of clothes and some books. Liz got up and walked to the corner of the dark room and pushed the door closed.

"They say they need it quiet so they can hear em coming this time."

"Hear who coming?"

"The White folks. They tell me that the White folks come and take them away."

"You see em?"

"Sometimes, but I don't like lookin. Their skin is all black and peeling."

"Peeling?" Then I remembered what Mr. Archie told me. "Why you come here? Why?"

"Cause I have to."

"Why? I mean you got a place to live at, wit a momma and a daddy."

"Yeah but... I need to come here. You ever run away?"

"Thought on it."

"Why?"

"My mom and Mr. Travis like each other."

"The store Mr. Travis?"

"Yeah. But cause of me she can't take his offer to marry. I think it's my fault, but Mr. Archie say that she got a lot of stuff inside her that cause her to not wanna marry again."

"What kinda stuff?"

"She still love my daddy, and she say she promised not to forget him."

"You don't need no daddy no how."

"How come you say that?"

"Cause?"

"I wish I had a daddy. Smoke and them go on vacations sometimes with they daddy. Tiger moved in with his. You got a daddy, and everything seem okay."

"I wanna run away. That's why I come here. That's why I come here and talk and sleep sometimes."

"But you got a momma and a daddy, things can't be that bad."

She started tearing. I could see the light catching her eyes more. I scootched over by the bed and looked her in the face. She wasn't crying yet, just tearing up.

"Sometimes a daddy ain't good for the family. So I come here."

"But what about yo sister?"

"She too little."

"Yeah, but she can walk, so you should bring her too."

"No, she too small and he don't bother her none. Momma don't talk much."

I didn't understand what she was saying. But whatever it was she felt like she needed to be away from the house. I could hear the rain hitting against the outside walls. The door to the room creaked open and then closed.

"Shhhsh, be quiet. She can hear the White men coming. Every time it rain she can here em coming. She the littlest one. She heard em coming the first time too."

I still didn't see nobody. But I heard the noises. Sounded like ten big feet kicking in the back door and a lot of scraping. Then the back door slammed shut. The candles moved like they was going out and then quiet.

"They gon with the White folks now."

"Where?"

"I don't know. They don't never tell me nothing else."

"What they tell you?"

"They always tell me that the White folks coming to get em, to scare everybody else. But they don't never say where they going. They just end up back here telling me that folks is coming to get em."

"Didn't you say they was peeling?"

"Yeah, like hot dogs on a grill. That's why I come back cause I seen the clouds. I was hoping they'd tell me where they was going. I came back too because you said they was burned. I didn't want them to go with the White folks no more. I want em to stay with me and be okay."

I just sat. Thinking.

"It sound like the rain dun passed."

"It always pass when they leave. Like the thunderstorm take them. What did Mr. Archie tell you bout this house?"

"How bout we go back to Ms. P's. I don't really remember what he said." I did remember but I didn't want to say. I wanted to get out of the house. I was too doggone scared to sit still. I didn't like the sounds and the drafts. Why would Liz go in there by herself? I kinda hoped that I would be tough enough to ask Liz for a kiss, but as much as I was shaking I figured it wouldn't be no good. Besides, everytime I looked at Liz I saw the books from Stack's house, and I heard Mr. Archie saying that we don't need to do nothing but hold hands. So I let it go and thought about how much I wanted outta that house.

"Come on Liz let's go."

"Hold on, I gotta put out these candles." She straightened the sheet on the bed and blew the candles out. She grabbed my hand and started walking through the blackness. It wasn't so bad going back through the kitchen. Liz was steady as she walked. Her hands still felt soft and funny.

"You okay Liz?"

"Yeah, I'm okay. You?"

"Yep, I'm okay?"

"Are you? No lying or I'll pop you." She held her fist up as we made our way into the dark green and out of the backyard.

"I didn't like being in there."

"You were scared huh?"

"Naw, I wadn't scared just couldn't see nothing."

"You were afraid."

"I was okay. I just don't understand what you needed to go in there for." I began to duck under the gate and stopped. I let her go under first and then I followed. The gate's rusty, silver, wire left brown, orange marks on my shirt. I brushed at the dirt. Liz walked and kicked at rocks. Our feet sunked into the mud enough to cake up the edge of our shoes. We kept walking. She looked straight ahead without ever answering my question.

"Why you gotta go in there?"

"Cause."

"Cause what?"

"Sometimes it makes me feel better, is all."

"Oh." Mr. Archie always told me when a woman don't answer the question the third time, just leave it alone. He talked about how this man name Racy was always bothering women for a date, but didn't nobody ever go out with him.

"Ummm Hum Buck, that boy wit his big ol grinnin face nevah got a date. I mean nevah. Would walk around wit the cleanest outfit on from Sunday to Sunday, but nevah no date. Some folks said it was cause his feet was so big and he was short. But he was alright far as I could see. He use to wear his hair in a twisted up conk, jet black. He had a sharp lil moustache and one gold tooth. Boy he thought he was an item walkin round North Memphis. Not quite sure what he did to get all that stuff he had, but long as he wadn't bringing no trouble to our street nobody give a care. He had these high polished pointed shoes that slid from under the pants leg for days. All the time he step up to women on Friday evening, struttin. Swingin and smooth, justa struttin. Boy acted like he was on Beale Street all day long. This what he say to the ladies, "Missy I declare I seen you in my dream last night. I ain't lyin I swear on it. How's about you and me make like the stars and shine together." And everyday, every woman would look at him, tilt their heads up and keep on walkin. He jus kept on struttin, didn't shake a bit on the outside. I seen him one day and he stopped me.

"Say Mr. A, I need a word witcha."

"Yessuh, Mr. Racy. How ya doin son? You lookin sharp as a tack as usual."

"Mr. A, it ain't doin me no good though. I get's me all these fine threads and the women don't even pay it no mind. Why in Chicago-"

"Ah Ha, in Chicago huh?"

"Yeah, in Chicago the ladies love these kinda threads."

"Well, whatcha stoppin me for?"

"I..need some advice." He looked all over like he didn't want nobody to hear him. "I.. need some help wit these here women."

"First thang is that they ladies, not women. Second thang Racy is this ain't Chicago or Beale Street or Bourbon, or whatever. This here is North Memphis. We simple folks, you know that. You ain't been gone but a year up North."

"Mr. A, I ain't disrespectin ya, but what kinda advice I'm needin is how I'ma get me a date? The clothes ain't workin and my words must be too slick for these here women."

"Son, when I was your age, and I ain't that far from ya, I use ta say to the women: Good Morning, an Good Afternoon, an Good Evening." Racy sat on the curb and blew out.

"Nah Racy don't be blowin your breath at me, jus listen."

"Yes sir."

"Alrighty nah, what I'm tellin ya is that I use ta be kind to em. Carry they groceries and help do thangs round the neighborhood. I wadn't no real flashy guy but I held my own. But women like to be purty."

"I'm listening."

"A man ain't spose to be purtier than his woman. Lookin at you like being in the big city, they fraid of that. They like thangs simple."

"Alright man, alright, I gotcha," he jumped up slapping his hands together. "I gotta tone it down a bit."

"Ya gotta be yoself..well be respectful."

"I gotcha Mr. A."

"My name is Mr. Archie."

"Sorry Mr. Archie."

"That's already bettah. And Racy, when a woman say no or don't answer three times in a row, let it go and ask later. Much later. Ladies don't like to feel like they being bothered too much. You just be yoself and stop that big city stuff and git back to simple thangs."

"Thank you Mr. A... I mean Mr. Archie. I'ma work on it."

"Well, lo and behold Buck, that young Racy found himself a purty lil lady who like him without the conk and fanciness. This all jus ta letcha know that when a woman say no, jus let it be, she come around."

So I let Liz have her peace. I let her keep in her thoughts. Well, I didn't let her, mom would say that I didn't let nobody do anything. It was their choice.

"You still wanna go to the store?" I asked.

"Nah. We can go back to Ms. P's. Buck, you don't tell nobody bout my place."

"What about Mr. Archie?"

"Nobody Buck. Swear on it."

"I told you my momma don't let me swear on nothin. I won't tell." She looked me in the face and kept walking. We went back behind the other house with the fence pulled up and stayed in the alley til we reached Bickford. I let her lead pretty much. I didn't want to intrude on her space. Something was on her mind and I really wanted to know so I could talk to Mr. Archie about it and help.

"Liz, why you gotta go to that house?"

"Sometimes it's safer in there. Sometimes it's better than being home. That's why."

"Okay." I kicked muddy grass onto the drive in the alley. The drive was concrete all the way up to about twenty feet into the dark trees. Then it stopped, like nobody wanted to finish it. I reached for Liz's hand. I didn't care if it was soft and all. I wanted to hold it and squeeze it like my momma did mine. I wanted her to feel better. The rain hadn't done nothing for her. It didn't take away her pain. It brung it on. I guess some things work different for some folks. We can't all be the same, so I guess the rain only do good by some folks. We headed up Bickford and turned left onto Sixth Street. No one was out on the stoops. The rain had made everybody go in. I liked it when it rained at night. It made it cool. But during the day it felt like hot air fogging up the kitchen window in the winter. Sticky and wet. We walked. I had drops of water making designs around my cheeks and eyebrows. Ms. P still had her door open and I could hear music coming out of the house. It sounded like Mr. Archie with a band. A old voice drug in with the plucking of the guitar, *"Whose makin luv to yo ol lady while you was out makin luv."* It didn't sound much like Mr. Archie. I knocked on the door.

"Who is it?"

"Liz and me, Ms. P," I yelled back.

She walked up and pulled the hook from the door.

"Yaw'll get caught in that rain?"

"No mam. We was fine we-" Liz bumped me with her shoulder and turned back to lock the door. She looked at me in, 'the shut up' kinda way. So I did.

"You went where?"

174

"To Bucks' house on Fifth. We was gonna go by the park, til it started raining," Liz said.

"Is that so? Well, long as you wadn't out in the street none. You can still get sick from the summer rain."

"Yes mam." I said. "Mr. Archie-"

"He in the kitchen lookin through the icebox for something to snack on."

"He still hungry? Mam, he told me you wadn't supposed to eat a lot at a ladies house. He said it wasn't smart cause folks would think you ain't got no home training."

"Did he say that when he made ribs?"

"That's the only time he say it."

"I figured on that."

I didn't get it. I looked at her with my question face. My eyes squinted and cheeks raised up, my head tilted to the left a little. She took me and Liz by the hand and started walking.

"I take it yaw'll didn't make it to the store?"

"No mam," Liz answered.

"Well, we gon haveta fix that growling in your stomach Buck."

"My stomach ain't growling."

"Coulda fooled me. I thought you might want some of this here um, lemon pie that's in the kitchen."

"Lemon pie? I didn't see no lemon pie at brunch?"

"That's cause it had to stay in the frigerator. I plain ol forgot about it."

Liz brightened up, I was about to take off. Until I felt the hand on my collar snatching me backwards.

"Don't you run in this house nah."

"Yes mam." Ms. P smiled and let me go. We all walked through the dining room and into the kitchen. Mr. Archie was sitting at the small table with a fork eating away at the pie. He jumped when we walked in and started cutting the pie with a knife like he was making pieces for everybody.

"Ummph, I was just cuttin this here pie for us, heard yaw'll comin."

"Mighty funny the pie got pieces gone."

"I do declare that is strange. Strange indeed. You see, I was looking in the icebox and I seen that a sliver was gon too. When you reckon it happen?"

"I reckon it happen when I went to the front door."

"You know it jus may have happened then. Me, myself, I was in the bathroom. Anythang coulda happen while I was in there."

Ms. P picked up the pie and carried it into the dining room shaking her head. "Just a mess that man is." He laughed loud and clicked his finger at me. I clicked back. Liz followed Ms. P with plates and forks. She was being real quiet. I was thinking about her. Thinking about how I was gon tell Mr. Archie. We followed them in.

"Buck, whole day dun passed without you being with them boys of yours. Look like you and Ms. Liz doin mighty fine." He stopped walking and looked at me. "Got anythang you wanna tell me Mister?"

"Not right now I don't, and it ain't been a whole day."

"Not right now huh? Well if'n you been wit them boys I ain't seen it."

"Well... something is botherin me."

"Go on speak up son."

"It was early on... Mr. Archie the old house on Fifth..."

He put his hand on my shoulder and leaned to my face. I looked around the corner for Liz and Ms. P. "That house, the one that jus sit , under them big trees," I stopped and looked again.

Mr. Archie straightened up and pulled on his shirt, "We'll talk on it later," he said turning through the the doorframe. We sat down to eat at the table.

Liz was actually eating now. I guess hunger'll do that to you. She looked a bit more comforted. Maybe being in that house brought her some peace. All I know is that her smiling face made me feel like one hundred dollars. The pie was sweet, and creamy.

"Ms. P, how you make this pie?" I asked. "I want my momma to start making it."

"Old family secret. My momma passed it on to me, with a sweet milk recipe and lemon juice. I changed it a bit. I pass it on to someone special to me." She looked at Liz. They smiled at each other and laughed, continuing to slice pie with the edge of their forks. We all ate two slices. Mr. Archie ate three, considering that one was already gone when we got to the table.

I still needed to speak at him. I needed to know some things. I heard noise out from the street. The kids were starting to come back outside. It was around three something. The whole day had flew by and really, it was just getting started. Ms. P and Mr. Archie was making faces at each other across the table. Liz and I glanced at each other and giggled at them. We ate pie.

Chapter 16

"Sometimes the dirt under ya fingernails mean that you dun placed a lot of time into ya work. Sometimes it don't mean nothin. It jus sho that you dun sat around scratchin yo head an lookin off in the distance at thangs outta ya reach."

"But momma say it ain't nothin outta reach if you try hard enough."

"Well, ya momma is right bout one thang, you sho nuff gotta try, again, again, and again. If'n you don't put no effort behind them thoughts then you jus sit scratchin ya head, fillin up your fingernails with lazy dirt."

"Lazy dirt?"

"Yessuh. Dirt that come from a sweaty head that ain't did no work."

"I ain't gon never have lazy dirt."

"And I ain't gon letcha have no laziness in ya."

Ms. P looked on Mr. Archie, she smiled. She didn't have no real expression. Her face was kind of a far off blank like she was seeing something inside of him.

"What yaw'll two speaking on?" she asked.

"Buck got somethin on his mind, but won't tell me nothin. Decided I was gon tell him bout Ol Stan from over on Danny Thomas."

"Nah Archie, ain't no sense in bringing that up. Whatever the boy got on his mind let him be."

"Yeah Mr. Archie, I feel okay."

"Umm Hum. How bout you darlin?" he asked Liz. Liz looked at me and then at Ms. P. She never looked at Mr. Archie. She slid her fork through the last piece of her pie.

"I'm fine Mr. Archie. I ain't got nothin bothering me."

"That so?"

"Yessir."

"I reckon I best leave well enough alone. I'll jus mind my own."

"Archie, can ya pick them plates up for me please."

"Why yes mam I can."

Ms. P walked off into the kitchen and Mr. Archie followed. He stopped before passing through the door. He looked back at me, then Liz, like he knew something. He looked, sucked his teeth and disappeared.

Liz looked over at me whispering, "You told."

"No."

"You did, you told him about my place."

"I ain't lyin Liz, I ain't said nothin. I wouldn't lie to you."

"You swear?"

"I promise you, I didn't say nothin." She sat back in her chair and looked at me. Her arms were crossed covering the smiley face on her shirt. Ms. P walked back into the room and sat at the table.

"Well, I set Archie to washing them dishes. That oughta keep him busy for a few seconds. That way he leave yaw'll two alone."

"Why he asking questions?" asked Liz.

"Well, Buck asked him bout the old house on Fifth-"

"You told, you told, you said you wouldn't tell," Liz pushed from the table and the chair fell backwards. The curtains flew up, from the air, as she ran by towards the living room. Ms. P jumped up after her.

"Liz, Elizabeth." She followed close behind her. I could hear Liz and Ms. P whispering in the living room. I sat at the table and held my head in my hands. I had made Liz cry and I never wanted that. I just wanted to know about the house. Mr. Archie had messed up everything. I didn't want him to bother me or say anything to me. I got up from the table and walked into the living room. Ms. P stopped talking and looked at me. Liz's eyes were red and lines of tears traced around her cheeks. She looked at me and dropped her head. I felt worse.

"I promise I ain't tell nothin Liz. I promise I ain't tell nothin." I put my hands in my pockets and walked out of the front door into the wet heat of the street. Some guys were playing football and yelling and stuff, but I couldn't see who they were past my own tears that sat in my eyes. I wiped them off so I wouldn't look like a punk. I walked down Sixth Street.

I thought about walking back down the alley and going into the house to see if I could hear something speaking, but I was scared. I walked up Bickford towards Fifth. As I passed the concrete walls of the gym, I could see up to the basketball courts. They were filled with the same guys that had been playing when that boy got killed. I couldn't have played there if I wanted to. But I guess for them it didn't matter. For them it didn't matter at all. I crossed the street, and turned up Fifth to go home. I figured I didn't want to be bothered.

Just as I stepped into the street about three houses down from my apartments I heard a loud screeching sound and something like another pop from the park. But the sound was muffled by the tires spinning. I looked towards the park and thought about running. Then I thought about falling to the ground. I didn't do neither. I stood in the middle of the street until the silver, front end of a long brown Cadillac shot towards me with smoke behind the wheels. The horn blew loud and I dove. The wind pushed my t-shirt up into my face. I scratched my hand up and the scab on the slice in my hand opened and blood came out real slow. My knuckles hurt and my knees were skinned through my pants. I sat on my butt looking at the tail end of the car disappear up the block. I climbed to my feet and wiped my hands on my shirt leaving streaks of brown, red blood. I looked around and nobody had come out of the house. I thought to myself if I'da been hit nobody woulda seen it. Nobody at all. I kept walking up the street, a little quicker this time. There was nobody out. Nobody was on the hill of the projects or on our steps. I looked up at the house and stared at the trees around it. The white paint peeling in sections and the closed off windows. The curtains moved. I ran to my house and up the steps. I fumbled with my key until it fit in the lock and opened the door.

I was breathing real hard as I sat on the couch. I didn't even think about how my hand was pulsing and the pain in my legs. I just sat on the couch thinking of how the curtains moved. I could hear the sound of police cars whirring down towards the park. Folks would start coming out when the cops came. More and more in the neighborhood the cops came. It seemed like Black folks had gotten so sick of staying in North Memphis that they just start doing crazy stuff to each other. Either way, I was glad the cop horns were loud. It took my mind off of the house across the street for a minute. No sooner than I settled down and felt the burning from the scrapes on my knees and hands, I started hearing stuff in the back of the apartment, like feet dragging and creaking the floorboards. I wanted to cry again but I got tough. I stood, walked to the edge of the hall and saw something disappear into the kitchen. I walked slowly down the hall looking into my room as I passed. I could see a shadow moving back and forth on the floor as I walked. I made it to moms door and it looked like it had been messed with. I reached the kitchen and started to peek around when, a flash of white like a streak, turned and water flew into the air. I shouted and looked, mom looked back at me with her frustrated look,

"Boy, what the hell are you tipping around this house for? Goodness you liketa scared my hair straight. Tippin an carryin on."

"You scared me to mom. That's why I was tippin around. I thought you was a ghost."

"A ghost? Buck?"

"I was scared cause-" I stopped. I didn't want to tell Liz's secret again.

"Gon nah speak up. What is it that scared you so bad?" She took the rag off of the oven door handle and bent down to wipe up the water.

"It wadn't nothin mom."

"It wasn't anything?"

182

"It wasn't anything at all mom. I was just scared." She finally calmed down a bit and that's when she saw my hand and knees. She put the pot down and pulled her robe tighter as she walked over to me.

"Baby what happened to your hands... and your... my goodness these pants are ripped up bad on the knee."

I walked to the table and sat down. "I'm okay mom. I jus fell down in the street." She looked at me and then she knelt down and picked my head up. She looked me in my eyes.

"Buck these ain't no simple fall down scratches. Nah you gon have to tell me the truth. What happened today?"

"Mom ain't you spose to be at work?"

"Boy don't you ask me no questions when I'm tryin to find out somethin. Now tell me what happened today."

"From the beginning?"

"Boy, don't make me get a switch."

"Yes mam." I said. I didn't want to say what all had happened. I wiped some of the dirt on my pants off. "Did you just hear the police cars?"

"That's what woke me up, them doggone horns." She got the pot, filled it with water, sat it on the fire and took out some tea bags.

"I think somebody got shot at the park again."

"What!"

"I think somebody got shot again. I was coming from Ms. P's house and crossing the street from Bickford to Fifth and I heard a pop. I was about to dive to the ground but I couldn't move."

"I'm gon get us outta here. Ain't no mo sick days for me. Ain't no mo coming home early. I'm gon get you out of this place.

This don't make no sense, no sense at all. I'm sick..." her voice sounded full of hurt. She leaned back in her chair and smooth her hair back with her hands. "So you scratched your knees up falling on the ground? Well, long as you alright."

"No mam."

"No mam what son? You hurting? Where you hurting at?"

"I ain't, I'm not hurting, just a little sore. Mom I didn't fall down. I dove to the concrete in the street."

"What happened?"

"After the pop, I heard tires squealing and peeling out. There was this big, brown Cadillac whipping around the corner that almost hit me." Mom stood up and walked over to the boiling water. She took the tea bags and dropped them in. She was speaking with her back to me.

"Don't tell me no mo. Don't tell me nothing. Long as you ain't hurt don't tell me nothing. I can't stand...I couldn't stand to hear that my baby..." her voice trailed off.

"I'm okay momma. I'm fine."

She reached over for a cup and picked it up. I could see her hands shaking bad. She leaned one hand on the countertop and turned the water on to rinse the cup. The old white cup slipped from her hand and broke into the sink.

"Goddammit," she pulled her hands away and rubbed them. She then put her hands back on the sink and stood there, crying. I had made mom cry too.

"I'm sorry momma."

She turned to me and looked, "What I don told you about apologizing when you ain't done nothin wrong. You ain't done nothing. I just gotta get us outta here, that's all. Just gotta get us out... Lawwd, just get us out of this place."

I walked out of the kitchen down to my room. I closed my door. I could hear the water still running, and I could hear mom crying soft.

Momma looked tired. Not regular tired, but worn from the inside, like bad blues. That's what Mr. Archie woulda called it. Bad blues bring on tears, old memories that hurt to think on. I slept for only two hours the night that car darn near ran me down. I don't think it was the fear from being hit that kept my eyes from finding rest. I think it was the way momma said, simply, "I'm tired."

We was gettin outta North Memphis and I felt it. But I felt like something else too. I felt like a string on a guitar. I felt tight and twisted round something I couldn't see. Kinda like when a junebug gets tied to a string and a kid holds the string in front of a noon day sun. The sun make the line disappear, and the junebug fly not knowing why he can't get away. The junebug keep flying, around and around like the kid is pulling it closer like the sun do the Earth. I keep feeling like if I go, then thangs jus gonna get worse for the neighborhood.

Like I was important enough to make things go bad.

But momma always say, "Buck, baby, one person move ten cars, if she put her mind to it."

"One car at a time?"

"Naw, she can find a way to take all ten cars and move em out her way if she got to. One person can change everything."

"I guess."

"No guessing, that's truth." She'd tap me on the nose and smile. I look for ways to make her smile. But lately I ain't brought on nothin but more problems. It ain't my fault though. It's the neighborhood's. I ain't never supposed to make up no excuses, but when things start happening real fast it ain't no excuse. Problems come in plain view, all you got to do is stop for a second and look. The problem wasn't no secret. Fifth Street was dying.

Chapter 17

"If'n the wind pick up at night and blow real hard you can hear music and words come from the trees. It's like them trees holdin spirits. Cept for round that house on your street. Ain't no music in the wind round that house, jus bad howlin sounds. Angry sounds. That house got a lot of grief, an ain't nobody live in it since them folks got took off.

Weather sho was bad that day. It was like the clouds had fell from the sky and was sittin thick on the streets. It wadn't quiet winter, but fall was winding down and leaves was on the sidewalks, and all down that hill in front of that house. Lemme see, it was a momma, daddy and a lil baby girl bout five or so. Nice young family. That boy had gone to Fisk to get him his teachin degree. Fine young man he was. Named Clifton, his wife was named Celia and the lil girl had the prettiest name. She was named after the color, Violet. It was cold and late. I was visitin some folks, Lonny and Chelle that useta live down your way. That's when it happen about thirty-eight, forty years ago now.

But I recall one night while visitin yo dad... that scene from then, like a spell, came and climbed on me... took ahold ah me, like cold sweat after dreamin. Me and your daddy was sitting in yaw'll living room. We had the door open cause the breeze wadn't freezin cold, but it made the house feel okay. Diane was in the kitchen when the clouds opened up and the storm got loud. We looked out through the screen door as the door rattled from the wind.

"Wind done picked up a bit Mr. Archie. Bet's be gettin on back yonder to the house."

"I'll be fine V. I'll be jus fine. Ain't no lil wind gon stop a man from walkin."

"This Memphis wind'll take you on away from here fast."

"Boy, I done been in this here wind for a lifetime longer than you been livin."

"Excuse me for lookin out for your best interest. I was jus tryin to give you a heads up."

"Mmmm Hmm, if you don't mind I reckon I'll sit for a spell and sip on some mo of that fine tea Diane done made. How she feelin?"

"She feelin alright. She come back from Clarksville visitin with her folks. Her momma makin due pretty good."

"I'm sho she is. Strong lady, she been taking care of that man of hers. What's wrong wit him again?"

"We don't right now, but momma assume it's all that drinkin and working the land he done did all these years."

"Hmph, that sound bout right. That alcohol a terrible thang. But we drink like the Indians."

"Watcha mean?"

"We drink to forget. So much happen to us... our folks, hell V, you gotta escape somehow."

"That so? You don't drink Mr. Archie?"

"My body don't set well wit it. My reactions real bad."

"Yeah I here you on that. I feel awfully sick myself when I get that stuff in my system. Feel like my head sitting on a heating lamp. I gets to sweatin and my head hurt somethin terrible."

"That's the same way I feel son. Some thangs don't nevah change none I tell ya. We can pass on some terrible stuff."

"Watcha mean Mr. Archie?"

"Parents pass on thangs. Yo daddy the same way."

"That so?"

"V, son, some thangs we need to speak about. Somethin me an you gotta address."

"I'm listenin."

"Victor can you come help me with this big pot? I'm tryin to put it in the shelf over the stove."

"I'll be right there Diane. Mr. Archie let me do this for Diane, I be right back."

"Maybe you was right. Maybe I should be makin my way on."

"Thought you wanted to talk sir."

"Different occasions for different thangs. We speak on it sooner or later."

"I'll hold ya to that - I'm coming baby - You be careful nah."

"I'll be fine V. I'll be alright." I hugged ya daddy an walked on out the door. I stood on that ol gray porch and looked out into the wind. The trees had done lost they green but them orange and brown colored leaves looked like they was trying to paint words in the air. A couple of cars rolled down the streets, but it wadn't many folks moving around outside. Folks was gettin ready for the storm. I pulled my coat up to the bridge of my nose and folded my arms to keep my hands kinda warm. I walked down the steps from under the hangin trees and made my way to the street.

The darkness was coming from the clouds, late afternoon darkness. Shadows of charcoal and light shot through thick steel clouds. I walked up Fifth in front of that house and that's when I seen it. Clear as day. Like someone put some glasses on my eyes that showed thangs different. I couldn't move no further. Legs wouldn't respond to nothin my thoughts said do.

The rain started, small drops and lightnin. Then big fat drops like God opened the bottom on heaven's well. I stood looking at the house. A group of men in long flowing white sheets, like angels. The sheets was flapping in the wet wind. Hands barely crawled from under them cloaks. Lightnin flash. They had the daddy face down in the mud. Lightnin flash. The little girl was kickin an being held under one of the white sheets arms. Like she was wrapped in linen protectin her from the rain. Lightnin flash. They was in the back of the house. The screen door was slammin open and shut. The momma in no clothes caught the first flame and it crackled like pork skin on an open fire. Thunder, thunder, thunder. I fell to the ground. My clothes stuck to me and I could feel the warmness of tears with the cold of the rain rollin down my jaw. I walked over towards the house and stood lookin at the frame. Wadn't no wind on that house. Wadn't no rain. I began walkin back to my home."

Chapter 18

"What a little moonlight can do." Ms. P always said that to Mr. Archie. But with her it seemed that it meant something good. To me, the nighttime was filling up with different noises. Crickets and locusts was getting ready to fade cause September was coming. What was really different was the sound of what Stack's uncle called, "Nigga desperation."

"Niggas, youngbloods, niggas like cancer. Yaw'll lit brothers ain't gotta be no niggas. Yaw'll gotta change this here," he'd point around and up the street.

I always found myself looking down at the flap of his pants leg tucked underneath his butt. Sometimes he made sense. "I know you cats ain't ol enough to thank on such thangs, but I'ma give ya a rhyme. Integration brought nigga desperation, and ain't no hesitation in the way we strive to make us dead. Ya see, we can't fit in so we try to forget. Use ta be alright but nigga desperation catchin up."

That's what the sound was at night now. No nice Ms. P moonlight, just folks shouting, horns blowing and the crack of guns drowning out the wind, crickets and all the natural sounds. I waited for morning like each day was Christmas Eve. It wasn't a waiting feeling of getting a gift or something good on them days, it was just a blessing not to hear bout something bad happening. Mom looked as if she could feel the desperation. I guess it wasn't a real thing you could see in her, nothing on her face at least.

I could see it in how momma moved. She moved like something was making her walk stiff. Her eyes looked dark, even with makeup. When she dropped that cup I think she did like that woman in the park did when her son got killed, she snapped. That's what Mr. Archie called it. Snapped, when thangs get to be so bad that all you can do is cry and pray. Pray and cry and everything that come with it.

I figured on how to make momma feel better. I figured I'd wake up earlier than her and make her something to eat and clean up some if needed. Besides, I wasn't sleeping much in the morning anyway. I mostly stared out the window towards Liz's apartments even though I couldn't see the building. But looking over that way made me feel nice about her.

It wouldn't be so tough wipin the sleep out my eyes and gettin thangs set for mom. Boiling water, and frying eggs would be the hardest thing. Making toast was as simple as putting four slices of bread in the slots, pushing down on the silver lever and making sure that each piece was good and buttered. I went ahead and got up around 5 o'clock and walked slow around the house, so I wouldn't make no noise. Momma slept with her door closed mostly but she had stopped doing that since her and Mr. Travis had the falling out. So I had to be extra quiet. Everything was pretty easy, but not as simple as I thought. I messed up two eggs trying to tap them with a knife the way mom does. I finally used the edge of the counter.

The only thing she would have to do was use the hot water I boiled for her coffee. I wasn't supposed to mess around with anything that could burn me. But mom was starting to let me do a lot more. She was letting me cut onions and peel potatoes without watching me. It seemed as if my going into junior high school made her think that I was gonna be able to start taking care of a lot more things. Then again, all the guys my age did more than they was supposed to according to Stack's uncle. He said that all the boys was gettin raised like women cause they had to help around the house and clean up all the time. I told mom that, and she said that he was crazy. Then she said that everybody should always have chores. I ain't never really known it no other way. I don't think I could live without having something to do.

Anyway, all the food was cooked and the dishes was put up. I even pushed the broken cup to the bottom of the trash so she wouldn't have to deal with last night. My knees and hands hurt a bit after doing everything but it wasn't any worse than falling on the concrete during street football. Besides, I didn't really get that cut up or nothing anyway from that stupid car. My jeans was just ripped.

Momma got up at like 5:15. She still had to catch the bus to get out to Whitehaven. She always laid her clothes out at night so she didn't have nothin but bathroom stuff to do in the morning. She walked in the kitchen and jumped.

"Boy, what you doin in here?" She put her hand over her heart like Fred Sanford did when he get ready to have the 'Big One.' I laughed and moved from by the table. I had the toast buttered and the eggs was in the skillet. I didn't stir scramble the eggs cause I didn't want to make any noise. So I just let them cook flat. They almost looked like omelette eggs. All they needed was cheese, peppers and ham. That's what mom woulda put on em. But I wadn't supposed to mess with the real sharp knives so I wasn't gonna be cuttin anything. Mom came over to me and kissed my forehead.

"Bless yo heart. You made your momma breakfast and hot water."

"Mom, it's for your coffee."

"I know, I know, I'm just playin with you." She rubbed my head. I hate it when anybody else rubs my head. Cause it makes me feel like a kid. I was twelve going on thirteen and I was the man of the house so I didn't want nobody rubbin my head. But when mom did it, I felt good. Mom pulled her robe closed and sat down at the table. I grabbed some orange juice and poured myself a cup before scraping the eggs out of the skillet onto our plates.

"So what's with the special treatment son?"

"This ain't special mom. I'm just being helpful from now on."

"Well, I think it's special treatment. You gon be doing this for that lil Mumford girl real soon?"

"Mom?"

"Just askin is all. Just askin...Vincent,"

"Yes momma?"

"I'm... we ain't said grace yet. Gimme them hands. Lord thank you for another day. For lettin us fall in your good graces. Thank you for this food we're about to receive for the nourishment of our bodies to be used in your work. Amen"

"Amen."

"Buck, I'm sorry you had to see momma do that last night."

"Do what momma?"

"Son, sometimes it's alright to feel hurt and let it out. It makes you see things clearer. It makes you understand. I needed to feel that kinda fear and anger cause it's gonna make me work harder. I don't

194

want you to never see me not working. You need to know what struggle is so when you get something in your way you can use what ya seen. You my only reason for waking up and I ain't gon let nothin-"

"I know momma and I ain't gon let nothing happen to me or you."

She smiled. Her smile paid for the cooking and boiling water, more than any money or allowance could have ever done. She ate and talked a little before going in the bathroom and gettin dressed. She left the house at close to 6:00. I cleaned up the kitchen and figured I'd get back in the bed til the sun was all the way up.

Chapter 19

At 10:30 I heard a rattle at the front door. Waking up at 5:00 o'clock made me more tired than I thought. I could hear the door rattle, then knocking, and more knocking.

"I'm coming...I'm coming..dang." I walked towards the front door wiping sleep from my eyes. I could see dark light coming through the windows. Dark like thunderstorm clouds had just finished and the sun was tussling with the clouds to reach the grass. "I'm coming, who is-"

"Buck, we going to Stack's. Open the door, stupid."

I really hated Smoke's voice. It always seemed like he was trying to whisper but just couldn't figure out what the volume was supposed to be to make it right. Him and his brother both had that problem. That's why we didn't never tell them no secrets. I opened the door.

"Uuughh, he got on Aquaman underoos," Smoke yelled. I looked down and realized I'd answered the door in my drawers. I was tired. I pulled up the latch on the screen door and started walking towards the back.

"Buck that was Smoke trying to rattle the knob to death. He figured your mom probably left the front door open."

"Your brother is stupid. I'll be right back." I shouted walking to my room. "Hey, why yaw'll wanna go back to Stack's house after yesterday?" I couldn't hear what they was saying, but I figured I'd just ask again when I got back to the living room. I grabbed a pair of pants and walked to the bathroom. Smoke was right behind me.

196

"Why you walkin through my house?"

"This ain't a house it's an apartment."

"Skillet, get your brother."

"Smoke stop being dumb."

"You the one that's dumb. I was jus tryin to hear what Buck was sayin."

"You just nosey Smoke and I don't appreciate you walkin round the house." I pushed him in his chest and he stumbled back a bit.

"Dawg Buck I was jus playin." He shrugged his shoulders and walked back down the hall. I guess I was kinda mean to him. I grabbed my toothbrush and dipped it in a crusty box of baking soda that was stuck to the rusted white in the mirror cabinet. I scrubbed the gummy powder back and forth in my mouth and walked back to the front. I could see Smoke standing up by the radio looking in mom's album crates. He was flipping and reading off the names that he could. Skillet was sitting on the couch quiet. I spoke through a mouth full of baking soda, "My bad Smoke."

"Huh?"

"My bad."

"Huh?"

"My bad, my bad. He said my bad Smoke."

"I know I was just playin."

"Stupid," Skillet and I both said. I pulled the toothbrush from my mouth and headed back to finish cleaning myself up some. I started thinking how much I didn't want to go back to Stack's house. But I knew the guys would tease me about something or another so I thought about not saying nothing. There was something on my mind though. Something that didn't feel good. I walked into my room, changed shirts and slipped on my shoes. I could hear Smoke and Skillet laughing and talking about album covers.

"Look at this one. It's got a spaceship on it. What's that say?" Smoke asked.

"Parleemint Funkladic."

I walked in and interrupted them, "Funkadelic, Skillet."

"I know that. I jus missaid it."

"Whatever. Hey," I really didn't want to go to Stack's so I needed to think of something cool to do so they wouldn't think I was a punk. "You know the house across the street?"

Smoke stopped looking at the albums and looked at Skillet.

"Yeah, we know the house across the street," Skillet said.

"Our momma said that house ain't right. Folks had got a bunch of stuff done to em up there. That's why it ain't nobody live in it no more."

"Yeah, dad said that folks should come and tear it down, or clean it up and sell it or something."

"What else yaw'll hear about it?" I asked.

"Well," Skillet started, "I heard that the house ain't got no walls inside. I heard that it's held up by one pole in the middle that ain't no bigger than two inches thick."

"That's right and that if somebody broke that stick the house would sink down in the ground."

"It ain't nothin like that wrong with the house."

"Yaw'll ready to go to Stack's?"

198

"No Smoke. I ain't ready to go to Stack's. Listen. That house got walls. A lot of walls. All covered in red and black. Stained walls. The wind whistle through it and make noises that sound like voices too."

"Skillet, I'm ready to go to Stack's and look at naked women."

"Be quiet Smoke. You went in Buck?"

"Yeah. I went through the whole house. All on my own."

"He lyin. He lyin he ain't went in that damn house."

"Shut up Smoke."

I knew gettin them to go into the house would take they minds off of Stack. But some ideas are better left in your head. I had to face some fear though, and the guys wouldn't have let me get away with saying I just didn't wanna go to Stack's house. Besides, them books of naked women ain't do nothing but make me think about Liz, and I didn't want to think on Liz that way. She was a lady, like Ms. P. She was like my mom. She wadn't no woman in a book with her legs pulled over her head. And I jus wadn't ready to see no man in army clothes wit needles, and shadows running round him.

We left my house and crossed the street. We stood in a sideways line looking on the old white frame.

Chapter 20

I hoped that Smoke didn't see the fear in me. The darkness inside the house done it. Made me shiver, like how it feel at the end of September. Beyond the wall in the kitchen, the dank smell of old wood and bleeding oily paint was stronger than when I followed Liz inside. I stood in the frame of the kitchen door. We didn't take the back alley to get there. We walked up the long front driveway, cracked and gray, overgrown with weeds. Mud and grass pushed up the slabs of concrete like hell was tryin to get from underneath it. The drive was real tall and couldn'tna been used anytime, not even when the house was new. It just didn't look like somewhere folks wanted to enter. Mr. Archie always say when something is good, or pretty, or new, folks gotta have it, use it, they need it.

"When thangs git ol folks don't look at it the same. They thank ol thangs ain't got much use. Not needed ain't a real good feeling son. Look here in this garden. Ya see how I dun let it get smaller?"

"Yessuh."

"Why with the cornerstore and that big ol supermarket, folks don't come by for my greens, yams or tomatoes, much no mo. Ain't got much reason to. So I cuts back on planting a lot nah. Only folks come by is-"

"Ms. P, Mr. Taylor from up Seventh Street and-"

"Umm Humm. You ain't gotta run down no list to me nah." He stopped and took his hat off. The cloudy tufts sprang from beneath. A few traces of sweat curved over his eyebrow. He took out his handkerchief and dabbed at his forehead and cheek. He looked up

200

through the trees. The sun caught his eye and I could see brown in the dark part. He smiled.

"That's right some folks do come by. But most folks only think on me as jus an ol man. But them that come by knows." He looked at me and patted my knee. He pushed himself up from his crate, placed his hands in the low part of his back and pushed his stomach out. "Them that come by know." His smile spread out into a slice of moon, no teeth just a quiet smile. "When thangs get ol Buck, folks forget about it. Don't need it no mo. Like a Christmas toy buried in a box gather dust, that's what happen to something that ain't new."

Mr. Archie walked into the house without looking back to wave me in. He left me sitting in the backyard staring at the rows of greens that wadn't picked and green tomatoes hanging over fallen ones sitting on the ground. I picked up as many as I could and brought them with me to the backdoor. I could see Mr. Archie sitting at his kitchen table taking skin off of potatoes. His hat sat on the edge, tilted up from his cane laying against the side. I fussed with the door for a moment, trying to hold the green tomatoes in my arm and pull at the black door handle. He looked back at me and stood, walked over to the door and pushed it open. He looked at the tomatoes and then at me.

"Figured mom might want to fry some, figured she might need em."

That slice of moon smile came again and he took a few of the tomatoes from my hands and carried them to the sink. He placed them in a basket and turned the water on. I followed and put mine in. The water ran over the top of the green flesh and trickled into the drain. Small pieces of dirt and fuzz sat on the whiteness. I hadn't seen any dirt before, they looked clean. He let the water run over them and he rubbed the tomatoes with his thumbs smoothing off whatever unseen things was on them. I grabbed a couple and did the same.

"Figure ya mom might need em, huh?"

"Yessuh. Fried tomatoes, macaroni and cheese and pork chops. That's what she make wit em."

"That sounds purty good. Well, I guess that ol garden back yonder do serve its purpose... still."

"Long as somebody use it then folks need it Mr. Archie."

"Yeah, but when folks let thangs sit, thangs get spoiled. When a garden or toy spoil, ain't much can fix it Buck."

"If it's worth fixin, then you gotta try. Momma say that all the time."

"Seein as that's your momma tell you that, I can't argue much on it. But if something ain't new no mo, the need kinda goes away." He walked back over to the table and left the water running. I kept washing the tomatoes.

"Sometimes the old things is what we need." I said looking over my shoulder. I heard Mr. Archie exhale. His shoulders moved a little and I could see the corner of that silent smile. He kept shaving potatoes.

The house was old. But maybe the house needed somebody to want it. Maybe Liz made the house seem better. It wasn't quite as scary when I was with her.

"Buck, go all the way in. You the one wanted to come here," Skillet nudged me in the back.

"Smell like ten Stack uncles in here." Smoke said looking at each corner of the room.

"It ain't that bad, come on."

I walked into the kitchen just like I did when Liz had ran in. It wadn't so bad as long as it wasn't raining. With the rain, the storm clouds blocked out the sun which made the house darker. At least we could see a little of the outside brightness through the wood and old curtains on the windows. I stepped over the same spot in the kitchen into the hallway and I could see the light fading from the backdoor. I was praying that the door wouldn't slam shut again. At least not until we'd made it into another room and couldn't hear it as well. Floorboards moved and squealed as the three of us walked on through the frame of the kitchen door. The shelves was all closed in the kitchen, and things looked okay.

As we made it into the splitoff hallway. I could hear the back door. Smoke looked back into the kitchen.

"Yaw'll," he said real soft, "The door closin." We all stopped moving. I stood in front, Skillet was behind me. Smoke was holding on to his brother's shirt.

"Stop holdin me."

"Shhhssh." I wanted it quiet so I could hear the door. Sure enough I heard the small tick, tick, tick, click-clunk. It had closed and locked. The house groaned and I could hear shuffling in the room straight ahead of us. I guess it woulda been the living room. I looked back towards the guys.

"Probably jus a cat yaw'll."

"That ain't no cat. Them was big steps."

"Shut up Smoke, dang. Stop actin like a punk. I'ma tell dad."

"I ain't no punk."

"Shhssh. Be quiet, listen." There were no more sounds. "That noise wadn't nothin but a truck going by shakin the house. Come on." I pushed the door open to the room where Liz had been. Darkness. The little light from the other parts of the house didn't help in that room at all. I held my hand out to start feeling my way through the blackness. A cold touch moved across my fingertips. I sucked in air and pulled back. Smoke took off to the kitchen. I pulled the door closed and followed him and Skillet. My fingers were still cold.

"I wanna go to Stack's house and look at books. At least we ain't gon get killed."

"Smoke, we ain't even went to the other end of the hall yet."

"Yeah and I wanna go back in that room. I ain't scared."

"I'm with you Buck. And you with me Smoke cause I'm older and daddy told me to stop lettin you be a punk."

"Okay, okay, aight, I'm jus kinda worried."

"Let's at least go to the other the end of the hall and look in the other rooms then we can go," I said.

We started walking again. I pushed the door back open to Liz's room and looked in. I guess my eyes got use to the light cause I could see a little better. It wadn't nothin inside. Nothin. No mattress, candles, books, nothin. It seemed like Liz had never been in there. Maybe I picked the wrong room. I closed the door and moved quicker down the hall.

"Why you look like that in the room? Why you stop and look?
What you see?"

"I don't wanna know what he seen. I wanna go to-"

"Shut up Smoke," I said. I kept walking. I got four feet down
to the next room. The door was closed there too. But it felt warm.
My momma always told me that if it's warm in a empty place then it's
got a good spirit. When it's cold something bad happening. I touched
the door. Long, brown wood splinters hung off of parts beneath
patchy stain.

"Touch the door yaw'll."

Skillet rubbed the door and humped his shoulders. I didn't
even bother with Smoke.

"I ain't feel nothin."

"Don't feel hot to you?"

"Nope, regular."

I touched the door again. Warm. I went to open it and the
house started to squeal again. Whine, click, click. I heard a clap and
the light at the end of the hall started to fade. From the windows,
small plinks echoed through the rooms. My heart started. I heard
another crack and rumble. A thunderstorm.

'They only come when it rain.' At least that was what Liz said.
I didn't tell the guys. I wanted to feel and see it for myself. I needed
to know what Liz needed. The plinking got harder and then the fat
drops started beating on the roof. Small drops fell into the hallway
from a puddle sitting on the ceiling.

"I think we should go yaw'll. Somethin don't feel right."

Skillet looked at me and agreed with his brother. Skillet turned to walk towards the back. As he stepped his foot fell into a dead spot in the hallway and shot through the wood. He trapped his foot almost up to the ankle. His jeans were pushed up and I could see his skin scratched open by the wood. He screamed out. When he screamed it seemed to startup the house. The door at the end of the hall opened back into its wall and a cry came out from the deep corner. I couldn't see anything but Skillet's leg. I didn't want to look. I heard a dragging sound from behind the warm door and a dull crack like a broken old chicken bone in a dog's jowls. Skillet shouted. The door opened on Liz's room and then closed. Smoke was pulling at the floorboards. Every time he pulled a board from around Skillet's leg, Skillet yelled. I reached down to help. Once we got his leg out he took off out through the kitchen. The door was already open. We all jumped down from the porch instead of taking the steps. We splashed into a mud, water puddle and slipped our way to the drive. Drops of rain covered my eyes. I wiped as we ran under trees to get to the street. We kept running to my front door, not looking for cars or nothing. I fussed with my keys trying to pull them out of my shirt and off of my neck. I finally got the door open and we fell inside onto the floor. Rain and sweat rolled down our faces. I looked at Skillet's leg. His jeans were just high enough to show the scrapes around his ankle.

"I'll go get something."

I got up to go get the Mercoorachrome and some tissue paper, I also grabbed a towel to wipe his ankle off with. Skillet looked down at his leg and shook his head. Smoke sat on the floor with his hands around his knees, quiet. The cloth part of Skillet's shoe was ripped on one side. The rubber had brown scratch marks. I came back with the wet towel and told him to lift up his pants leg more.

"It's your fault Buck my brother got hurt. I told you somethin wadn't right."

I didn't respond. I rubbed the blood from the scrapes with the wet rag. Then I pulled out the brown bottle. Skillet looked at me.

"Man you ain't puttin that stuff on my leg. You ain't my momma. That stuff burn."

"But it keep out infection. I used it the other day all by myself."

"The cuts ain't that bad no how."

"Yeah but you can get gaingreen, and they have to cut your leg off if it get infected."

"You ain't puttin that stuff on my leg." He stood up. "Let's go Smoke."

"My bad, yaw'll." I felt like I'd gotten Skillet hurt. I didn't want the fellas mad at me. "Yaw'll goin to Stack's?"

"I guess," said Skillet.

"I'll see yaw'll later then."

"Later Buck."

"Yeah, later...Buck."

They walked off into the sprinkling rain. The sun had started to drift back through the clouds. Another messed up start to a day. But for some reason I felt that something good was gonna happen.

Chapter 22

It ain't what happened in the house that had me kickin the bottle all nervous when I left to walk to Mr. Archie's. It was the feelin that Liz went to the place cause her pain was big. Her pain was like the look in Stack's uncles eyes almost, but it had something not right in there too, like a confusion. I figured at least Stack uncle was scared cause them shadows was real to him. Liz was scared cause I guess her daddy was her shadows. I don't quite get what coulda happened on her to make her have that look. And like my momma say, she too pretty to always not be smiling.

I had done kicked the bottle all the way up the street and was about to hit Bickford and the park, when I thought about Smoke and them. I wanted to make things right. I expect they had already told the guys about the house stuff since Skillet's leg was all scarred up. Wadn't that they was gonna be mad at me for some reason or another, I just assumed they would talk about me too much and make me mad. But I had to go over and be with em for a little while cause that's just what we do. I flipped the bottle around back towards the South side of Fifth Street and started kicking back towards Stack's house.

"Buck, hol up. Buck."

I looked back and Lil Tony was running up from the park from where the old heads by the court was. He was yellin and waving his arms. I stopped.

"You goin to Stack's?"

"Yeah, for a minute."

"Why you turn back around at the street?"

"Huh?"

"Why you turn around when you got to the street? You act like you ain't see me."

"I didn't see you. I was thinkin on stuff."

"You ain't see me, how I was waving my arms and stuff?"

"I said I ain't seen you T. Wadn't nobody spectin you to be over in no park. Specially over by them. What you doin over there anyway. Mr. Archie say them cats bad news."

"They cool."

I kicked the bottle off to the side by the curb and kept walking. Something stunk bad, I mean for real stank. "What's that smell? Smell like smoke."

"What smell?" I leaned towards Lil Tony and sniffed at him. He jumped back.

"What you doin Buck?"

"That's your clothes stinkin like that."

"Shut up, my clothes don't stink."

"Mr. Archie say them guys smoke all kinds of stuff an drink and-"

"Ol Man Fishstick don't know nothing."

I looked at him and kept on walking. I looked at his eyes. They was scar blood red.

"You smell and your eyes is messed up T. Somebody hit you?"

"Naw Buck dang. Why you got so many questions. You ain't my daddy."

"Forget it then T. Let's jus walk down to Stack's."

Tony hadn't been with the group much in the last few days or so. Especially after that dude got killed with the gun. He was amazed by it. He wanted to see the body and everything, from what Stack was saying. He had even started dressing like those guys in the park: fishnet and plastic caps on his head, tank top t-shirts, and carrying a rake for his hair. He wasn't even talking the same. And when he came around he always smelled like smoke. Not regular Kool Filter King smoke, but smoke, *smoke*. He wouldn't run and play football much none either, was always short of breath. But he was one of the fellas. It wadn't my place to make no big issue of it. I wadn't his daddy. We kept quiet all the way across Chelsea and on to Stack's house. The door looked closed to the house when we pushed the gate open. I could hear something like giggling and music from the inside. Ton and I walked up the steps and the door was cracked. We pushed the door open soft and walked in. The light at the end of the hall was off which meant Stack uncle musta was gone. We looked off into the living room and it was dark in there too. We got by Stack's room and Skillet and Smoke was standing outside the door. Man was close to the bathroom with this silly look on his face. Skillet looked at me and held his pointing finger to his lips. He ducked back down and looked through Stack's keyhole. He waved for me and Ton. I stepped on a floorboard and a squeal jumped up into the air. The music drowned it out. The squeal sounded like a whistle from the Gap Band song that was on. I put my head down and Ton turned to get his head down to the keyhole and headbutted me hard. I rocked back some. He kneeled down some more and looked through.

"Dang."

"Lemme see T," I whispered. He moved over a little bit. I looked into the hole and I could see Stack on his bed. His shirt was off and some legs was coming out from his side. I could hear a girl saying, "Ouch." and "stop." and "It hurts a little." I could see Stack moving around like he was swimming. Then he jumped up and yelled, "Why you pinch me?" Stuff was dripping from his ding a ling and Bigfoot Ann got up quick and started yellin. I took off down the hall. The guys followed me out the front door. I don't know if she saw any of us, but what I saw was nasty. Skillet ran fast even though he was limping a lot. We was all laughing. She had big ol tittees like in the book. I just couldn't get outta my head what was wrong with Stack's ding a ling. We slowed down when we got up to Chelsea. We sat on the bricks outside this old recording studio and rested for a minute.

"What happened Buck?" Smoke asked. He sounded like he wasn't mad at me no more.

"Whatcha mean what happened?"

"Yeah Buck what happened? Was it like the book stuff?" asked Man.

"Worse."

"Worse good or worse bad?" asked Skillet

"Worse good I bet," said Ton.

"Naw worse bad. Stack had some stuff coming out of his ding a ling."

"It's a dick Buck," said Ton.

"I don't say that word."

"Me neither Buck," said Man.

"Anyway, she jumped and it was Bigfoot Ann."

"Ugggghhhhh," all the guys said.

"Stack was doing it with Bigfoot Ann?" asked Ton.

"I guess. Did he know yaw'll was in the house?"

"Nah. The door was kinda cracked so we snuck in like yaw'll did," said Smoke.

"That was nasty," said Man.

"I got me some too," said Lil Tony.

"You lyin, you lyin your butt off."

"Shut up Smoke. When you get some?" asked Skillet.

"Last week."

"From who," I asked. I knew he was telling a story.

"From Elizabeth."

I got quiet.

"From fine Elizabeth. Dang Ton," said Skillet. "How was it?"

"She was saying she love me and stuff. I told her to shut up and we did it."

"You lyin," I shouted. "You a damn lie. What day was it on?"

"Why you so worried about it? It happened on that day it was raining real hard. We was looking for you and I left the guys. I saw Elizabeth over by that old house. We went in there and did it." He pulled his rake out and start combing through his big nappy afro. I wadn't as mad cause I knew he was lying.

"You lyin," I said.

"I don't believe you either," said Man.

"I believe you T," said Smoke.

"I don't even care if yaw'll don't believe me. The old heads put me up on how to talk to a girl so I can get what I want."

"They teaching you how to do a lot of lying."

"Buck you got a problem wit me?"

"You lyin is all."

"You callin me out."

"You jus lyin."

Ton stood up from the brick. He was bigger than me by like a hand. But I wadn't no punk.

"I bet you won't say I'm a lie in my face."

"Don't need to, I jus know."

Tony reached into his pocket. I stepped back by the door of the studio. He flipped out a shiny blade and held it still with his thumb.

"You callin me a lie?"

"Tony what you doin?" Skillet walked over by him. Him and Skillet was the same size. We was all kinda scared of Skillet cause he looked rougher. Ton looked at me and started laughing. "Fuck yaw'll, I'm going back to the park." Ton turned and started trotting across Chelsea. I leaned against the big blue door into the spider webs in the corners of it. Tony wasn't one of us no more. I was glad, cause he was gonna start a lot of problems that we was glad we wadn't a part of.

"Hey, yaw'll wanna go back to Stack's?" asked Man.

"Why? You wanna see Bigfoot?"

"Shut up Smoke."

"Both of yaw'll shut up," said Skillet. "Hey, you cool Buck?"

"Yeah."

"He smokin and drinkin and stuff with them guys in the park. He be alright though," said Skillet.

"I guess. Let's go back down to Stack's." We walked back up the street until we got down bout a half a block from Stack's fence. Bigfoot Ann was walking towards us. She had on a big collared shirt with her stomach out. The shirt was tied in a knot over her belly button. She had on some cut off jeans that was real tight too. She was walking and swingin her arms real long. We all stopped walking and looked at each other. Smoke had to be the first to talk.

"Heyyyy BigFoot." We all laughed.

"What yaw'll laughing at?"

"Nothin," I said. "You seen Stack?"

"Naw, I ain't seen no Stack wit his fat self. Why I seen Stack and why you askin?"

Skillet stepped up, "We jus going down to Stack house is all. Figured you mighta seen him coming out since you coming from that way."

"Well, I ain't seen him." She turned and started walking. We started giggling. I was gonna start saying, 'BigFoot and Stack sittin in a tree,' but I figured against it. "Hey, you seen Liz?"

"Naw she been sick since yesterday so she ain't been outside since the afternoon. She didn't even come to majorette practice at the gym last night."

"When you see her, tell her I said hi." I had no regard for the fellas at all.

"Whatever Buck. She don't like you no mo anyway. But I'll tell her when I see her." She kept walking.

"Why you askin bout Elizabeth?" asked Man. "You like her still?"

"No wonder you was shoutin at Ton," said Smoke.

"I know Ton was lyin is all. Cause-"

"Cause what Buck?" asked Skillet.

"Just cause. I know he smokin and stuff and I know he telling stories... Forget it, let's walk." We started towards Stacks house again. I could see the Black car pulling up to the front.

"Hey yaw'll maybe we oughtta wait some."

"Why?" asked Man.

"Cause there go that Black car pullin up."

"And," asked Smoke.

"Yaw'll know that car always there when Stack uncle there."

"You scared of his uncle?"

"Naw Skillet. I ain't scared." I was scared but they was too. "Yaw'll ain't bothered by what you seen him doing."

"Yeah, but he gon be in the back. We can jus go get Stack and leave."

"I ain't scared Skillet. I wanna look at the books."

"Shut up Smoke."

"You shut up," Smoke said and turned to run. Skillet snatched the back of his shirt. "I was just playing. Let me go, I'ma tell mom." Skillet let him go.

"Let's jus go get Stack and then leave."

"I don't feel like it. I think I'ma go home for a minute."

"Buck you ain't gon go home. You going to try and find Liz."

"Smoke you talk too much. I'm going home for a while. I jus don't feel like going back down to Stack's."

"I think Smoke right for a change Buck, you is mad at T and you gonna try and find Liz. If you know it ain't true then why you going home?"

"I know it ain't true cause... I know it ain't true. I jus don't feel like lookin at no books right now. Besides, I'm kinda hungry anyhow."

"Me too Buck. Can I go with you?" asked Man.

"I don't care."

"Okay then. I'm going wit Buck yaw'll."

"That's' fine we goin down to the house anyway. We'll catch up wit yaw'll in a bit."

Smoke and Skillet started walkin back. We turned to go across Chelsea. I brushed spiderwebs off my shirt. We stood at the street corner and waited on cars to pass.

"Buck, you like Liz a lot?"

"I like her a little. She okay for a girl."

"You like her like Stack like Bigfoot?"

"Naw, what you askin stupid questions for Man?"

"I was just wonderin?"

"What?"

"I ain't never touched a girl, let alone do that."

"So? We ain't spose to touch up no girls. Ain't yo momma told you how you treat a lady?"

"No, you know she ain't home much anyhow," he stopped. "Go," Man shouted as he jumped in the street and took off across without looking. I looked both ways a little before I ran. He kept running when he got on the other side.

"Race you to the house," he yelled back and kept running.

"You cheating." I ran swinging my arms, huffing and puffing moving fast. I even rocked my head side to side cause Lizard did that when he ran, he was always the quickest. Man had almost a six line on the concrete lead on me, but he had short legs. I figured as long as I tried hard enough and kept running I'd catch up. The parked cars flashed red and brown and blue in the corners of my eyes. I was pumping and hissing between my teeth. I got about two lines back from Man by the time we got to the house. I got close, real close.

"I beat you."

"Cheater."

"I beat you."

"You cheated Man. I wasn't even cross the street when you started and I still almost caught you."

"My momma always say that almost ain't good enough. That's what's wrong wit Black folks. We always almostin."

"Yeah, but you cheated Man."

"I ain't cheat, jus had a head start is all."

"Whatever." We sat on the concrete steps in front of the apartments. The five steps was clean as usual. Nobody never used it no how cause of the dirt paths that went up the hill to the same concrete walkway. We used the steps more than anybody, jumping down and seeing how far we could land. I leaned my elbows back on the steps. It was hot, but not a blazing hot normal day. The air was thick as usual and junebugs was bumping into trees and flying crazy. The tree on the side of the building threw a big enough shadow that it wadn't much sun on us. A couple of folks was walking by, but not many. Most folks was at work. The one's that wasn't, was either still sleeping or smart enough to stay inside during the heat. Man starting asking about Liz again between us playing, that's my car.

"Smokey and the Bandit Trans Am, that's my car...Buck you an Liz ever kiss?"

"No, General Lee, that's my car."

"Everybody know you like her, Starsky and Hutch, my car."

"Everybody don't know nothing, you gotta pick real cars now."

"My Cadillac, we know she like you."

I sat up, "You seen Lizard?"

"You like her don't you?"

"I ain't seen Lizard since last week. Let's go in mom made some lemonade and left it in the icebox."

"Forget it then Buck."

"Forget what?" I laughed.

"I jus wanna get some girls too. Even when we play Catch a Girl, Get a Girl, I don't catch no girls. Some of them girls let yaw'll catch em. Cause they like yaw'll."

"But we jus catch em and hit em or somethin, we don't kiss or nothin like that."

"Stack them do. And Liz always let you catch her, then she hit you and run off again. That's how we know she like you."

"Mr. Archie say that some folks jus gotta be themselves and things work out okay for em. This one guy use to act all rich cause he came from Chicago, but wasn't no women that would go out with him. Mr. Archie said he told him to jus be himself. And guess what?"

"He got a girl."

"Yep. Come on Man, let's go in and get some snacks."

Man and I went inside, ate molasses sandwiches and drank lemonade. We leaned against the table in the middle of the living room so we didn't have to move that far to change the teevee. I had the bag of white bread sitting to my side cause Man always ate too much, but he ain't never get no bigger. We looked at Good Times and kept talking about girls and stuff. He seemed pretty bothered bout not having a girlfriend. But didn't none of us really have girlfriends I thought. Then again, after seeing Stack and BigFoot, I assume they was going with each other. But Stack was always talking about how he had to quit a bunch of girls. By the time Good Times was going off, me and Man had finished a half a loaf of bread. Mom was gonna be mad. I wasn't supposed be in the house during the day. She always made me go outside and do something.

"Don't make no sense for a boy to be inside during the summer. Yaw'll need to be outside, running and playing and such."

"But it's hot out mom. We get tired too fast."

"Go to the public pool."

"Too far."

"Go to the community center and play ball."

"Too crowded."

"Boy if you don't get outta this house," she'd chase me slapping at my behind. We would laugh as I took off out the door. She just didn't think it was right for kids to be in the house when we wasn't limited to staying in one place.

I picked up the bread and molasses. "We better get going. Figure the guys be coming this way in a minute."

"Oh well... Buck," Man said looking at me.

"Hunh?"

"Can I use yo bathroom." He was leaning and clutching his stomach.

"Number 1 or number 2?" He looked at me and took off down the hall. I could hear the door slam. "Man don't be do-dooin, in my house Man." I stood outside the door til this smell came from beneath the crack. "Dang Man. Hurry up."

He came out after about three minutes, holding his stomach.

"I think I'ma go home. I don't feel so good."

"You shoulda went home before you had to do it in my bathroom." He waved me off and started walking to the front.

"I'll see you later Buck. Tell the fellas-" he stopped talking and took off running holding the seat of his pants. I could smell the same do-do smell from the bathroom. I left the front door open and put the latch on the screen door. I walked back to the bathroom to open the window. I could see from my first step onto the white of the floor that Man hadn't flushed good. There were pieces of it floating around the toilet still. I reached over the tub and pushed the window open. I pushed the lever on the toilet. It gurgled and groaned as the last few pieces circled the inside and left brown marks. I knew I had to clean it before I left. Mom would be home in a couple of hours. She liked everything to be cleaned up when she got home. She only had a hour and a half to rest up before her second job. I went to open the back door so the smell could get out faster. Just as I made it to the door I could see through the kitchen window. Lil T and some of the old heads from the park were walking the dirt trail behind the

220

apartments. They was talking and carrying shiny pieces in they hands. One guy had something that look close to black coal sticking from his back. I kept peeking as they walked by. I made out what the coal piece was when the guy pulled his t-shirt up for a second before pulling it down. I figured on trouble the way they was walking. But I didn't want to see nothing else so I didn't open the door. I went back to clean the toilet. I knew from the direction they was going that they was headed towards Frank's store. The old White man had been in the neighborhood forever. He had the cheapest lunch meat. You could go and get a quarter or fifty cents worth of souse, or bologna from Frank's.

I thought about how they was walking down the alley and something in my stomach knew what was bout to happen. But it wadn't none of my concern.

I cleaned the toilet and sprayed some freshener. The smell was fading. I figured I'd go down to Ms. P's or Mr. Archie's to sit a spell. If there was something about to happen, I didn't want to be around the guys or out and about. Besides, I wanted to know if Liz was doing better. I wanted so bad to go over to her place and see her. But didn't nobody ever go over to her house. The girls said that her folks didn't speak to nobody and as far as I knew they was right. I had never got no parts of a hi from her dad. And nobody never saw her mom unless she was shopping or hanging out laundry. Her little sister was always with the mom. Liz came and went only when the dad was gone or if he was there, she was always back before the street lights came on. Not *when* they came on. I wondered how she had got so much stuff over into the old house I followed her into. It seemed to me that she woulda never had time to go and be there.

I closed up the window in the bathroom but left a crack. I put the stick in it so it couldn't get pushed open no farther. I left outta the house and headed up to the park. I walked fast down Fifth. When I made it to Bickford Street I stopped. I didn't want to go by the courts. I could see the old heads over there talking. They wadn't playing no ball or shooting craps or nothing. They was just talking and smoking. Some little kids was over on the sliding boards and swings inside the fence behind the court where the old heads hung. I looked both ways before crossing, still thinking about Liz and then about the guys in the back alley. Lil T looked small compared to them other guys, but he looked like he fit. I was starting to sweat from the heat. It still hadn't heated up real bad, but it was enough. I stayed still until one of the cats leaning against the pole holding up the backboard looked over at me. He moved from the pole and walked over to the table. I realized then that I had been staring. I know they didn't think nothing of me, but none of the old heads liked to be stared at. A small line of sweat rolled down my left cheek. I put the back of my wrist up to my forehead and wiped. I looked at the street again and started walking. I crossed going towards the back of the gym. I knew the side doors were open because they was having a free clinic. So I trotted a little faster. I tried not to look over at the old heads. I knew if I did they would probably call me over. They was always trying to talk to us about stuff. I kept trotting with my head straight and my eyes cutting towards them. The long guy that was leaning stood up straight and looked at me sharp. I could feel his eyes going over me, like he knew

222

I knew. I felt more of the heat and more lines of sweat pushed out and down my chin. I pumped my arms like I was playing basketball and jumped in the air. As I made it to the side of the gym, almost out of sight. I could feel them moving towards me. Just as I opened the door I heard, "Hey lil daddy, hey." I let the heavy gym door fall shut behind me. Kneeling over inside the white and blue painted walls of the air conditioned part of the building, I held my knees. I finally stood up straight and let the coolness go over me. It wasn't right that I felt so scared, but seeing as folks was getting shot almost every week, I didn't know what would set them guys off. I walked nervously through the hall past the library and dance room. I pushed the double doors open and made it into the part of the gym that didn't have air conditioning. But it was some real big fans pushing the heat around enough to make it decent. There was a drink machine at the end of the hall by Melvin's office. Melvin opened and closed the gym. He was kind of chocolate colored, light brown with a little afro that was always real neat. Some of the girls said he looked like an old Marvin Gaye with muscles. I didn't see it. All I could see was that missing tooth he had. He wasn't even embarrassed about it though. He was always smiling, even when he got tough. He must've had about three hundred pair of those tight coach shorts, cause that's all he wore. He sat in his office probably like thirty minutes out of the day. The other time, he was walking around talking and joking with kids and old heads. The only time he didn't joke was when he had to stop a fight in the gym, which was at least twice a week. Melvin saw me walking through the double doors looking back.

"Whatcha say nah! Lil Buck. Took anybody to the scoop today?"

"No sir." I looked back again.

"You ain't playing no ball today?"

"No sir Mr. Melvin." I looked back. He stopped and looked down the hall with me.

"Say lil bruh, watcha looking back yonder for? Something on your mind?"

"I'm fine, just was hot out there."

"So you looking back to see if that heat followed you through huh? That whatcha looking for? Come on nah, watcha say youngblood?"

"I think I will go play a little ball."

"Hold up nah. Something on your back, ain't no getting it past me. Come on in my office. Want a coca cola?"

"I was going to Mr. Archie house."

"Well, seeing as you made it my way, I get you a coca cola and rap with you a spell. Then you be on your way. You only a stone toss away from Mr. Archie."

I didn't want to go with Melvin, but he wasn't gonna take no. Especially when he could see something in me. We walked to the soda machine. He put in fifty cents, opened the glass door and pulled twice to get the bottle out of the slot it rested in.

"What kind of coca cola you want?"

"Orange be fine Mr. Melvin." He dug his hands deep into his pocket and pulled out another set of quarters. He reached in, tugged twice, and pulled out an orange soda. He sat his on top of the machine. He put the lip of my bottle on the edge of the top opener and popped the top off. He passed me my drink before doing his. We walked into his office. The squeaks and pounding of basketballs was loud. Inside there were old heads playing at one end and some young guys playing at the other end. A bunch of little kids ran back and forth from the back of the gym to the back hallways where the arts and crafts was set up. We sat inside of Melvin's office.

"So how your mother doing?"

"She's fine."

"Alright, be straight wit me now... What was you looking for to come through that door? I done seen that face in this gym too much not to know something ain't right."

"The-"

"Don't you lie to me Buck," he said pointing the tip of his bottle towards me.

"The guys over by the court-"

"Go head."

"They was just staring at me is all. I was looking at them and they started staring back hard. I'm jus kinda scared of them I guess, specially after last week."

"Look here Buck, them niggas is gonna catch theirs in due time. If not from God's hand then from another niggas hand. You don't pay them niggas no mind, just don't be making no scenes about them. They looking for trouble from anybody they can get it from. I'm working on getting a police car to come by here every few hours or so. Hell, they messing up my damn park hustling and drinking and carrying on over there. They leaving piles of cans and cigarettes all over. You don't worry about them okay? I'm figuring out on how to get em to somewhere else."

I thought to myself before speaking, 'If anybody could get rid of them it would be Melvin.' If he couldn't do it then wasn't nobody getting them away from our park.

"Mr. Melvin, Mr. Archie say that they squeezing the air from the trees in the park."

"Hmmmph," he looked at me and kinda nodded. His look seemed odd. His mouth turned up almost in a question. He blinked a few times before saying, "You see how on that court it got lines and some colors on it?"

"Yessuh."

"Around that court it use to be some small bushes that divided the horseshoe court and the ball court. Everything was painted on the court. Lines, designs, names, it was real bright and pretty." He leaned back in his seat. "We had to take the bushes out cause we kept finding needles in em. That was round 70-71. After that, not too many folks wanted to come and help on the courts. Too many guys hustling there. Pretty soon the winter cold and the rain washed off most of them colors. I ain't had the heart to go out and paint it no mo myself. I kinda done give in to the notion that stuff changing to quick round here to keep up." He looked me in the face, "Gon and get over to Mr. Archie, I reckon I see you with them boys of yours up here playing ball a lil later, right?"

"Probably."

"Right on then. Go head on I'll see you."

226

I took the last sip of my soda and threw the bottle into the trash can, "Thanks for the soda." Melvin kinda waved at me, looking right past me. He had his hand up to his forehead, a little smile came to his lips for a second.

I didn't feel as nervous but I could see in him the same thing in Liz, and in that lady's face who son got killed. It was that same look on my momma's face after she dropped the cup. I walked out the front and the sun hit my eyes. I squinted and looked up the sidewalk towards Mr. A's. I looked back towards the court and I could see the guys over there playing ball again, loud. I could see Tony sitting at the table laughing with them. He had a brown paper bag beside him and the two cats that was with him was passing something back and forth. Ton looked up. Through squinting eyes we saw each other. He looked at me for what seemed a minute. I began to turn away. I could hear a junebug zip past my head. I looked for it. I caught the small zig zag of it as it dropped and dipped across the field, into the sun, and outta my vision. I couldn't hear it or see it anymore, I decided to go home instead of Mr. A's. I kinda didn't want to be around nobody else.

Chapter 23

"If it ain't one thang it's another." Every now and then mom said and sang, "If it ain't one thang it's another," when she got home from work and had to do something around the house. "If I ain't runnin out to a different job then I gotta deal with the mess on this street. Boy, we gettin outta here real soon. Real soon. Your momma got something good happening."

"What you know good momma?"

"I know God is good. He taking care of things in due time."

"You been say-"

"You have been?"

"You have been saying that since last week mom. *I know when something is a hint.* That's what you always tell me around Christmas when I keep talking about a gift or something."

"Let's just say Christmas coming pretty early this year."

"Good. It's these shoes that-"

"Child-"

"Just playing mom."

Mom always talked about moving on up. We used to look at Good Times when she came home. She would prop her feet up and rest her head on the couch. I'd get her something to drink so she could rest. Her waitress clothes would always be hanging on the back of her door, cleaned and pressed. All she had to do was relax for a minute then get dressed. The cafe was only about a mile and a half or so. She could walk if no buses were running that way.

228

When Good Times was on mom looked at the teevee with a smirky smile, like half laughing and half angry. It seemed more of a false smile every time James and Florida was about to get out the ghetto. More than that, momma would turn the teevee off. I didn't right understand it. It seemed to me that she would've wanted to watch it. But it wasn't that she didn't want to see the happiness. It was more or less that she had seen all of em and she knew what was going to happen. I didn't get it then. It took me some time, but after seeing that every moment when J.J. them was gonna get out, something bad happened. Somebody got killed or somebody got laid off, or somebody got hurt. But there was always a chance for good, at least mom always told me that.

A couple of days after Mr. Travis had stopped taking mom to work, mom started talking more and more about getting out. But the afternoon I left the community center talking to Mr. Melvin, I'd decided to go back to the house instead of to Mr. A's. That was about 4:15. Mom made it home from her temporary job at 4:45 or 5:00.

"Mom, why you turn off the show today?"

"Seen this one. Don't make no sense to watch it again."

"But they movin-"

"They are moving?"

"They're moving mom. They're going to leave the projects. Sides I ain't- I haven't seen this one."

"Re-runs son."

"Mam?"

"Re-runs."

"The guy on 'What's Happening' that be lockin?"

"Excuse me?"

"The guy on 'What's Happening'. You know?" I stood up and twisted my wrists and pointed at the sky, humped my shoulders and jumped.

"That was pretty good."

"Mom."

"Sit down baby. A rerun is another word for repeat. Except when a teevee station shows a repeat of an old show, they shorten the words repeat showing to rerun."

"So that's why they call Re-Run on 'What's Happening' *Re-Run*, cause he always making the same mistakes."

"I would assume so. You know that show better than I do."

"So you turned the station cause you seen that Good Times. But I ain't seen it. I wanna see them move."

"You want to see that Jackson girl."

"No mam I wanna see Thelma." She reached towards me and popped me on the shoulder.

She turned the show back on. It was only five minutes left but I could tell by the way that everybody was sittin on the couches and standing that something had happened. Michael was telling his mom that when he became a judge that they would be okay and Thelma talked about dancing. James wasn't even in the picture, but when Florida said, "He was working so hard they shouldn't have laid him off like that." Mom got up and walked out of the room. I didn't get it then. I just didn't get it. But something deep in my stomach burned.

I walked with mom to the busstop at Chelsea before heading over to Mr. A's. We stood and talked a bit more before she climbed on the bus and headed off to her six o'clock job. She waved at me out the window as the cough, grind and whistle of the bus moved down the block. I ran back down Fifth figuring I'd hit the guys somewhere along the way. I walked up the big hill to the parking court in the middle of the small brick projects across from me. I could hear a ball bouncing and feet shuffling. When I got around the side of the building I saw the guys playing ball. They wasn't really playing yet. They was dribbling and passing waiting on Stack to break out the bottom of the crate with his feet. He jumped down on the blue bottom of the box until it popped once. Then he took a pair of vice grips from off the seat of his bicycle and starting tearing out the rest. I ran up behind the guys and popped the ball out of Lizard's hand. They all turned and looked at me before saying, "Where you been?"

Skillet grabbed the ball back and bounced it between his legs, "Where Man?"

"He got sick and went home. What yaw'll do?"

"Nothing."

I walked up to him, "Stack talk about BigFoot some?"

"Yeah," yelled Smoke. Stack turned.

"My uncle told me I'm a man now. Yaw'll still some lil boys. But I'll teach you the game."

I thought to myself, 'That's why you still in the seventh grade.'

"Aww Stack," I waved my hand.

"What you been doing? With Elizabeth I bet."

"Better than Big Foot," I said.

"But Liz ain't puttin out."

"So Stack, don't nobody care about that."

"You care. I heard what Lil T said."

"He was lying. You *would* believe him-"

"Hold on Buck, I ain't say I believed. You puttin words in my mouth."

"Forget you Stack. Finish with the crate."

He laughed and finished tearing out the last pieces in the bottom. Smoke had popped the ball away from his brother and was dribbling behind his back. I went over to the fence by the back alley behind the old house and wiggled a loose nail out of the wood. Stack was holding the crate towards Smoke.

"Your turn to hang it," Stack said. Smoke took the nail and the vice grips. Skillet took the crate and held it against the light pole. Smoke pushed his hands into the empty space and held the nail to the plastic. He tapped it once to get it started. Then he pulled back as far as he could, inside of the crate, and smacked the head of the nail. He did that about six more times before the nail was all the way through. Lizard had ran over and grabbed two more nails and passed them to Skillet.

"You know Stack always wanna think he Dr. J. He always wanna hang on the rim and stuff," Lizard said. We all agreed and put two more nails in the same area as the other one. Smoke and Skillet played first. I let Lizard go with Stack cause I didn't like playing with Stack. All Stack wanted to do was stand near the basket and dunk it in. He didn't never move, not even on defense. By the time the first game was over the locusts and crickets had woke up. It wadn't many lightnin bugs cause we wadn't by the field. The, "rrrrooonnn rrrrooonnn," of the bugs was enough to let us know we only had another thirty minutes or so before the street lights came on. We played until then, not worried about Liz or Lil T or nothing. We just played ball.

Chapter 24

Mom made it in the house around ten fifteen that night. She was still in her singing mood. She didn't look all tired like she usually did. I heard her keys jingle as she walked up the stairs to the door. I jumped off the couch onto the floor grabbed my book and flipped through the pages. Ran to the teevee and turned it off. She walked in just as I got back to the floor and my book. My chest was heaving a little, I hoped she wouldn't notice. She walked in humming before she started talking to me.

"Well, Mr. I hope you wasn't too lonely here tonight."

"I was alright mom, just reading."

"Just reading huh?" She looked around the front room, then at me. She looked at the teevee and then at me. "Just reading huh?"

I didn't look up, "Yes mam."

"Awfully funny that spot in the teevee still there."

Yep, it sure was still there. That one little drop of light in the middle of the blackness of the screen was still there. It was like a little halo on an angel. That dang light always stayed on an extra five minutes after the teevee was off.

"Yessir, awfully funny." She put her bag down fast and came over to start tickling me. I laughed and rolled around on the floor. She exhaled loud and sat down with this goofy smile on her face. She rubbed me on the head pushing my hair down. Mom looked around the room at the little pictures on the tables. She smoothed out the cloth draped over the arms of the couch with her hand and I could see a tear in her eye.

"Son, God is good. Your mother done worked and worked to make this a decent life for us. Day in, day out. Sun Up, to sun down like a slave, I done work two, three jobs but God is good." She held her hand up like she did in church when she felt the Spirit. I didn't know whether to try and comfort her or let her be. I wanted to cry too. "I mean... since your father passed, I just prayed and let God work through me. That's all you gotta do, that's all. He works in mysterious ways he does." She was still waving her hand. I figured that something bad had happened at the job. But that didn't make no sense. She was smiling when she came in. I could see happiness in her face.

"Momma, what's, what's wrong?"

"Ain't nothing wrong son. Come up here and sit by your momma."

I got up and made my way onto the couch. I sat up under her arm and she hugged me tight. She looked down at me.

"Tonight, I walked out of that cafe like a leaf on the wind son. I glided out and felt high as a kite. I told Mr. Dan that I wouldn't be needing to continue with this job. I thanked em and put in my two week notice son. That's right."

I knew from her other jobs that that meant she was gonna leave. But what I thought was that we needed the money. I didn't say nothing.

"Listen," she got off the couch and started rolling her head and showing with her hands. "I was going on my second hour of work, taking orders and such. Nah, I know you ain't never heard none of these names son but listen at this. I was doing my rounds and Mr.

Foster walks in. I don't see him at first cause I'm kinda use to White men being in the diner at night. So I didn't pay much mind of it. I makes it to his table and he looks at me with them big blue eyes and says, 'Well, if it ain't the hardest working temp in data processin. How you doing mam?'

'I'm fine Mr. Foster and you.'

'Thought I'd come on down here and get me some of this good Soul Food is all. Nah I ain't bein rude at all, but why you serving tables?'

'I do a little extra to make ends meet.'

'Well, hmph. You know we been in the process of increasing our company size. Was figurin on addin a few mo folks down there in your area. Even figured on openin a new division for data entry, maybe even use some of them big new computers.'

So son I'm standing here talking with the manager of the data processin area at my temp job, at my second job. Nervous as I was, I forgot I was supposed to be working. I stood with my pen in my hand.

'We is gon bring on a few mo workers and put em in at Level 5 and start em out at 10.00 dollars a hour and then move em on to salary.'

'Yes sir?'

'Now we don took notice of all you doin round the department, your Saturday and Sunday workin, an I been thinkin on makin you permanent. How that sound to you?'

'I, I,' Son I was so choked up and surprised, I couldn't answer. I just held my hand up to God and thanked him. I just thanked him.

'Sir I truly appreciate this opportunity. This is just what I been looking for sir. Let me get you your peach cobbler on the house.'

'Now listen, it's a lot of training gon have to take place, an a lot of paperwork. You up to comin in earlier tomorrow so we can take care of the process?'

'Yessir!'

'Then I see you in the mornin.'

He smiled and put his head down into a magazine. I rushed to get him his cobbler. I worked the rest of the night in a cloud. Made myself an extra 25.00 dollars in tips, that we gon go out to Big Boy's with tomorrow. Son, we gettin on out of this place. Your momma not sad. These ain't tears of sadness you looking at. These tears come from the proudest place in my soul. I can't praise Him enough."

Mom walked from the front room singing, having her own Sunday worship, "Jesus is oooon de main line, tell em whatcha want. Jesus is on de main line, tell em watcha want." I clapped a little bit and felt good. But then I thought about Good Times and I felt scared for us. I wanted to ask mom, but Mr. Archie had told me that you don't take nobody sunshine. Mom was lightin up the world with hers.

Chapter 25

That morning mom left the house around 4:30 instead of 5:45. The buses didn't start running til a little after then, but I guess she just wanted to get there as early as possible. I didn't wake up to wish her well, cause I felt like I woulda jinxed her. So I stayed in bed and said a short prayer. I fell asleep and got up around 7:30. It wadn't no sense in trying to lay in bed longer, cause the light from outside always found a way to get past the curtains. Sides, mom say any Negro that sleep past 8:00 o'clock is shiftless.

I got on up, ate some cereal and looked at the Great Space Coaster. I don't know why I looked at it. I was too old for that show and that Gary Gnu stuff, but I turned it on anyway. I decided to head out the house to see if anybody else was up and getting ready for the free ones truck to come. If the guys was up I know they was down at Stack's, so I was gonna go that way but I figured I hadn't seen Mr. A in a whole day. I never missed a whole day in the summertime. I turned and headed back up the street. I crossed to the other side just in case I had to walk around the back. But it wadn't likely that anybody was out, except for maybe one person trying to do some early morning hustling. The sun was hotter than the day before. That's the way it usually is anyhow. You get one day at eighty-nine degrees and then the next week you can cook eggs on the sidewalk. Mom said that it was the kinda weather that make Black folks in Africa melt.

I went ahead and walked in front of the gym between the kid's park fence and the gray, white brick wall of the community center.

The sun sat low in the blue and pushed off a few white clouds. Everything seemed good in the morning right after dawn. The air even smelled different early on. North Memphis was good at this time. It was the hours between sundown and sunup that made the neighborhood bad. I got across the park just fine. I was walking up to the street right across from Mr.Archie's when I heard it. It was like what Mr. A called sassy blues. The twang from the strings wasn't loud but it could be heard at just the right moments. I walked across the street. I looked over to Caldwell school and saw cars sitting in front. The teachers were back and getting ready for the new school year which was less than three weeks away now. I hadn't even thought about how the seventh grade was gonna be. I guess it was too much going on. I got to the gate and unclipped the hook. The front door was open and the screen door was like black glass. At my angle I couldn't see through it at all. But I could hear.

"Weelll, fine timin babah, fine timiiin indeed. I said ya got that, fine timin babahh, ya got jus whuuut I need. An when I'm stahvin babah ya know jus what ta feed. Lemme see nah, weell, ya got them red beans an rice, fried chicken an collard greens, ya got them yams and corn bread, somethin spicy in between, you know what I mean. Ya got the good eatin babah, an everythin I need. So uh, come on over here girl and fix me somethin real sweet. Umm Hummmm, un huh, uh hun, hun hun, huuuuunnn."

"You a mess Archie, I do declare."

"Mess cause a you Ms. Mam. You make me sang them kinda songs cause of that fine cookin you do."

"Fine cookin?"

"That's right, cookin. I know you wadn't thinkin I was addressin some other foolishness in that song was you?"

"Nah Archie."

"Ms. Mam I have to say you have got a dirty mind."

"No dirtier than that there song you sanging."

"Dirty songs all in the mind. Folks make out words to mean what they want em. Jus like you doin mam."

"Archie please. Sides, you spose to be upstanding for that boy of yours. Now what if he come over here. He gon hear you sangin that kinda stuff."

"He ain't gon hear me cause I'm finished. Got somethin else that's messin with me anyhow."

"Speak your mind."

I was about to knock and go in but I wanted to hear what Mr. A was about to talk on.

"You and that there Mumford girl was private a lot the other day. Nah ain't none of my business, but I seen how the girl acted. I also see them long sleeves. It's summertime."

"Summertime it is, and what's that got to do with anythang?"

"She awful defensive is all I'm saying. I dun heard some thangs, an yesterday give me some insight."

"Keep it to yourself. I ain't listenin to your explanations."

I didn't want to be nosey by listening in on the conversation, so I went back and closed the gate hard. I jumped on the porch and called out, "Mr. A you up yet?" I figured that give him time to kinda quit speaking on Liz. I heard another couple of words and then Ms. P said, "I reckon you oughta leave it be til he gone."

"Well, well, there is somethin to my worries and thoughts on that girl. The way you gettin all defensive make me feel awfully suspect. Awfully."

I could hear Mr. Archie sittin down his guitar. I knew he was either wiping his brow, or looking with them questioning eyes. It was quiet. I walked all the way up to the door where they could see me and I could see them. "Mr. A, you-"

"Well, if'n I wadn't I expect I would be now don't you think?" Mr. A smiled and lifted the latch on the door. I knew they was feeling kinda weird so I broke the peace.

"What yaw'll doing so quiet and all?"

"You shoutin and yellin, nah you come in asking questions, I was gonna get you something sweet to drink and a cookie-"

"Archie it's too early for that kinda stuff."

"Aww ain't never too early for some goodies. But seein as the boy got so many questions, I reckon he got too much energy. Whatcha say bout you goin in there and put them vegetables up in the icebox for me Buck."

"Archie you terrible putting that boy to work."

"Awww, hush it."

"Excuse me sir?"

"Uh, well, Buck get on in there and put them vegetables up. I'll help ya."

I got up to go to the kitchen but stopped in the hall to hear if they said something else.

"No you won't help. You gon sit here and tell me what you just told me to do."

"I didn't say a word Ms. Mam. I wouldn't say a word against yo kind soul mam. Let me fix you something to drink."

"How bout you come over here and give me a kiss on the cheek. I'll forgive you that way."

"Why yes mam, I can do that."

I got away from the door fast after hearing the gross old folks kissing sound. I finished putting everything away in no time.

"Nah Buck did ya finish putting them vegetables in the icebox?"

"Yes sir, even wiped off the counter and put the cookie box-"

"You been in that box?"

"Un Un. I jus put it back over by the toaster is all."

"I'm jus foolin wit ya. Come on over here by me."

"Buck you come on over here and sit by Ms. P. We can send Archie back in the kitchen to find us some snacks since he worried bout his oatmeal cookies."

"I ain't worried, jus know the boy ain't sposed be eatin no lot of sweets."

"Now Archie, you just said you thought the boy should have some sweets. I tell you what, you go get us something like some cookies and milk. Just go and find us some sweets."

"Yes Miss Mam. I get right on it fast as possible. Sorry mam."

"Stop it now."

I liked seeing them flirt. Kinda like looking at something that was supposed to happen but not in front of you. It felt private. It felt like the quiet talk they was doing when I was in the kitchen. I leaned back against the couch and tried to avoid putting my head on the white cloth over the middle part of the high back. Ms. P looked at me.

"So how you doing young man?"

"Mam?"

"I know you been thinking bout Elizabeth since she ran off day before."

"Yes mam. But not like nothing nasty thinking."

"I know. Well, Elizabeth got a few things that bother her but she like you."

"She do?"

"You know that. Don't start acting."

"Yes mam. What you think is wrong with Liz Ms. P?"

"Son, ain't nothing wrong with that girl she just going through some woman type things right now is all. She's fine."

I knew better. I knew she wasn't fine cause of how she go to that house and sit with them ghosts. But I didn't say nothing against Ms. P's words. She looked me in my face after she started talking. I guess she saw that I didn't believe her words. She stopped talking.

"What's on your mind?"

"Mam, if Liz okay why- I think something bothering her. I kinda got this feeling the day before. I think something on her mind that's bad."

"Ohh, Buck quit it. That girl is fine. I can't believe how much you like that old man in your statements. I mean jus like him."

"That ain't no bad thing is it Ms. Mam? I mean if you got a problem with me and the boy I reckon we can get out the cards."

"Archie how long you listening in on us?"

"Long enough to know you think the boy act like me," he laughed and walked back over to his chair. The floorboards moaned a bit as he moved across the planks.

"Seein as how the boy talk like me, let's find out what he share with me. What you two addressin?"

"None ya."

"Mam?"

"None ya business Archie. Now where our milk and cookies?"

"Mmmph, I knew I was missing something."

"I sure would like a cold glass of milk and a cookie Mr. Archie."

"I bet you would," he got up grumbling under his breath.

"What's that you say there?"

"Nothing," he disappeared behind the wall. Ms P let out a hollow laugh. It sounded empty and fake.

"Buck, what is it that make you think on Elizabeth that way?" She jumped right back to the questions.

"Well, we-"

"We who?"

"Us kids all see how her daddy, not to speak bad of a grown-up mam, act to her momma. And I was with Liz day before-"

"Yes, yes," she said urging me to speak faster.

"I, she, well, I went, she went into that old house on Fifth."

"What you mean she went into the old house. Son what that got to do with anything?"

I felt nervous and bad for telling Liz's business. I didn't wanna snitch and have Liz hate me. So I tried to hold off on speaking so much.

"I gotta use the bathroom." I tried to stand up and Ms. P held me tight by the arm. So tight it hurt. She squeezed and squeezed.

"I reckon you need to keep on speaking before you go to the restroom Buck." She had this look in her face, like an angry dog that questioned you being in his space. I sat down quick so she would let go. "Tell me what you know," she said.

"I followed her in there when it was thunderstorming. She had all kinds of stuff there. Like she was there a lot."

"And?" She moved her arm to fix herself on the couch and I jumped. Mr. Archie had walked back into the room and saw me moving from Ms. P, scared.

"What's going on in here?" He asked. His voice sounded different. It sounded straight, almost the way mom would correct me. His eyebrows arched down and he held the tray still.

"Sit down Archie. I think it's time we talked about some things."

He put the tray down and sat beside me. I felt bunched in. It felt too hot between the two of them. I started sweating.

"What she have in there?"

"She who?"

"Hold on Archie, hold on. Tell me, what kinda stuff Buck."

"It was a mat big enough to sleep on. Some books, and some stuff like make-up and deodorant stuff."

"Who we talking about here? The Mumford girl?"

"Archie be patient. Go head Buck."

"She had a little lighter and some candles and a pillow. It look like she was always there. And she even said that she talk to the ghosts there." I don't think Ms. P heard the ghost part. She had stood up and walked around the table. She sat next to Mr. Archie and leaned to his side. I heard her whisper. Mr. Archie was already leaning up towards the coffee table trying to hear and understand what I was speaking about. When she stopped whispering he slammed his hand on the table. The table shook. The glass rocked and milk jumped over the rim onto the row of cookies. His hand looked like the fist of some giant. He hit it again and the glass fell spilling milk all over the tray. He lifted his hand again and Ms. P stopped him. She put her hand over his and held it. He got up and walked towards the front door. His steps were smooth. No limp or slow steps with a cane. He moved fast and it made me afraid. He had taken his hat off when Ms. P leaned into him. His hair was a gray scramble on his head. The white of his shirt showed stains at the armpits. He swung the screen door open and stepped onto the porch. I couldn't see him from the couch but I could hear. He shuffled along the wooden deck, swishing from one end to the other. He was talking to himself. Ms. P walked to the door. I stayed in my place. Grown folks business ain't a place for a kid, although I felt I was a part of it all. I had snitched and whatever I said seemed to click on a switch in Mr. A's head. Cause I had never seen him look or sound the way he did. Ms. P stood, about to go outside, and Mr. A spoke.

"Gimme a minute please, jus gimme a minute. I'll be alright jus gimme some time."

"Don't go to thinking too much now Archie. Keep ya head and lets sit down and talk some more."

"I said I be fine dammit."

Ms. P pushed the door open and walked out. I heard her mumbling with peaks in her voice like a mother to a child. She was being kinda quiet, I guess as quiet as she could be but Mr. Archie, "These our kids Patricia whether these damn parents want em to be or not. We raise them. The neighborhood suppose to raise em and make it safe. But we failing Patricia, we failing."

"Archie, we ain't failing nobody. The neighborhood ain't the way it was. We can't make things stay right forever, sometimes you gotta do what you can and close your eyes-"

"Can't close em, cause they open even when I sleep. I see that boy layin there in the park with his guts hangin out and I here the gunshots. I can't sleep no more Pat. I ain't sleep right in years and it's heavy, it's heavy on my soul. It hurts my heart Pat and this is jus too much now."

I could hear Mr. Archie. It sounded as if he was crying, but that couldn't be. He wasn't supposed to cry. He was supposed to tell stories, and sing good blues, not cry. I felt my eyes getting warm. I looked around the room at the walls, not really fixing my eyes on nothing. I walked over and pushed the door open. Ms. P looked at me. Mr. Archie was sitting on his wooden bench with his head hung. His hands were in the middle of his thighs pressing hard. His lower lip shook a little with every bit of air he took in. I ran over to him and put my arm around his neck and put my head in his shoulder.

"Don't cry Mr. Archie, don't cry. Momma say don't cry cause it just make it worse. Please don't cry." I put my head further in his shoulder. He sat still and didn't respond. His head was still hung low. He finally lifted his arm and patted me on the back. Ms. P was looking on holding her hand to her mouth. Her eyes was like small rain puddles. She stood beside us looking down on us crying, not with us, but with different tears. Her tears and her eyes looked like knowing stares from somewhere else. Mr. Archie pushed me up and put his hand on my shoulders. I knelt a little to be face to face with him.

"Men ought to be men enough to do right by us."

He got up and went in the house. The door closed behind him. I sat on the bench in his place. Ms. P sat beside me.

"Buck, let's go on down to my house and get some more of that icebox lemon pie. Come on now, let's go."

I knew I needed to go. Just like when mom was tired, I think Mr. Archie was more tired than anybody. I knew he needed his quiet time so I left with Ms. P. I hoped that Liz would come by. Her dad left for work early on in the morning. That's when she usually came out and spent time with the girls. I hoped she would come and see Ms. P.

Archie's Psalm

Chapter 25

The day moved on pretty fast after leaving Mr. Archie's house. I ate pie with Ms. P at 8:30 in the morning. What mom didn't know wouldn't bother her too much. I wasn't supposed to eat pie or sweets too early but the pie was making me feel better about telling. I still hoped that Liz would come by but the longer I stayed at Ms. P's, the more the street filled with the sound of kids and still no Liz.

"What you thinking on there Buck?"

"Liz mam."

"Pretty straight shooter."

"Mam?"

"Usually you take a minute to say anything when it's about Liz. You came out pretty quick with that one. She must really be on your mind."

"Mam, I ain't old enough to really, well, I'm too young to-"

"Son don't be nervous, tell me what's on your chest."

"Mam, I can't find the right words to speak about it."

"Aww shoot son, I know what your problem is. I can see it in your eyes when you smile at the lil girl and when you say her name."

"Mam, but, see, I'm not old enough to be like that with Liz."

"Well, I'm gonna assume that you addressin something else, different from what I'm talking about. Love ain't something physical."

"Mam?"

"When your momma hug you, how you feel?"

"I feel like she wouldn't let nothing hurt me. Almost how I feel with you and Mr. Archie."

"Thank you for saying that, but let me explain a bit more. That feeling is love Buck. It ain't a touch or word that can really explain it, but you know it."

"I kinda get it."

"Jus listen, sometime you can share a bond with a person from the moment you look on em. That feeling like you wanna have them around is what love is. Love ain't got to be no touch or words, no sir."

"But I still think that I'm too young."

"Buck sometime we love too late. Most of the time we don't know when and how to love. When you a young man and a young woman, it's simple. You just have to be a friend."

"What else is there mam? Ain't being friends the only thing that matter?"

"Hmmm, I reckon you might be right on that one."

"Can I be excused mam? I'm going down to see if I can find Liz."

"Buck listen, don't ask too many questions of her. Let her be. She'll tell you what she want you to know, the rest ain't important. Just listen to what she tell you."

"Yes mam." I took my plate to the kitchen, came back, kissed Ms. P on the cheek and left out the house. It was still an hour or so before noon, but the sun was high, hot, and beatin down on the concrete pushing up heat out of the cracks and making the top of cars create wavy lines of heat. There were a group of girls including Rabbit, jump-roping under the shade of a tree. A lot of the littler kids were jumping curbs on their bikes. I walked down Sixth. I started coming up on the orangish-red brick building and then I got scared. What if I ran into her dad? I was gonna turn around when I heard my name yelled.

"Buck, Buck, come help me."

I saw Liz standing in the walkway of her apartments. She turned and went back to the inside of the breezeway. I could see when I reached the steps in front of the apartments that her door was open. She was already back at the other end of the building hanging clothes.

As I walked by, it was the first time I'd seen their front door open. Her mom sat on the couch with her little sister. She looked at teevee without moving. Her eye was thick and puffy. Her face was lighter than her neck, like powder. Liz had a long sleeve shirt on, in the heat, hanging laundry. I kept walking her way.

"Can you grab that basket next to the door?"

I had walked straight past the clothes, hadn't even noticed them sitting there. It was sheets and towels. I picked up the heavy basket and carried them to her.

"Thank you Buck."

"What you doin?"

"What does it look like I'm doing?"

"Oh, my bad." I stopped and thought about what Ms. P had said. I got quiet and stood watching her.

"What's with the quiet?"

"Nothing, just waiting on you to talk is all."

"Waiting on what?"

"Nothing."

"You silly Buck." She kept hanging the laundry. I looked at her face to see if it looked like her moms anywhere. It didn't, but I still don't know why she was wearing that longsleeved shirt. I looked around the apartments and saw two older women walking the trail going to the store on Kell Street. They was looking over at Liz staring and talking. One of the ladies shook her head in a shameful way and then spoke, "Lil Ms. Mumford you tell your momma we said hi. If she need anythang you be sho to tell us now." The other lady was spitting into a can and carrying her purse draped over her left arm. The speaking lady had a rag in her right hand and dabbed it at her forehead. Her purse was hung in the same way. They kept looking and talking. Liz stared at them, she had stopped working. She never answered them back. It wasn't like she wasn't respectful she just looked like she didn't want to hear them. Liz mumbled.

"Always walking by... nosey and stuff."

"What Liz?"

"Nothing." She popped out the last towel and hung it. "Gotta get this stuff hung before the afternoon so won't nobody steal it."

"Yeah."

"Thank you for bringing the basket down for me." She picked up the empty, twisted straw handled laundry basket and started walking back up the steps. I followed her. She made it to the door and looked back, "I'm coming to Ms. P's in a lil bit, you gonna be there?"

I stood outside the door seeing just her head sticking out and answered, " Yeah I'll stay there for a while."

She smiled at me and shut the door. I walked back to Ms. P's house.

It was close to noon and the guys would be at the community center playing ball in a minute. I was fixin to go back to see Mr. Archie, but I thought against it. I walked down Sixth and listened to the yells and giggles of the kids playing. If we was gonna be moving on up, I bet it wasn't gonna be no bunch of kids in Whitehaven. And if it was, it was just gonna be White people. I made it to Ms. P's and just like at Mr. Archie's house that morning, I heard talking.

"If'n I don't do something bout this one Pat, I couldn't live with myself."

"What can you do, huh?"

"I can make sure he don't touch them women no mo."

"Ain't none of your-"

"It is Patty, dammit it is. Been my business before this and I'ma make it my business now."

"How so Archie. I done lost you once on the count of you not thinking thangs through. Ain't gon lose you no more. I'm too old to have to worry about you and your stubbornness."

"So you think I should just let it be."

"I ain't say that Archie. My God, you just gonna have to let it be until you think it all through."

"Can't do that this time mam. Might take too long."

He couldn't do what and what was he gonna do? I stayed on the porch for a minute and it was silent. I went ahead and left to sit on the curb. Then I walked back down to Liz's. I figured at least that way I could see her when she came out and I could meet her halfway. I was sweating bad by the time she came walking out through the brick

254

pathway. I wanted us to run straight to the gym and sit on the cool side, in the library. Liz was walking with her head down. She crossed the street and headed into the gate. I knew where she was going. I called to her.

"Liz," I waved my hand and yelled. She looked up at me and came back from beneath the fence. She still had her head down.

"What's wrong?"

"Nothing, Buck. Just sad is all."

"Why you sad Liz? You shouldn't be sad."

"Why shouldn't I be?"

"My mom say that God got us all in his good graces. Each day-"

"God done forgot about my house Buck."

"Don't say that Liz."

She stopped on the dirt hill in front of the burnt down house at the corner of Bickford and Sixth. We sat on some dry grass between the patches of green and dust.

"Buck, if you had a daddy you think it be better?"

"I don't know. I figure it be okay."

"Sometimes, you can't explain things and, and, when you can, it don't matter much. I wanna run away."

I didn't say nothing. I just listened and like Ms. P said she kept on talking.

"I wanna go down to Mississippi. I went there to visit my Big Momma and she had these long grass fields, with honeysuckle, trees, and it was quiet. At night you could hear crickets, and the wind was still hot but it had a smell so different than here. She say my momma use to go out and pick cotton with her and it wasn't nobody that would bother them. Not even after my momma daddy died. She say my grandaddy was a good strong man. Big Momma never liked my daddy. She said he wanted to be a man too much."

"I don't think you should run away," I cut her off. I hoped she didn't get mad at me, but if I was being selfish or not, it didn't matter. I just didn't want to hear her talk like that. I wanted to talk about other things like kissing and BigFoot and Stack. We needed to talk about stuff that wasn't so important. We was kids living in a grown folks world and that wasn't right. But she had things she needed to get out.

"If I run away, things get better."

"What things?"

"I know you guys know what happens at my house Buck. But I'm glad you don't act no different towards me."

"Ms. P told me that a friend is the best thang to be. I'm your friend Liz I love you a lot, like I do my momma." She moved close to me and put her head on my shoulder.

"I love you too Buck."

Some of the little girls jumping rope pointed, laughed and giggled at us. We sat on that dirt hill for a while. I didn't say much and she talked every now and then about being in Mississippi and being away from North Memphis.

"What do you dream about Buck?"

"Whatcha mean?"

"You know when you dream about stuff, what do you dream of?"

"I wish we was rich-"

"Not that kind of dreaming. Real dreaming, you know?"

"I don't get it."

"I dream about taking my momma back to Tunica. I dream of getting her and my sister to a better place away from my dad."

"Liz can I ask you somethin?"

"Yeah," she picked her head up off of my shoulder and looked me in the face. Her skin was soft and smooth and brown. I could smell her and it was like fresh clothes hung up outside after the wash. Her hair was pulled back into two ponytails one on each side of her head. She looked at me again and spoke, "You can ask me, right after you catch me." She kissed me on the face and took off running down towards Ms. P's. I chased her wanting to catch her so she could kiss me on the cheek again. My face felt all hot and warm. Her lips felt like my mom's only smaller. I laughed and hoped that she was feeling better now. I caught her as she made it to the gate at Ms. P's.

"I quit, I quit."

"You kissed me, now I gotta punch you."

She stopped and broke down in the yard, crying. I walked over and she backed away pushing with her hands and feet across the small green yard. She put her hand around her knees and rocked.

"Why you have to say that? Why Buck?"

"Say what, what I say Liz? I'm sorry, what I say?"

Ms. P came to the front and walked down the steps fast to get Liz. Mr. Archie was behind her. As Ms. P reached for her, she moved back more.

"No, no, no, no, no."

"Darling what's wrong?"

"Boy what you done to the girl?"

"Nothing sir, I, we was jus playin and she start cryin and actin when I said I was gon-" then I knew. Mr. Archie grabbed me by the shirt and took me in the house.

Ms. P looked at us and then knelt back down to Liz, "Sweetheart stop them tears, you okay here. You know that."

Mr. Archie opened the door and pushed me towards the couch, "Whatcha say to that girl Buck?"

"I said I was gon punch her."

"Nah I know you know better than to hit a girl. I know we done taught you better, boy if I was in my right mind I'd take this belt to your behind."

"But Mr. Archie she kissed me and she ain't never done that before. Anytime I play with her she run away and we punch each other. She just started actin when I said it this time."

"Why you expect she jumped so?"

"I don't know, but I think somebody told her them words before. I bet-"

"Go on and say it."

"Mr. Archie please don't tell Liz I said anything. I tol Ms. P already and she said she wadn't gon say nothin." I was starting to cry.

"Son just say it, I gotta hear it from you."

"Her momma had a swole eye and I done heard you talking about her longsleeves. I even heard some old women speaking peculiar about something."

"You listen up, I ain't gon let nothing else happen to that girl. Nothing else. You believe me son, that's it."

258

He walked out the back way through Ms. P's kitchen. Ms. P was bringing Liz into the house. I stood up.

"I'm sorry Liz. I don't wanna see you crying."

"It's alright Buck she just a little warm. That heat'll make you tired and bothered real easy. That's all wrong wit her."

"Yes mam. You want me to leave?"

"No Buck, don't leave," said Liz. She looked weak, tired and ashamed. "I was just actin is all."

"Okay Liz. I'm sorry about what I said."

"It wasn't nothing. That ain't what bothered me. It was the heat like Ms. P was saying."

Ms. P rubbed Liz's head, smoothing out her ponytail and picking small sticks of dry grass out of her hair. I didn't wanna say much else to her. I did feel like I wanted to be close to her, touch her hand and make her know that she was alright. But I didn't move. Maybe for fear that she would jump again, or just cause I thought my moving would make her think I wanted to leave. There was no way I woulda left her that day and I didn't. I stuck around at Ms. P's until late afternoon.

Ms. P and her cooked some cheese sandwiches and talked a lot in the kitchen. I stayed in the living room and read from the books Ms. P had laying around. The books was big and hardback. They looked like they was old as me. One book was named Native Son, the other was by some man named Zora. I figured it was where Zorro came from, so I picked it up. It was hard to get cause the words was spelled bad. I couldn't get past the first two pages. Even in those two pages I knew it wasn't about Zorro. It was about Black folks.

I knew Black folks wrote, but I didn't think they wrote whole stories. I know my mom read poems though. Anyway, I put that book down and flipped through the other one. I didn't read much because it seemed to be too much anger on the pages. Then again the man in the book was actin like Lil Tony, so I guess the anger was how we act sometimes.

When Liz and Ms. P finished cooking and talking they came out carrying some food to the dinner table, Liz was smiling a bit.

"Yes mam, if anything happen. Yes mam," she giggled.

"Now you don't do that no more darling. You save them kinda thangs til you older."

"But I do like-" she stopped talking and looked at me smiling real funny.

"Shush up nah. Buck get on in here and help us eat these sandwiches."

"Yes mam."

We all sat at one end of the table and stacked crispy brown, gold bread with cheese falling from the slice down the middle, onto our plates.

"Lord in our troubling times give us the strength to make it through. Bless this food we bout to receive, Amen."

"Amen," we both said. I thought on Mr. Archie but after a while it passed. I would see him later on. We enjoyed our afternoon.

Around four Liz began getting herself ready to go back home. I felt worried that something would happen when she got there. I didn't want her to go back but what could I do? I kept quiet and walked into the kitchen with Ms. P.

"Mam I worry about her when she home. I don't like her being there."

"Buck that-"

"Mam, I know it ain't none of my business but I like Liz a lot. I wish I could watch out for her like a man supposed to."

She rinsed out a dish and wiped it with the towel draped from her shoulder.

"Thangs gonna be alright for her. Her father about to get laid off is all. Sometime a man take his frustrations out."

"But why a man gotta be that way with his family?"

"Buck don't speak on this no more. Let it be. Just be a good friend for that girl. That's the best thang for her right now."

"Yes mam." I left the kitchen and walked to the front with Liz. We called back to Ms. P and let her know we was leaving. Liz and I jumped down the steps and ran out the gate. I could hear Ms. P yelling as she made her way to the porch.

"Yaw'll be careful walking up this street. Watch out for them cars."

"Yes mam," we shouted back.

Liz held my hand for a second before letting go and telling me what was on her mind.

"I'm glad you walking me home."

"I like walking you home, you my friend."

"I know. Buck?"

"Huh?"

"Don't think I'm weird and please don't tell nobody bout today, kay?"

"I promise I won't."

"Cross your heart, hope to die?"

"Yep."

"You don't have to walk me all the way. I'll be okay. See you tomorrow?"

"Yeah, God willin."

"He willin and able," we both laughed hard. She took off across the street and disappeared behind the brick. I turned and went back down Bickford to the park. I tried to look up the street to see if them old heads was at the park but they wasn't. I figured that the cops must've come by and made them move. But the closer I got to the gym I could see different. Mr. Archie was sitting at the table speaking to this big guy who was darker than Skillet and Smoke put together. The big guy had been around every now and then. He looked familiar, but not seein him much made his face like someone in a dream.

I walked to the side of the gym and hid so I could see them. It didn't make no sense to me what Mr. Archie was doing. The big guy had on a straw hat with a feather in it. There was a guy standing on the side of a long, blue Cadillac Fleetwood. And I mean there wasn't none of the regular old heads around. Mr. Archie was half sitting and half standing most of the time. He was moving his arms around like he was explaining. The oil colored dude was nodding and shaking his head. I kept looking on.

The big guy by the car got waved over by Straw Hat. Straw Hat leaned his head up to the kneeling guy and the big guy shook his head. He then reached his hand out and shook with Mr. Archie. Mr. Archie got up from the table and looked around. His eyes stopped towards me and he put his hand up to his face to block the sun some. I moved back into the corner out of sight. I couldn't see him no more, but I could see Straw Hat and the big guy getting into the Cadillac.

I waited a little longer before going out to get to Mr. A's house. I didn't want him to know or figure out that I'd seen him at the table. By the time I left from the side of the gym, Mr. Archie was at his front gate. I looked down and I could see waves from the heat rising outta the concrete. He looked like he was melting into the waves, almost like a blur. I went home knowing that mom would be getting in soon and wonderin why Mr. Archie was talking to that man.

Chapter 26

I made it to the house as mom was walking up the block. She had a little dip to her strut. She had on her church clothes, it looked like to me, without a hat. She held her arms out for me and I ran up to give her a hug and a kiss. We walked back down Fifth Street. She held my hand, which made me feel kinda funny cause I was too big to be holding hands with mom, especially where everybody could see. But seeing as how I felt she was in a good mood, I just didn't care.

"Guess what?"

"Mam?"

"Your mom got a job out there at the new division of Air Mail."

I thought to myself, 'Wow Air Mail, I don't know what that is but it must be good.' I kept my dumbness to myself and asked, "What's that mean mom?"

"Well, son it's been a long time coming, but we gonna finally be able to get out of North Memphis."

"Soon?"

"Real soon, like in seven days soon." She opened the door and walked in. I sat on the couch with her. She threw her bag in the chair and moved the coffee table up closer to the couch. She lifted her heels up and put them on the table and lay her head back. I sat up, legs apart, hands together making circles with my fingers. I still hadn't said much at all. She spoke into the air.

"Yes Lawd, yes indeed. I'll be getting paid per hour for the first six months then we have a chance of getting salaried. But that ain't the good part." She put her feet down and sat up, "They also found apartments in the area that will allow move in specials for new employees. You know what that means son?"

"No mam."

"During our orientation today we went to each apartment complex. I already put my name on the list for these nice apartments off of Winchester, just five, ten minutes away from the company. I'll be able to move in next week." She clapped her hands and held them high. I just sat there.

"Boy do you here what I'm saying? We can finally get outta here. No more gunshots and sirens at night. No more cars zooming too fast down the street. No more son."

I sat, still, quiet.

"What's wrong baby, something happen today?"

"No mam, I, I just-"

"What is it?"

"I don't wanna leave mom? I ain't gonna have no friends out there and we start school in less than three weeks. I ain't gon know nobody."

"Son, the schools out there are all new and got air condition and they have little league football. I promise you'll like it."

"But I like it here. If I leave then I can't see Mr. Archie no more, and Man, and the guys." Really, I could handle not seeing the guys, but Mr. Archie and Liz was on my mind the most. I felt Mr. Archie was a part of me, and Liz too. I knew I was letting mom down and that she was gonna get mad at me, but I couldn't hold my tongue. I didn't want to leave North Memphis cause it was all I knew. There wasn't nothing that was real to me outside of Chelsea, Greenlaw, Caldwell, Bickford and Seventh street. It wasn't nothing that mattered to me. It wasn't no way I could get use to being out there. It would be like I was getting put on another one of them big yellow buses and being sent to them schools out in Frayser again. I was so happy when I didn't have to go out there to go to school. But if mom was gonna move us, it wasn't nothing I could do about it.

"Son, I know it's hard to leave friends but it's all for the better. You don't understand me now but in due time you will." She patted me on the leg and got up singing, walking to the back, "This lil light of mine, I'm gonna let it shine. This lil light of mine, I'm gonna let it shine. This lil light of mine..."

I sat on the couch sad. I felt like crying but I had done cried enough the last couple of days. It wasn't no sense in being sad over something that made mom feel so good. But I couldn't help it, I just didn't want to leave. I stayed in the house and looked at teevee. I didn't really watch anything, I just stared. Looking into the tube seeing nothing and thinking about nothing but Liz and Mr. Archie.

Chapter 27

The night mom told me we was moving was the last time I felt comfortable in the apartment. For her, leaving held all these dreams she'd wanted for us. I didn't see or feel nowhere near that way. It was like taking a dog away from a little boy after he had raised it up from being a puppy. I started thinking like Liz. If I ran away then she would know how bad I wanted to stay. If me and Liz both got together and ran, then we'd both be better off. It wasn't nothing we could do against our folks, but be kids, as long as we were at home. If we went off and left then we could be grown-up. We could show them they wasn't always right.

I thought about leaving all night. I figured I would let mom go to work the next day and me and Liz could leave, since her dad would be gone too. But in getting a good plan together you don't think something can stop you from somewhere else. You just want so bad for things to be the way you want, you forget how things keep going on around you.

I finally felt sleep coming down on me around ten-fifteen or so. That night I heard two shots, about fifteen minutes apart. The first shot came in loud and stinging, and then the whine of the sirens was loud like a guy with his fingers in his mouth whistling five feet from your ear. It must've been around 11:30 or so. I hadn't been sleep long and the crack of the shot was loud, too loud. I was thinking it was a dream cause there was a big bright flash in my eyes. The flash came right after the first crack split the air like thunder. I felt something burning in my chest. It was warm like a flame jumping up from a stovetop. I sat and rubbed my chest hard. Smoothing out my pajama shirt in little circles. I rubbed and sat looking at how the window cast shadows of trees on the wall from the crack in the curtains. I tried to rub the burning away, but it just sat high near the bottom of my throat. I looked down and felt to see if something was there making my insides burn. But it wasn't nothing visible. I wanted to call out to mom but my breath and voice was caught up in the air. I could see floating letters. Words drifting in a circle, not strong enough to get past the dark spaces in the room.

The second shot came soon after and bursted the mountain of cries floating around. I cried, cause that second shot was like a flash of lightning and everything that Mr. A and I had done was real close behind my eyelids. Kinda like looking at a picture and closing your eyes. The picture was still there just like it was, in gray shades, with patches of colors here and there. All the walks, the chasing, the stories, all of it was like playing 1,2,3 Red Light... like frozen snapshots. Then the light changed from being a picture in my head, to a flash shooting through my window. The glass broke forward like a rock hit it in slow motion. I could see the slices of window snap from the frame and fall piece by piece into dark patches of wood and colored carpet. I looked at the glass on the floor and then out the window. I could see a bright morning star flicker. Mom opened the door and rushed in to see if I was okay. She stepped over the big cuts of glass. There weren't any small pieces at all. Slivers was on the place carpet and on the floor. The star that was flickering out reflected soft off the glass. Mom held her robe and walked to the window. As she looked out, her head turned in a way that I could see each muscle straining in her face.

"You okay baby?"

"Yes mam."

"I'll be damned if some bastard done threw a rock through this window." She looked around on the floor as she pulled her robe tighter and looked back and forth from the floor to the window. "You see the damn rock?"

"No mam. The window jus broke I think."

"Boy please, I ain't in the mood now. Did you see the rock?"

"No mam." I pushed my hands under me. I looked down at the glass and at the window. It wadn't no hole or nothing. The glass had just broke and fell in. I didn't say nothin though.

"You stay put. I'ma go get a dustpan and stuff."

Momma didn't seem worried about me. She just looked angry and that look of when she said she was tired was on her face. But it wadn't no tears there. She was mad. As she walked into the hall, I heard different sirens. Just like Mr. Archie said, there was a thunderstorm. Not a long one, just enough to push everything bad out for a minute. I could hear momma in the kitchen saying, "Great, just damn great." I reached over and pulled my curtains closed so the water wouldn't get in too bad. Mom came back in and kneeled to sweep up the mess.

She mumbled, "So damn glad we gettin the hell outta here, hell. This don't make no damn sense." She stopped and stood after she had gotten all of the glass. "You alright?"

"Yes mam."

"I figure I done got it all. We might as well get up. I have to pay for this window outta my deposit."

That night it seemed as if everything was creeping like a sunset. I wasn't sure of what time it was. I thought it was close to midnight but mom had started to get ready for work. Hadn't she heard the shots? How come she was thinking it was a rock? The cracks was loud, both of em, and all she did was think it was a rock getting thrown through the window. She couldn't see past her happiness I supposed, or just didn't want to think that there was gunfire. I don't even think she seen the glass wadn't in pieces at all. Not one tiny piece. It was all in long slices. It wadn't no kind of rock could do that. But it was 11:30 for me and morning for her, and maybe, we just wasn't able to see the same thing.

I heard her sweeping the glass into the trash and starting to get ready. I wanted badly to go back to sleep, but I had to figure out on how me and Liz was gonna leave. You can't really start no plan and then back out of it. That wouldn't be man-like.

Mom hadn't come back to check on me again. The house fell quiet. I couldn't hear her moving in the bathroom or the kitchen. All I could hear and feel was the warmness from outside. I guess the sun was coming up, but I couldn't see it. All I could see was Liz crying as I left her behind. I didn't want that. I rolled over in the bed away from the warm air and to avoid any rain if it started thunderstorming again. I felt sleep coming down on me even though I wanted to be up so I could plan. It came down on me soft and slow.

Thinking I'd been awake most of the night I figured the late sleep would do me good. I found that I was still tired when I finally

270

decided to get up. It had been bad dreams that had taken away all of my nighttime hours. The window was still there. It wasn't no draft of warmness or rain drops on the window seal. I never had nightmares so real until mom told me we was moving. But that had to be what I had, cause nothing really happened. The gunshots I heard probably took place but had mom come in the room that night? I wasn't sure of much, except that I didn't sleep. I climbed out of the bed and called for her. It was Saturday morning and she didn't usually leave for the cafe or her temp job until around 7:30. My clock read 7:25. The sun had come up and mom was gone. She hadn't come in and said rise and shine or kissed me on the forehead. I guess she was in a rush. I walked down the hall to get cleaned up before grabbing a bowl of frosted flakes.

Saturday morning used to be kids time, cartoons and cereal, Kung Fu Theater and Super Friends, but I was feeling old. Leaving North Memphis, for momma, seemed the best thing to do. I felt like it wasn't so good, but like Mr. Archie sometimes say in between his singing, "Even a dog see when his master ain't right no mo. Sometimes you gotta make decisions that's good for the bigger picture. What you want and need, take a backseat to them feelins ya have. Yessuh son, even a dawg know when his master ain't right. Sometimes ya gotta move on down the line," he'd strum his guitar.

'It wouldn't be no more of his Saturday morning stories,' I thought to myself. I sat down in front of the teevee and flipped the channel to thirteen and watched Fat Albert. I couldn't even laugh at Mushmouth when he came on. I usually woulda spit out my milk from laughing so hard. But I didn't get much humor out of nothing that day. Not even when the guys came by to tell me about Stack getting caught with BigFoot Ann the night before. Smoke wouldn't let nobody say a word.

"Naw Buck, naw, this what happened-"

"Smoke you gon mess up the damn story. You don't never tell nothin right and always wanna talk."

"Shut up Man damn-"

"Yaw'll stop cursing in my house."

"Yeah, no manners Buck," said Skillet.

The guys had come over earlier than usual. Most of the time they didn't come by til Kung Fu was on, but whenever something big happened and I wasn't around they always came over early, too early.

Skillet kept talking cutting off his brother. "Buck, man, it was a trip for real. We was looking for you cause Stack had said that he was gon let us look again. He kept on talking bout how fine Big Foot was. We jus couldn't tell she was cause of the clothes she wear."

"Tell the story Skillet," said Man.

"Alright, alright. Stack had told us to-"

"We waited outside his window Buck and then-"

"Shut up Smoke damn," Lizard faked a punch, flinching at Smoke's face. I laughed at how hard Smoke jumped.

"Anyway Buck, we'd tol him how we was tryin to see through the door at his house. He was actin like he was a pimp or something. He said he could get Big Foot whenever he wanted."

"And, come on what happened?"

Skillet had been sitting with his back against the couch when he came in. Everybody else was sitting on the floor behind the table, leaning back with their arms holding them up. I was in front of the table as usual, still in pajamas, eating my cereal. When Skillet started talking he moved to the floor beside Lizard and put his elbows on the table and used his hands.

"Stack was like,

'My uncle said he could smell us in the house. He said that's why he left to gimme some privacy. I guess he musta left the door kinda cracked.'

'Yeah, that's how we walked in and heard your music playing and your door closed.'

'Aight then, yaw'll caught me but yaw'll don't even know what's up.'

I knew what was up though Buck. So I figured I'd dare him. You know he don't like getting challenged. 'Stack since you the Mack and all, I bet you can't do it no more.'

'Skillet, I ain't gotta do nothin for you. You seen it already.'

'Yeah, but you a Mack."

"Yeah Buck, and then we all was like, you a punk you can't do it anytime," Smoke interrupted. Skillet folded his finger deep on his thumb and popped the hell outta Smoke's ear.

"I'm tellin mom for real this time."

"Shut up Smoke," said Lizard again. Man was sitting leaning towards Skillet with listening ears.

"Damn, always messin up a story. Sorry about cussin Buck. Now you know Stack always gotta win a dare. He told us he could get her again late that day. His mom was gon be out at another job. So we talked on it and he said he would leave the bedroom window curtain cracked. We went to the side of his house right before it started getting dark. Sure enough Big Foot came walkin down the street. We all was looking through the window waiting. Stack let her in and when he got to his room he gave us a wave. He didn't kiss her or nothing she just start taking off her clothes."

Man leaned in closer to Skillet. Even Smoke had shut up and was listening hard.

"She had on a big white bra. Stack was rubbing on her and she was taking off her pants. She still had on her shoes too. She got on the bed and pulled up his sheets. Stack climbed in and was looking at us. The music was kinda loud, we could hear it playin,

'Call me, when you need someone to talk to, call me, satisfaction guaranteed.'

Then like pow, we didn't even hear it. All we saw was the door bust open. The curtains flew back and Stack momma was in there fast with a big extension cord. She grabbed Big Foot up and popped her twice and then she got on Stack and was hitting him all in his ding a ling. He was yelling like a punk. She turned around and reached for Big Foot again but Big Foot had grabbed her stuff and ran out in the hallway. We was dying."

All the guys was laughing around the table. I laughed with them for a minute and then I stopped. Come next week it wadn't gonna be no more stories. No more of me hearing them talk about stuff at least. I felt my chest get tight and I wanted to cry cause I didn't want to leave.

"Buck that was funny, why you not laughing?" asked Man.

"I'm laughing, just not hard. I ain't laughin at nobody gettin hit in the ding a ling."

"We all cracked up again."

"Get ready, we gon go play against Greenlaw today," said Skillet.

I didn't much feel like playing. I wanted to tell them about me leaving but I still thought it was something I could do to make mom wanna stay. Besides, it wadn't no way I was gon not be around Liz. I had to tell her about my plan. The guys had started getting up to sit on the couch. I figured I better get outta my pajamas.

"I'ma get dressed. Don't be messing around in my house."

"We ain't," said Smoke. "Can we go get some cookies?"

"Yeah, but don't eat em all." Smoke and Man followed me down the hall. I grabbed my pants and a shirt and walked into the bathroom. I closed the door. I could hear them talking in the kitchen shutting and closing cabinets. I peeked out and yelled, "Yaw'll know where the cookies at, stop looking for other stuff."

"Okay Buck, dang," said Smoke. Man was walking back past the door to show me his cookies. I shoulda known it was just Smoke. I closed the door again.

I made my way back up to the living room and the guys was quiet. They wasn't looking at teevee or nothing. They was just sitting.

Skillet looked me in the face and then stood up, "So what's up Buck?"

"Whatcha mean what's up? I'm ready to go."

"Hey yaw'll let's roll," Skillet said. The guys got up and started for the door.

"Hold up yaw'll."

"Why? You ain't gotta go. You ain't gotta go no more."

"What you mean Skill-"

"We know what's happenin. You gonna keep on lying to us? Hell, we use to it nah."

The guys was eying me real hot. They looks was strong on me. Even Lizard was looking hard. Man was kinda between us staring.

"Why you actin like you don't want me to go? You think I don't wanna hang wit yaw'll?"

"We know you ain't gon hang wit us no more."

"Damn Skillet, why you actin crazy?" I asked.

"We saw your momma letters and stuff and her papers on the kitchen table," Smoke said. "We saw her letter talking about yaw'll moving next week. We saw it on the table and you ain't even tell us about it."

"Yeah Buck, we knew Tiger was gon leave. We knew he was gon leave a long time before. But you ain't tell us nothing. You ain't tell us nothin," said Man. He was looking at me from under his eyebrows. Like he was crying or something. I felt my chest getting warm like in the dream.

"Bloodbrothers? You wadn't gon never tell us huh?" Skillet was angry. When he got mad his jaw would clinch and make muscles.

"I don't even know what yaw'll talking about, what letters and papers?" Then I thought on it. When I went in the kitchen I saw the papers but it wadn't none of my business so I didn't look at them.

276

Smoke was nosey. He was always looking at stuff he ain't have no business looking at. I knew then, it was him. I was heated. I lunged at him fast and caught him with a stiff right hand on his cheek. He fell back into Skillet.

"Why you reading my momma stuff, you bastard." The guys caught me and Skillet didn't even help Smoke. He held him up and put his arm on his shoulder. "Let's go yaw'll." Man and Lizard turned and opened the screen door and walked out. Smoke walked out next. Skillet looked back at me, "You coulda at least told us early like Tiger did. You coulda at least acted like you was gon miss us."

"But Skillet I jus found out last-" Skillet turned his back on me and walked out.

Man had put his cookies on the table. Pieces of the brown chips sat on the edge. I walked over and turned off the teevee. I picked up the cookies and walked back to the kitchen. I threw the cookies in the trash and pulled out one of the chairs to sit down at the table. I looked on the letters laying there:

> Tenant will vacate this apartment on August 29th. Any things needed can be taken out of renter's deposit.
> Thank you.

It wasn't much in the way of what the words said. According to the letter we was moving on Saturday, seven days away. It was some other letters with pictures of apartments on the table too. All of them was saying this good stuff about Whitehaven. Beside it sat mom's regular numbers scribbled on paper. Usually the bill numbers was real small at the bottom. This time it was circled with an exclamation mark beside it: 100 dollars. I sat at the table for a while longer before I decided to walk to Mr. Archie's. I figured telling him would make up for not telling the guys. But hell, I didn't even know about the move myself. I shouldn'tna felt so bad about it, but I couldn't help it. I had never seen them looks on their faces. I had never seen that kinda face from folks my age at least.

Chapter 28

The house was pretty much packed away. The pictures and little stuff was in boxes by the front door and mom had kept a clothes bag for us to dress from in the morning. The days had ran by like a rolling rain cloud in the middle of July. The things happening followed it in the same way, loud, and angry, hot like coals in a pit. The neighborhood was on fire with licks from the devil's tongue. I wanted to make it alright, but wadn't no way to stop a tire made of bricks rolling downhill. To make it worse, the tire was on icy stares and looks from people on every corner. I knew then mom was right, Fifth Street had cancer. It had been eating itself up since 68 and it wadn't nothin nobody was gon be able to do to fix it. It wasn't so much that I didn't know or see it for a long time, I guess it was the fact that I was moving away that made it so obvious.

Folks had been standing on the corners for as long as I recalled. Standing, on corners, and on porches like they was all waiting on something. I just hadn't noticed it this way before. Mr. Archie called it God watchin.

"De river not wide enough, nooo Lawd. It ain't wide enough, naaaw Lawd. I'm jus gon float on over on yo wangs of prayer, dis river ain't wide enough, naaaw Lawd. Folk got a way about em. Always watchin an waitin. God watchin," he'd said.

I'd look at him, and ask, "God watchin, huh?"

"Yessuh. They lookin for somethin on every street corner, in every park round here. They jus watchin and waitin. See'n as how God only move on his time ya think they go head on an move bout they business. But Black folk dun perfected God watchin, an that ain't gon change."

"Things change Mr. Archie, some folks get better."

"Be careful witcha words Buck. I say this always, thangs don't change, people do."

God watchin. I saw it now, how puppies grow to dogs, and kittens to cats, but they still what they is. With people, we ain't got no real reaction to something cause all of our answers is inside us. We change but only in shape. We create actions and make thangs happen, for good and for bad. In my whole life I'd seen shootings, fires, people killing themselves with needles dangling, folks dancing cause they got they monthly food stamps. I had seen any and everythang you coulda seen, all by the time I was twelve years old. It wasn't no way I was gon fit in with nothing else, but mom kept on moving, packing, and cleaning until every part of our apartment on Fifth Street was disappearing. It was almost like the more we packed, the more folks was wandering the streets.

I hadn't been to Mr. Archie's or Ms. P's since the week before cause it seemed like they could melt ice with the air they was breathing. Honestly, I didn't go cause I didn't want to have to tell Mr. A, I was leaving.

I was sneaking off with Liz everyday though, and had already told her that I was going. On Wednesday, we really spoke with everything inside us like mother and son. It was the last day I was gonna see her. I kinda felt that some things had been taking place for a few days and she wasn't gonna be able to see me off cause of it.

We went to the old house. Inside them gray walls it was bright, not from sun or outside light shining in, but from the peace. It wasn't no sounds or cutting eyes staring longways at folks for no reason. Me and Liz was free. It was almost like we'd runaway for a while.

"Buck, if there ever a time I can come visit, can I?"

"Yeah. I told you I wish you could come wit us. I don't wanna go still. I wish you wouldnt'na talked me out from running away. I still don't get what your reasoning was."

"Buck," she talked and made stick drawings in air with the handle of a broken branch. The branch left long shadows on the wall as the small candle Liz had lit, flickered to the push of several different drafts happening in the room. "I'm gonna miss you for more reasons than I know how to explain, but it's good you leaving."

"Why come you say it's good? You wanted to leave just like me."

"Well, seein as my folks really need me, I don't think about that so much no more."

"How they need you? Your daddy mean, and he ain't right."

"When the last time you spoke to Mr. Archie or Ms. P?"

"Been a few days. I ain't figured out how to be upfront with Mr. A. He like my daddy and I don't know what to say to him."

"I reckon you ain't heard nothin from them friends of yours either huh?"

"Like what?" I sat up on the mat in the room and I could see the afternoon light starting to settle into the sky. It was a glowing red out behind the wood planks and old curtains. Liz's right side of her face was dark almost like it wadn't there. She talked smooth and without hesitation. If I wouldn't have cut her off, she woulda for sure just came out and said everything. But I cut her off every few words trying to get her to go straight to what she was hiding.

"Liz, what I shoulda heard? I ain't seen them since... I told you why I ain't seen the guys."

"I'm not scared no more Buck."

"What you mean?"

"I ain't scared, don't have to be. See, my daddy been off work the past few days. He talk to us now. He don't shout much as he use to."

"That don't mean he changed. He still probably go back to what he was doing."

"I don't think so Buck."

"How so?"

"Buck, you ain't heard *nothin*?"

"Naw Liz, dang."

She stopped twisting the stick and sat it down. She got up and walked out into the hallway. I blew out the candle and followed her. She'd made it through the kitchen and was looking back on the house. I could see in her eyes this satisfied look, complete look. I ran and caught up with her.

"Liz, what you speaking on? Just tell me what done happened."

"I don't need to be running away from nothing again Buck. He sat down and told us he was sorry."

"But folks always apologizing for thangs and don't mean it Liz. He gon do bad stuff again. Mr. Archie say we all creatures of habit. We do thangs the same way our whole lives until something drastic come along. We can't and won't change til we feel some particular joy or pain that make us think."

"I guess it was pain Buck."

"What?"

"My daddy ain't touched none of us in three days. He usually tear into momma every other night. Sometimes he do it twice a day. But not no more since Saturday."

"That's only four days Liz."

We walked down the trail to her apartments. The street light had come on and she wadn't running or nothing.

"When the wind blow too hard you get a rattle and these sounds in your house. Sounds like something moaning with deep pain. It's that sound from a window that ain't quite closed and the wind fighting it's way through that crack." Liz talked and kept walking. She had her hands in her pocket. She was pretty as a Sunday lady going to church. I kept staring on her hoping she didn't mind. "On Saturday it wadn't no wind or nothing in back of the apartments. It ain't getting that cold yet. But I heard moaning like November trying to walk through the walls. Then I heard pounding, thick pounding trying to get through the bathroom window. I figured somebody was out back in the alley doing dope or fighting. But the noises was getting louder. I walked to the window. Momma was in the kitchen, but I don't right know if she heard nothing. She was moving pots around and frying chicken. I moved closer to the wall and looked through the gap. I could see Lil T standing with his knife open. His arms was wide and his eyes was screaming big."

She stopped walking across the street from her apartments. "He was with them guys from the park. I could hear the moaning. I could hear it low and then in short bursts. Then I saw...

'Please, please I ain't gon do it no mo. I ain't gon touch em jus leave me be. Please, awww Laawrd, awww Laawrd. I promise I ain't-' Then another thud. Two of the bigger guys was standing up over him. His working overalls was half down making, and pulling, his arms tight to his side. He was rolling all in the muddy part under the window. His face was swollen. Blood was coming from his mouth. His words was mixed with spitting, and that... low ... moan. He was rolled over in a way that they couldn't kick him in his stomach no more. So them guys kicked em in his arms,

'We hear you put yo hands on em again... we hear anythin true or false, we gon fuck you up good nigga. Dem is women and girls,' one of the guys said pointing at our window.

'Awww please jus leave me be, jus leave me.'

Buck I ain't seen nothing like it. Lil T looked up and caught my eyes. I ain't move or nothing. He walked over and put the knife in my daddy's face, right here." She pointed beside her ear and made a line. "He sliced my papa's face real slow. Papa didn't come in after that. He ain't come in until late. We was in bed. I ain't move cause if he hear any stirring, that's usually what set him off. I pulled my little sister close to me in my bed and held her. She was shaking. Mom didn't move at all. I didn't hear the bed twitch, or creak through the

284

wall. She was still." I could hear dad breathing hard in the front room.

When we woke up to get ready for church, he had started on breakfast. He was good on Sunday mornings anyhow. But he was usually lying. He'd do stuff to make himself feel better. It was never really for us. But it look like he was making things right for him this time. He had on a clean change of clothes for work and a white bandage on the side of his face. Momma didn't ask about it. I didn't look at it much." Liz walked across the street holding my hand and pulling me. I looked into the hallway at the steps next to her door.

"We might be going down to Mississippi pretty soon. I might be gone when you leave," she stopped. "I'm gonna miss you."

I couldn't look her in the face for a second. I wanted to cry. She kissed me on the lips and the locusts sounds and whirring died down. She held her lips, so soft on mines like, forever. "I'm gonna miss you Buck."

Her mom was sitting outside and playing with her little sister. Her mom had on a bright dress and her hair was down, hanging at her shoulders. Wasn't no make up, just a little darkness under her right eye that wasn't really there if you hadn't seen it before. Liz ran over and hugged her neck. I called out to her, "I'ma miss you to." It was hard to do but I walked away, down towards Bickford. It was just dark enough to still see the daylight and the moon. The street lights was on and Liz had stayed out past her time.

Chapter 29

The week was almost gone and I hadn't seen nobody but Liz. I knew I had to say bye to Mr. Archie. I was dreaming of it every night. I was dreaming good dreams, like Mr. Archie's good blues. I could hear him singing deep from inside and telling me stories. It was so much I needed to do still. Most of all, I wanted to be bloodbrothers with the guys.

Wednesday had ended too fast. Mom was getting folks to help her take stuff out to Whitehaven every day. So she wasn't home when I got there that night. I sat on the couch, looked at some teevee and ate cookies and milk. At around nine, I felt like something was making me leave the house but I ignored it. I figured on not getting into trouble before saying good bye to folks. I slept okay after saying bye to Liz. It wasn't nothing like I thought it would be. I wasn't sad that I wasn't gonna see her no more, just empty.

Mom made it in around eleven. She walked in the room and woke me up.

"You sleep?"

'What do you think mom the light's off.' I thought. But then I replied, "Nah jus thinking."

She came and sat on the bed. "I know you been feeling kinda down about the move and all. I been listening to you. In our times of sorrow we get lost and we get hopeless, but leaning on the everlastin arm-" I tuned mom out. If it was one thing I didn't want at eleven at night from mom, it was a prayer meeting. I think she saw it in my face. Even though she had only turned on the small lamp on my dresser, I think she could see it in my face. "Baby, how about I let you come back and spend the weekend with Mr. Archie, maybe once a month?"

"I guess."

"Well, I figured you'd be happy bout that."

"It's just that, the guys, and Mr. Archie, I - I ain't told them yet how I feel about leaving. The guys mad at me cause they thought I wasn't gonna tell them, and I'm just scared of leaving Mr. Archie."

"Well, this your chance to say good bye to Mr. Archie and let him know you gon be able to come back and visit him. You can also tell the guys that you gon be staying with Mr. Archie every now and then."

"But how Mr. A gonna feel about me staying with him?"

"He thinks that's a mighty fine plan. That's the way he say it, 'Hmph, well well, that's a mighty fine plan there, yes indeed,'" she mocked his voice.

"You already told him we was leaving?"

"Of course I did son. He mean jus as much to me as he do to you. Maybe more."

"Yeah, but I was supposed to tell him mom." I rolled over. She touched me on my shoulder.

"Well, now you know you gotta tell em soon."

She got up and turned off the light.

I could hear dishes rattling and skillets being scraped, morning had come fast. As of late, mom didn't find it necessary to come in and wake me with the, "Rise and Shine" routine. She just went about her way leaving me be. I think it's her way of saying, 'Time to do something on your own.' I was satisfied with that. I knew it wasn't cause she loved me any less. Pretty much that wasn't it at all. She just knew a better way to handle things.

I figured the best way to say bye was to reach out to everyone by just going and speaking. I got up and started getting ready. I wasn't in a rush seeing as it was already close to eight.

"Good Morning sleepy head."

"Morning ma. You ain't at work yet?"

"Had a few more things to get done today before heading out."

"Oh. Any breakfast for me?"

"Of course. You get in there and finish up and get back in here to join your mom."

"Yes mam."

Mom was sorting papers on the table. She had been on the phone. I could see the line stretched. I got done in the bathroom and put on clothes. She was on the phone talking when I made it back. The line stretched from the hall way to the kitchen table. She talked to folks about changing phone and light, gas and water services.

The sun was behind clouds making it bright gray out. It would be getting cool in a few weeks. Until the fall came, the guys would be sweating in a school out here, and I'd be in an air conditioned school. That didn't matter though, cause the cold would be coming soon enough. At least all schools had heat just not air. I got me a plate and scooped some eggs from the skillet, grabbed a biscuit, some sausage, and made me a sandwich. Mom continued on the phone. I looked at the papers and saw that there was a pool in the apartments we was gonna move in. A swimming pool in apartments. A park in the apartments. A ten minute walk and no buses or long walks to school. Everything was right where it was supposed to be in Whitehaven.

Mom hung up the phone, "Finished with that mess. I declare the toughest thang about this whole process is mail and light, gas, and water," she paused and laughed. "I guess that's everything ain't it?"

I shrugged my shoulders and kept eating.

"I'ma get ready to get outta here. Don't find no trouble today. Here go two dollars. Get you something to snack on and go see Mr. Archie nah."

"Yes mam." She never gave me money before she left. She just kissed me on the forehead and told me not to eat up everything. A whole two dollars. I could take Liz to get some snacks after I visited Mr. A.

I walked mom to the door and she waved as she kinda jumped down each step to the street. She walked up the block towards the bus stop. I went back and cleaned up the kitchen before I went outside.

The sun was still playing peek-a-boo with the clouds when I left, behind one second, out the next. I walked to the curb and looked towards Stack's house. I looked that way for a minute hoping the guys would be headed this way. But there was nothing. I walked back down Fifth. I could hear a few voices over at the park. The big Cadillac sat at the curb in the same space it was in when Mr. Archie was there talking to Straw Hat. One of the guys that was always in the park was there too. I kept walking that way anyway. Instead of hesitating and going to the back of the gym, I kept my head up and walked to the front. Straw Hat was standing with his foot on the table's bench. He had on a long, black, shirt that looked soft falling on his arms and chest. He glanced as he talked. He looked over at me and nodded his hat. The big guy was standing on the outside of the Cadi again. Straw Hat called to me.

"Hey nah lil pimpin, you tell Old Man Fishstick we even nah. Thangs been settled good. You tell em I ain't gon be round here much no mo either. Might consider movin on, just might consider it," he laughed and went back to his conversation with the guy. I had stopped walking, caught up in his words. I kept staring.

"What I gotta tell him that for?" They ignored me. "What I gotta say that to him for?" I started walking over to the bench. The guy he was talking to was sweating from under his plastic cap. His tank top was sticking to him with patches of wetness showing. He held his hand up.

"Hold on now youngblood. Stop where you is."

Straw Hat waved for me. "Naw it's okay. Come on over here lil daddy. I got somethin for ya. You movin ain't ya?"

"Yeah, why?"

"Aww you tough huh? You askin me questions and all. I tell you what. Seein as you so tough and smart, how's about you answer somethin for me."

"I'm waiting."

"You waiting? Boy I'll," he brought his hand up. I sucked air into my chest and straightened myself out. He lowered his hand and took his foot off the bench.

"Don't do that Arch. I'll smack his little ass if you want."

"Naw that's alright. That's alright," he turned his back on me and whispered to Plastic Cap something under his breath, " I swear if this lil mothafucka wadn't the old man's blood and that old mothafucka didn't have shit on me... Shit, man, I'm jus talkin shit." He turned back around. "Look here boy, I know you going to visit the Old Man. You tell him we square. I might leave, but I might not. Got a lot mo work to do. But we square now, and shit, we jus alike now anyway. Now more than ever." He took out a wad of money, "You give that to your momma. Hide it in the house somewhere so she find it, or do what ya want with it."

"Naw, that's okay."

"Suit yaself. Get the fuck on way from here."

I wanted to punch him, or kick him hard. But I knew better. He kept talking and I made my way down the sidewalk in front of the gym. I heard him yell at me again.

"Tell him we square."

I could see Mr. Archie sitting on his porch watching the park. I got closer and saw him leaning back on his stool. His guitar sat beside him. He looked like he was God watchin. I pushed the gate open.

"Buck, Buck, Buck, been missin ya on these past few days here. Thought ya wadn't gon come and say bye to me."

"No suh. I was jus worried. I didn't wanna leave you and the guys-"

"And Ms. Liz?"

"Yessir."

"Well, I reckon that's a valid enough excuse." He was slouched and had on some dark blue pants and a dark brown shirt. He didn't have no hat on at all. His hair was combed in a neat, little afro. "Well, I reckon that is a good enough excuse. I've been missin you though. Thought several times bought comin up ya way to sit and talk wit you a spell. But I knew you was having some issues."

"It wasn't against you Mr. Archie. I wanted to come and see you, for real."

"I know it. That's how it workout sometimes you know? All of what you do is a response to what you thankin. That's what make us different. We make these decisions and we gotta live wit em, even if they wrong. But sometime, wrong is the only way to make it right." He *was* God watchin.

I didn't say nothing. If he was gonna speak like Liz, I knew to keep quiet. I pulled up a crate and sat at the bottom of the steps. Then I thought about Ms. P. I moved the crate up on the porch by Mr. Archie.

"Whatcha thinking bout?"

"When the dirt get some grass Buck, it's still the same ol dirt. It just look better from the top, but it's still the same ol dirt. Buck, in a minutes time we can be all the best that God can offer. In the same minute we can be all the worst that the devil need."

"Sir?"

He got up and walked in the house, "Come on." He walked straight through, to the kitchen, and out into the backyard. His vegetables was still growing a bit. Tops of carrots stuck out and some tomatoes was still hanging on. He walked out into the yard and picked up a handful of soil.

"If you can hold the world in yo hands, then you can make it what you want it to be." His words was strong. "Buck...This man name Way I hadn't seen in a loooong time, come and visit wit me recently. He was a good man, for a long time, but then he got himself lost." Mr. Archie was speaking shaky. His voice rose up and fell down, but it sounded strong still. It made me feel the pain in my chest. In my heart that heat feeling came with each word. I rubbed my chest and tried to listen, but my mind wandered. I heard words but they didn't make much sense in my head cause my thoughts was on the warmness in my chest. He kept talking and the words was distant.

"Way was a healthy statured man, his back and hands was strong. Face was like a snapshot from a black and white magazine. Perfect shade of dark. He was firm in his thoughts but he was lost. He useta be a helpin man. See, what he done all his life was be there.

I remember a young man Way loved dearly. That boy was always thinking up stuff. But he didn't have the tools and thangs he needed to make his ideas real. Way saw to it that this boy could do and build anything he wanted. He went and worked and begged to get this boy hammers, nails, wrenches, whatever the boy needed. He helped the boy build and create... but mostly, he jus watched the young man. Nah there was another boy Way found himself taken to. But he let this boy fall to the wayside cause he was so ashamed of hisself. Not too far apart was these two boys born, both boys was born in sin and Way had a hand in both. But them women he brought this pain to kept it to themselves and raised them boys up in a way they daddies nevah caught on. One of the boys was here in Memphis where Way could see him anytime he choose. But the other boy left for the North with his momma.

Buck, Way was how he was cause of one thang I suppose. He knew that his wildness and his laying with them women was all a response to his not being able to be with the one woman he really love. He also knew that he ain't have no right to create problems cause he was lonely.

Ya see, them boys was his own flesh, but Way jus didn't have the heart to speak about thangs that woulda made an understanding to a lot of other folks.

Buck, Way had trouble with being honest when it counted most." When Mr. A called my name again, the burning started going away. I could hear him clear. His eyes was moist. He wiped the water with the bend in his knuckles. He continued, "Way made a lot of mistakes. For every good thang he dun, the two wrongs he made in his life, and Buck I mean the only two wrongs he made in his life, come back to haunt em. Now all he got is these memories. And these memories tearing his old heart apart son. Never having nothing to hold on to, make a loss that much greater."

Mr. Archie had been standing on the edge of his garden. He dropped down to his knees and looked out past the rows and cried. Not big tears, but small single line tears, that fell down his face when he blinked his eyes. It wasn't right for him to cry for another man. But in doing so I think he found some peace for himself. I hadn't never met Way. I don't quite know why. I figured I had met everyone that meant something special to Mr. Archie, but I guess everybody got secrets. I didn't know whether I was sposed to leave him be in that backyard, or hold him. So I just walked over to him and put my hand on his shoulder like mom did to me the night before.

"Mom said I can come and stay with you once a month Mr. Archie."

His chest heaved hard. He looked up at me from over his shoulder and one tear traced over his right cheek, and then he looked down again.

"I love you Buck, and when you see me cry like this it ain't sadness, no suh. These is merciful tears, like rain."

"Rain wash out all the bad things?"

"That's right. But this rain gone last a lil longer this time. Mmm Hmm, it's gon wash away these blues eventually though. You gon in the house nah. I be in directly. Gon on nah."

I walked backwards not taking my eyes off Mr. A. He stayed in that kneeled position for a few more seconds, then he pushed his hand into the ground to pick himself up. He looked around his backyard and started walking to the steps. I moved from the door and let him walk through.

"I'm fine, jus a few thangs on my mind is all."

"I really don't wanna leave, I don't wanna go."

"Sometimes you gotta move on, *move on down de line*," he sang, then talked. "Even when you don't know what's on the tracks, you gotta just move on." He reached in the refrigerator and pulled out a tray. "Gon in the living room, I be there in a second."

He took less than a second, and was right behind me with an icebox lemon pie.

"Ms. P made this for you when she find out from Liz you was leavin. Liz come an talked wit her fore she left to go down to Mississippi."

I was hurt. Liz was gone. She was gone that night. I knew she had told me, but ... I wanted so badly for her to be with me the last few days.

"Aww, Buck don't look so bothered son. She tol Ms. P she was sad about leavin. She also said she was glad you wadn't gon have to worry no mo."

"I ain't worried no more Mr. A. She strong."

"Jus like you. Nah get you some of this here pie. I reckon you gon hang with them boys of yours today?"

"No sir. They kinda upset with me."

"Why is that?"

"Cause I'm leaving."

"Hmph. Much as we don't like to say it, us boys and men feel a lot of pain. It ain't a woman thang to cry, but you wouldn't know that from how we act. You need to catch up with them boys today."

"I was thinking about it." I bit into the pie. The smell and taste made my mouth fill with water. I ate two slices before Mr. A. finished his first.

"Mr. Archie?"

"Mmm, hmmm?"

"In the park... That man in the Cadillac, told me to tell you something."

He stopped eating and sat his plate down.

"What he say?" Mr. Archie asked.

"He told me to tell you that yaw'll was square." I didn't hesitate. "What he mean by that?"

"He mean that thangs in the park gon be okay from now on."

"How, why come?"

"When a man feel he ya equal he'll make concessions. He'll do some thangs he wouldn't normally do. But only when a man feel equal. Sometimes it take something drastic to make things change. That's all Buck. That's all he mean. Finish ya pie." He sat with his plate in his hand for a moment and then he start eating again. "How bout we take a ride downtown on the bus?"

"Mom gave me two dollars."

"You ain't gotta spend no money. We'll get off on Chelsea and get us a Lot-A-Burger and then go on downtown."

"Okay. But I'ma get sick from all this food."

"Don't worry, we'll sit here for a while and let ya stomach settle... look at some teevee for a spell fore we leave."

"That sounds good to me."

Mr. Archie and I spent all day Thursday together. We went to the big fountain by the courthouses and then we went down to Beale Street. Mr. Archie told me about W.C. Handy and how Memphis was the capitol of music, not Detroit or Philadelphia, but Memphis. I listened. Mr. Archie even went down by the Lorraine Hotel. He said he hadn't gone by there in over ten years. I stood with him looking at the glass case around the room. He stood on the sidewalk quiet for a minute.

"Ain't been right since he left Buck, ain't been right at all."

I looked at Mr. A's face when he said that. He blew out and then his chest filled and went down.

I got home late knowing and thinking about the one day I had left. Mom talked to me for a while and started cleaning up some more.

I fell asleep on the couch until the roar and whine of sirens shook me from my sleep. Mom had run up to the front room to open the door. I could hear pops, snaps, moans, like the stove when the fire caught up to the gas. The moan wasn't like the whistle of the wind Liz talked about. It was a steady crackle loud enough to make sure everyone around know there was a fire. Mom pushed open the front door. I saw the time sitting close to twelve. The lights were still on in the back of the house. Mom was still packing. She hadn't even made me get in the bed.

I could hear people beginning to talk loud outside. Doors were opening and folks was standing on they porches. Mom and I followed suit. One big fire truck was outside. A thick yellow hose lay in the street full of water waiting to be sprayed but the firemen just stood and looked, like the rest of the people. The old house was aflame from the center out. It look like it wasn't even burning on the outside, just in the middle. High and tall flames, enough to singe the green leaves of the trees hanging overhead. It looked like the house was sinking back into itself. I kept staring on it hoping that Liz wasn't inside. But I knew she wasn't there. She was gone. To me, I think the house knew something. Folks was in the street talked and carried on.

"I wonder who dun it?" said a old lady with rollers in her hair.

"Hell, it's bout time anyhow," said Mr. Tucker the candylady's husband. He stood with his hands on top of his stomach.

"Wadn't nobody gon move in there," mom added.

"Been sitting so damn long, house probably jus set itself on fire," another old lady said holding her robe closed with long brown fingers. Folks kind of laughed about it and start walking back in they houses. It was white, and gray, and black, falling from the sky like snow... hot snow covered in a burnt smell. The house continued to fall in. The firemen finally turned their hoses on and the water beat at the walls of the house pushing, breaking in windows and wooden boards. Mom turned me around back towards the house. Then I heard it. A groan and moan, almost like wind through a cracked window. The sound pushed fire out towards the water coming in. The firemen dropped down to the ground and the people close enough, fell. And then nothing. Just smoke and ashes remained. No fire jumping up onto dead leaves or nothing.

The firemen walked up the hill and kept spraying though. Mom had stopped to look back at the noise. I don't know if Liz would ever know it, but I think that house knew she was strong enough without it. Mom closed the door so smoke and ash wouldn't get in. I went to my room. My mom walked to the back and turned out the lights. It was quiet in the house, only a few stray sounds of people floated in. They faded away, and after awhile, along with the sound of the fire truck, all the other noises was gone to.

Chapter 30

I woke up to find our house completely packed away. The only thing left out was the big furniture, most of which was gonna be hauled off that afternoon and in the morning. I walked to the front window to look out at the house. The front of the house was half up. Charred white paint and burnt black sat at the top of the hill. It was another part of the neighborhood that would just be there standing ugly and raggedy. Mom came in behind me and said, "It's a shame, but that house needed to burn. The bad thing is, it's gon be there and ain't nobody gonna tear it down. It's just gonna stay right there."

She was right. It would be just like the house over by Ms. P that had burned and nobody found the time to just clear it off of the grass that was growing up around it. Mom had already been out of the house. She had a bag of fries and burgers in her hands.

"You slept in kind of late today didn't you?"

"I can't tell what time it is. You packed away the clocks already mom?"

"It's a little after ten. I took the day off to finish up a few things before the moving men come out this afternoon and tomorrow."

"Dang after ten-"

"Watch it."

"Sorry mam."

"I got you something to eat here but you have to go get cleaned up first. It'll still be warm."

I went ahead and took a bath and got the clothes that was still left out in my room. Through the last couple of days I hadn't even noticed that mom had packed off my room to. She'd done everything. After I dressed, I sat on the bed and thought about being out of North Memphis. I wasn't gonna fit in out in Whitehaven I thought.

It wasn't like it was going to Greenlaw or to New Chicago, we was going south, close to Mississippi. It would be like getting bussed and staying in the school for the rest of my life as far as I knew. For the longest, I'd been afraid to leave. I didn't want to change no matter how much I heard that folks have to keep on moving.

That Friday, sitting on the couch with my mom, I grew up. I figured out that God does things to us because it makes us understand that he is working. Or, like mom always repeating, he working in mysterious ways.

I rode out to Whitehaven with mom that afternoon. Looking at the trees pass by fast on the freeway, passing streets like Union, Airways, Elvis Presley Blvd, was okay. I liked seeing all of the trees lining the streets and seeing the shopping malls and fast food places, Mc Donald's and Wendy's, Long John Silver's was on every other corner. Krystals sat directly behind our apartments. All the places on the teevee commercials were there in my new neighborhood.

I saw all these things as the truck bounced down a street called Winchester and turned off into our new apartments. Then I saw Black kids running around, throwing footballs. Some walking around with football pads and clothes on like they really played *real* football. Black kids with radios walking around. Black people in regular cars, not Cadillacs.

Black people in *White*haven.

I didn't feel so angry after getting out there and seeing everything. I did feel bad about leaving. I knew I would be going back for one more day, but that's when it hurt. Lizard and Stack and Skillet them, I wondered if they'd seen all the different stores and if they was gonna ever be able to come and see me. We finally stopped in front of our new apartment. It was kind of tucked away. To me it still looked like the projects, just cleaner. It looked the same until I went in with mom and looked out the big sliding window door and saw the swimming pool... with Black kids diving in it. I kept looking out for a while. Mom finally touched me and told me we had to go back with the moving men. I didn't want to go. I wanted to stay and just walk around. She smiled at me, "Nice ain't it?"

I shook my head. We climbed back in the truck between the men and went back to North Memphis.

No new streets. No Mc Donald's. No cool street names, just Dunlap and Faxxon and Fifth Street, just Lot-A-Burger and Frank's store. We pulled back into North Memphis and couldn't get right off the freeway and be home. We had to travel over potholes and all the way down Danny Thomas to get back to our house.

It had taken all afternoon to do all the stuff out in Whitehaven, and it was starting to get dark. All I could think about was Whitehaven. I hadn't thought about the guys much at all. I went to sleep thinking how wrong I was and I felt guilty. I hurt bad and that night I found the strength to cry.

Chapter 31

Saturday morning I woke up and found that the moving men were already there. Mom had finished helping them take all the living room stuff down. All that was left was the bedrooms. I got up and pulled the sheets off of my bed. I wrapped them in a ball and started getting ready. Mom peeked in when she heard me rustling.

"We almost done. Just a little bit more to go. Your friends in the living room." I went ahead and started getting ready. I finished in the bathroom and took down the towels. I got dressed and put the towels and sheets into a bag. Mom grabbed the bags and went outside to throw the sheets in the back of the truck. The men had started on her room. I felt weird. I wanted so badly to see the guys, but when it came time to say bye, face to face, I wished that they hadn't come at all.

"What's up yaw'll?" I tried to feel right. They all sat on the floor in the front room. They was quiet. Skillet got up and walked up to me. He pulled out his knife and hit the switch. The blade slid out like a silver light through a broken piece of glass. I looked him in the face. Stack, Smoke, Man, and Lizard all looked sad. But they finally made small smiles on their faces.

"Let's go to the back," I said. We all walked down the hall of the old apartment. The floors creaked and squealed. We walked through the kitchen, out the door, and into the back of the apartments. Down the trail, I could see the guys from the park. They hadn't been over there much anymore. In the middle of the group was Tony. We all turned and looked. Tony stopped for a second, and then turned to catch up with his group. Skillet took his knife and cut his palm. We didn't say a chant. We didn't say much at all. He cut, then Smoke, then Stack, then Lizard and finally Man. I took the knife last and broke the silence, "I'm gonna miss yaw'll," I said soft. We all shook. The same way they came in, silent, was the same way they walked off around the side of the building. Man broke the rule though, he looked back and smiled again. They disappeared around the side of my building and through the driveway alley. Mom called to me and I ran into the house. I washed my hand off and tore a piece of dishrag to wrap around the cut. It still bled a little, but not as much as it did before. She looked down at my hand and shook her head at me. She kissed me soft on my forehead.

"Come on, let's go."

"Okay mom."

We piled into the moving truck and mom looked out the window at the apartment. I looked over at the old house. We rode down Fifth Street towards the park and stopped at the corner. The guys were over by the court. The sun was in back of them. They sat on the table all holding their hands. Mom pointed. I could see Mr. Melvin painting the court. He didn't look up. I guess he didn't need to. He didn't know I was leaving and if he did, why should he care? He kept painting.

I thought I saw Mr. Archie standing with the guys blowing a kiss. I thought I saw a smile, one only a father knew how to give. I guess I must've looked like Tiger did when his dad took him and his mom outta North Memphis.

I looked into the sun shining through the window of the truck at the guys holding their palms. Almost like a shadow Mr. Archie stood next to them. From the movement of the car and the sun shining on him, it looked like someone was standing with an arm draped around his shoulders. As the car turned from Fifth Street and moved past the courts, I hung my head out and watched the figures grow smaller. It seemed as if I was leaving my life behind.

But, I wasn't really leaving anything. I wasn't leaving nothin at all. It was all jumbled up inside my head and I see that ain't no good or bad like Mr. Archie said. Everythang jus a chain, a big old link holding a dog at bay. Any link might break at any time, good or bad, just like people.

When we pulled off, as I kept looking back, Mr. Archie had changed some to me. Not enough that I ain't still hold him high, but enough that I know in me I got some bad. I just gotta keep my chain strong enough.

Author's Notes

July 2nd, 2008. I just sat down and reedited this book after making it a limited release and doing what I always do with my books, failing to promote it. After not looking at this book for so long it was like reading a book written by another person. I've been on a tear lately, reading a ton of non-fiction for personal reasons and introducing myself to Octavia Butler's Parable Series. Those are a couple of incredible books, frightnening actually.

I guess right now, I am using this note as an attempt at justifying my writing or maybe it is just my goal to end what I feel is a pretty important piece of fiction. Then again importance is based on time and the opinion of others, but I really did enjoy reading the book. As far as giving someone a reason for the book, outside of it being my thesis, I guess this book is about me. It is slightly different in several ways but it is very close to how my childhood was. I think the idea of setting the story ten years after the death of Dr. King is important but it is not reinforced in the narrative. What is reinforced is my desire to show how neighborhoods undergo very subtle changes. There are a ton of other symbolic things here as well that I didn't see or attempt to do when I was writing. They just came out that way. I won't say what symbolism is there, or hint at what things I consider important here because I may have been reading a lot more into the text since I created it.

Anyway, if you have read the book, possibly you feel the same way I do, that there could be more. I have been contemplating a follow up to see what happens with Buck next. I guess I know what happens since I am using a lot of personal information, but I have to find the time. I have lost the discipline that the MFA program taught me. I have become involved in too many other things and now the writing has taken a back seat. I hope that I find my voice again. I do think that I have a lot of writing to share. Life gets in the way, but I guess life has always been in the way and I wrote so I am making excuses.

I appreciate you spending time with these characters and in a sense with me. July is a month of memories for me. I was married in July, my sister was born in July and my mother passed in July. This book is dedicated to Barbara Jean Allen, my momma. I'm listenin still.

www.ingramcontent.com/pod-product-compliance
Lightning Source LLC
Chambersburg PA
CBHW021314250626
47155CB00002B/525